A KILLER CROP

A KILLER CROP

SHEILA CONNOLLY

This Large Print edition is published by Wheeler Publishing, Waterville, Maine, USA and by AudioGO Ltd, Bath, England.

Wheeler Publishing, a part of Gale, Cengage Learning.

Copyright © 2010 by Sheila Connolly.

An Orchard Mystery.

The moral right of the author has been asserted.

LIBRARY OF CONGRESS CATALOGING-IN-PUBLICATION DATA

Connolly, Sheila.
    A killer crop / by Sheila Connolly.
        p. cm. — (An orchard mystery) (Wheeler Publishing large print cozy mystery)
    ISBN-13: 978-1-4104-3643-6 (softcover)
    ISBN-10: 1-4104-3643-8 (softcover)
    1. Orchards—Fiction. 2. Murder—Investigation—Fiction. 3. Large type books. I. Title.
PS3601.T83K56 2011
813'.6—dc22   2010054068

BRITISH LIBRARY CATALOGUING-IN-PUBLICATION DATA AVAILABLE
Published in 2011 in the U.S. by arrangement with The Berkley Publishing Group, a member of Penguin Group (USA) Inc.
Published in 2011 in the U.K. by arrangement with the author.

U.K. Hardcover: 978 1 445 83714 7 (Chivers Large Print)
U.K. Softcover: 978 1 445 83715 4 (Camden Large Print)

Printed in the United States of America
1 2 3 4 5 6 7 15 14 13 12 11

ACKNOWLEDGMENTS

The poet Emily Dickinson's shadow still hovers over Amherst, Massachusetts, more than a century after her death, and it's hard to open a magazine or newspaper these days without finding a reference to her. I am not immune to her lasting appeal, and since I'm writing about that part of Massachusetts, I thought it right to include her in this book. Many of the details of her local family connections are based on fact, which is why Meg and her mother, Elizabeth, are drawn into Emily's story. I may as well confess: I can lay claim to being Emily's fifth cousin, five times removed — a distant connection, but I'm happy to have discovered it.

As always, I want to thank my agent, Jessica Faust of BookEnds, for making this series possible, and my editor, Shannon Jamieson Vazquez, who always manages to excavate the essential story from my piles of words.

Simon Worrall's compelling book, *The Poet and the Murderer,* sheds light on the lengths to which some people will go to possess an original work by Dickinson. Alfred Habegger's richly detailed biography of the poet, *My Wars Are Laid Away in Books,* which I read years ago, provides much detail about Emily's life, as well as a helpful family tree. And I treasure a copy of *The Complete Poems of Emily Dickinson,* edited by Thomas H. Johnson, which I purchased in the bookstore up the street from the former Dickinson home.

And since the reproduction of Emily's works is tightly controlled, the final words in the book are my daughter's tribute to the poet. She accompanied me on numerous excursions to Amherst that always managed to include one of the delightful restaurants there, which I've included in the book.

1

Meg Corey set a cup of coffee in front of her mother and sat down across the kitchen table. "Mother, what are you doing here?"

The morning light that flooded through the east-facing windows of the kitchen was not kind to Elizabeth Corey, highlighting the faint glints of silver in her carefully cut hair, the slight crepiness gathered at the corners of her eyes. She rotated the handle of the cup in its saucer, avoiding her daughter's eyes. "Meg, dear, why shouldn't I be here? Isn't it about time that I visited you and saw what you were doing with our house?"

She was stalling, Meg could tell. "Of course you should see it — although except for the kitchen floor, most of what I've done has been boring structural stuff and you can't even see it. I would have invited you sooner, but the place has been such a mess, and I've been so busy, with renovations and the orchard . . ." Meg stopped herself: why was she on the defensive? It was her mother who had shown up the night before without warning. Yesterday, Meg had been at the grand opening of Gran's, the new Granford restaurant, which had served an extraordinary meal for the group of farmers of Granford who had provided all the locally grown materials. It had been an unqualified success for owner-chefs Nicky and Brian Czarnecki, and Meg was looking forward to many more delightful meals in the converted house on the town green. Seth Chapin had brought her home after dark, and she'd been anticipating . . . well, some quality time alone with Seth, as a happy conclusion to a wonderful evening. Instead they had found Elizabeth sitting on Meg's front steps in the dark, waiting for her. That was totally unlike her mother, who usually planned things down to the last detail. "Why didn't you let me know you were coming?"

"I wanted to surprise you. I love what you've done with the floor — is that the original planking?"

Another effort to divert the conversation. What was going on?

Meg sighed. Seth had seen them into the house and disappeared discreetly, and Meg's mother hadn't even asked who he was. But for that matter, neither one of them had asked many questions. It had been late, and both Meg and Elizabeth were tired. Luckily Bree Stewart, Meg's house-mate, was off spending the night with her boyfriend, Michael, so Meg didn't need to worry about middle-of-the-night introductions. Meg had led her mother upstairs to the bedroom opposite hers in the front of the house, turning on lights as she went, and then scrounged up her one pair of spare sheets for the bed. She had pointed her mother toward the lone bathroom and retreated to her bedroom, shutting the door firmly. Morning would be time enough for questions — and some answers.

Now it was morning, and Elizabeth Corey was no more forthcoming than she had been the night before. Her mother had never "just dropped in" in her life, so why had she made an exception now? There had to be a story here.

"What would you like for breakfast?" Meg tried to remember what she had on hand. Ever since the apple harvest had begun a week earlier, she'd had little time for even basic things like grocery shopping. She barely got her laundry done, usually close to midnight, and then only because she needed clean jeans to wear in the orchard.

She hadn't had her hair cut in weeks — or was it months?

"Oh, a little orange juice, if you can manage it. Maybe an English muffin?"

Meg opened her refrigerator and checked. No orange juice. "How about cider? It's fresh — I think it was pressed last week." The first of the season, made from some of the apples that had been damaged in a recent hailstorm nearby — though not in Granford, thank goodness. Good, there was a package of muffins hiding in the back corner, along with the remains of her last stick of butter.

"That's fine, dear," Elizabeth replied. "At least you have decent coffee. You would not believe the swill that some places serve these days. So, you seem to have settled in nicely. How long has it been now?"

"Close to nine months, Mother. I arrived in January. You might have warned me that winter is a lousy time of year around here."

"I don't think I ever saw this place in winter. I'm not sure how many times I saw it at all. There was that one trip we made together — remember that, dear?"

"What I remember is two old ladies, and that I was bored to death. Didn't you tell me then that you'd visited here as a child yourself?"

Elizabeth nodded. "I did, several times." A brief smile flashed across her face. "To tell the truth, I think Lula and Nettie seemed ancient to me even then. That old New England blood, you know. Which we share, you and I."

"You didn't mention the orchard."

"I didn't remember it. I don't suppose I was ever here at the right time of year. You're managing it now?"

"I'm trying, with a lot of help. Speaking of which, Bree should be back any minute. That's Brionna Stewart, my orchard manager. She lives here, too."

"Oh, really?" Elizabeth raised one eyebrow.

"I can't pay her much, so I threw in a place to stay. And we kind of share cooking."

Meg's cat, Lolly, chose that moment to stroll in. She looked at her still-empty food dish on the floor, then wandered over to Elizabeth's feet to sniff her shoes. Meg watched with inward amusement as Elizabeth tucked her feet under her chair.

"I didn't know you had a cat," she said. "And are those your goats in that field over there?"

Meg sat down. "Yes, they are. Dorcas and Isabel. They were a gift, sort of."

11

"Goats!" Her mother shook her head.

Meg ignored her and went on, "Lolly here kind of adopted me a couple of months ago. I gather she had been abandoned by her previous owners and made her way to my house. Why didn't we ever have pets when I was growing up?"

"Your father didn't like animals."

"Oh, right." Meg got up as two muffin halves popped up from the toaster on the counter. "I thought you told me it was allergies." Whose? Her mother's? Her father's? "Where is Daddy, by the way?"

Elizabeth sat up straighter in her chair. "Your father went sailing. Or boating — I'm not sure what the correct term is. Mainly he's indulging in a midlife fantasy. He and some of his cronies are sailing down the Intracoastal Waterway — one of them has a yacht or something that he wanted to take to Florida. They left from New Jersey last Thursday."

Meg put the muffin on a plate and set it in front of her mother, then pushed the butter toward her, along with a butter knife. "And you weren't invited?"

"Of course not. This is just an excuse for them to drink too much and skip bathing. Why is it men never seem to outgrow the need for personal disorder?"

12

Meg refused to take up that challenge. "So you decided to come up here instead. If you'd let me know sooner, we could have planned some things to do." Even as she said it, though, Meg wondered if her mother had known that she'd probably have said no to a visit. Meg *would* have said no: this was her first apple harvest, possibly the busiest time of her orchard year, and no way did she have any time to take off and have ladies' lunches with her mother, or go shopping or leaf-peeping. If her mother had taken a minute to think, she should have realized that. "So you drove up last night?"

"No, I actually came up a couple of days ago." Meg's mother again evaded her eyes.

Something was not ringing true. Elizabeth had been in the neighborhood for a couple of days without getting in touch with her daughter? Meg was about to ask why when Bree burst into the kitchen through the back door. "Hi, Meg. We've got to . . . Oh, sorry — I didn't know you had company."

"Bree, this is my mother, Elizabeth Corey. She arrived last night, and Seth and I found her here after we came back after dinner. She was just about to tell me what she's doing here."

Bree extended a hand. "Nice to meet you, Mrs. Corey. Meg didn't tell me you were

13

planning to visit."

"That's because I didn't know," Meg said tartly. "Bree, you were about to say something?"

"Oh, yeah, right. Raynard says the McIntoshes are ready for picking, and I agree. We may have to juggle some of the boxes in the holding chamber, because the Macs hold better and longer than what you've got in there now. And isn't it time to make another delivery to the markets?"

Meg sighed. "Yes, it is. I know, don't lecture me — I got kind of caught up in the restaurant opening this past week. What did you think of it, by the way?"

Bree slid an English muffin into the toaster and helped herself to a mug of coffee. "I thought it went great. The food was terrific, and everybody looked like they were having a good time. Or maybe better than that — they looked like they felt comfortable, at home with the place. Betcha there wasn't much food left over."

"Good. Michael enjoyed it, too?" When Bree nodded, Meg went on, "And I know Nicky and Brian were pleased. It's a great start, and I hope they can build on it. Doing it right once is one thing, but doing it every night is something else."

Bree's muffin popped up and she buttered

14

it and put it on a plate. "I know, and I think they know. Hey, I'm going to grab a quick shower, and then we should head up to the orchard. Nice to meet you, Mrs. Corey." Bree clattered up the back stairs that led from the rear of the kitchen to her room above.

"So that's your orchard manager? She seems so young." Elizabeth tore small pieces from the muffin on her plate.

"She's smart, hardworking, and knows what she's doing. More than I do, at least as far as apples are concerned. I don't know what I'd do without her."

Elizabeth seemed to ignore Meg's comments. "You said there's only one bathroom?"

"Yes. I'd love to add another one in a year or two, once I get the hang of this orchard thing and make some money."

"Are you short of money? I thought your former employer was generous when they released you."

"You mean when they booted me out? Yes, they were, by most industry standards. But I've had a lot of expenses getting started here, both with the house and with the facilities and equipment for the orchard. I have to watch my expenses, and a second bathroom is pretty far down the list at the

15

moment. Besides, Bree and I manage just fine."

"Still, a second bath would greatly enhance the resale value."

Meg counted to ten silently. "Mother, I'm not planning to sell anytime soon, at least until I've seen if I can handle the orchard as a business. I told you that."

"Yes, you did, but I had hoped you would change your mind. Meg, you aren't cut out to be a farmer! And all those years of education and experience . . . I'm sure you can find something more suitable, if you look."

"Mother, this is not exactly a good time to look for a job, certainly not in the financial sector. Besides, I happen to like what I'm doing. I'm learning a lot. It's an honest profession with a long history. I like this place, and the people around here are great. What more should I want?"

"A husband? Or do they call them life partners these days?"

Why was it her mother always managed to push all her buttons? In the space of the last few minutes, Elizabeth had managed to disparage Meg's home, her current profession, and her lack of romantic relationship.

"You met Seth last night," she began.

"Oh, that man who brought you home?"

"Yes. He's a neighbor, and he lives over

the hill. He's using space in my outbuildings for his renovation business."

"He's in construction?" Elizabeth's eyebrow inched up a fraction.

"Mother, you don't have to say it like that. Actually, he was a plumber when I met him, but he's wanted to branch out into restoring the old homes around here for a long time, and I offered him the use of my building for his business when his was demolished for the local shopping center." She thought she'd save the news that he had also attended Amherst College, one of the most prestigious schools in the country — and that he loved what he did. *Everything* he did, which included serving as a town selectman and unofficial supreme facilitator for just about anything that needed to be done in Granford.

"Ah," Elizabeth said.

Any further comment was forestalled by a knock at the front door — which was odd, because most people Meg knew came around to the kitchen door. She checked her watch: barely eight o'clock. Who would be coming by this early? "I'll get that," she tossed over her shoulder as she headed for the front of the house.

She checked the peephole of her front door and was astounded to find Detective

17

William Marcus of the state police standing on her doorstep. She opened the door quickly. "Good morning, Bill . . ." At the expression on his face, she surmised that the camaraderie of the prior evening, when they had shared a table at the restaurant opening, had evaporated. "Detective Marcus. What brings you here so early? Everything okay over at the restaurant?" Nicky and Brian had had enough trouble getting their new business under way, and she didn't want to see them suffer any setbacks now.

"Meg." He nodded once in reply. "Is your mother's name Elizabeth Corey? Mrs. Phillip Corey?"

"Yes," Meg said, mystified. "Why do you ask?"

"I need to talk to her on a matter of official business. Would you happen to know how to reach her? There's no response on her cell phone."

"As a matter of fact, she's sitting at my kitchen table at the moment. What's this all about?"

Detective Marcus relaxed almost imperceptibly. "I need to speak with her. Her phone number was the last one dialed by a dead man."

2

For a moment Meg wondered if she'd heard Detective Marcus correctly. The "dead" part came through loud and clear. But where did her mother fit in? Why would anyone local have her mother's phone number? Obviously, the simplest way to find out would be to ask her.

"Come this way," she told Marcus, who followed her toward the back of the house. When they entered the kitchen, Elizabeth looked up, mildly curious. "Mother," Meg began, "this is Detective William Marcus of the state police, from Northampton. He's asked to talk to you."

Meg watched her mother's face carefully, but saw no more than slight confusion and gracious composure. "I can't imagine why you would want to talk to me, but I'll be perfectly happy to answer any of your questions. Please, sit down." Elizabeth waved a hospitable hand toward an empty chair.

"Meg, perhaps you could pour some more coffee?"

Meg was silently amused at her mother's automatic assumption of the role of hostess. She looked at Marcus, who nodded slightly. She took the pot, filled a new mug for him, then refilled hers and her mother's before sitting down.

"What would you like to know — Detective Marcus, is it?" Elizabeth asked.

Marcus pulled a small notebook from his pocket. "You're Mrs. Elizabeth Corey, correct?"

"Yes," Elizabeth acknowledged.

"And you and your husband, Phillip, live in Montclair, New Jersey?"

"That's correct."

"When did you arrive in Massachusetts?"

"I drove up Saturday morning. I arrived in time for a late lunch."

Detective Marcus went on in a neutral tone of voice, "What was the purpose of your trip, Mrs. Corey?"

"May I ask why you want to know?" Elizabeth parried.

Marcus paused, choosing his words — or letting Elizabeth stew. "Your phone number was found in the recent-call list on a cell phone found in the pocket of a Daniel Weston, whose body was discovered early this morning in Amherst."

Meg watched with apprehension as the color drained from her mother's face, but Elizabeth's gaze never left Marcus's face. "Daniel? He's dead? Oh my God, what happened?"

"I take it you knew Mr. Weston?"

"I did. For more than half my life, in fact. How did he die?"

Meg's radar pricked up: Marcus wouldn't be sitting in her kitchen now if this Daniel Weston had died a natural death. But where did her mother fit in the equation?

"I'll get to that in a moment. How were you acquainted with him?"

"I've known him since he and my husband were in graduate school together."

"Have you seen him recently?"

Elizabeth's chin came up slightly. "Yes, Detective, I saw him this weekend." Her gaze flicked briefly to Meg.

"When and where was that?"

"As I said, I arrived in the early afternoon on Saturday. Daniel and I shared a late lunch in Amherst."

"Was your husband with you, Mrs. Corey?"

"No, Phillip is currently traveling with some friends. I'm not exactly sure how you could reach him — I believe he's on a boat, although perhaps one of his friends has a cell phone with him. But the point of his trip was to get away from such things, so it may not be turned on."

"We'll come back to that. You say you had lunch with Mr. Weston on Saturday. Then what?"

"He showed me the Amherst campus, where he teaches. We drove around a bit after that. This is what the locals consider prime leaf-viewing season, isn't it? The roads were rather crowded, I thought."

"Yes, there are quite a few tourists around. Where did you go after you went driving?"

"He drove me back to Northampton — I was staying at that lovely hotel in the center of town. We made plans to meet the next morning."

"You didn't have dinner with him?"

"No. He said he had a prior engagement, and in any case I was tired from the drive. I ate at the hotel, and went to bed early."

"Did you see him after that?"

"Yes. He picked me up Sunday morning and we had a late brunch. Then he said he had to prepare for something — a class or a college event, he didn't elaborate — and then he left. We came together again for dinner that night. He saw me back to my hotel afterward, and then he left. He had said he would call yesterday morning, Monday, but I never heard from him. Oh, God," she whispered. "Was he dead by then?"

Meg remained silent, but she was doing the math. What had her mother been doing all day yesterday, before she had appeared at the house? "When exactly did this Daniel Weston die, Detective?"

Marcus seemed startled by Meg's interruption. "His body was discovered yesterday morning, and he'd been dead a few hours. He died late Sunday night. What time did you finish dinner, Mrs. Corey?"

"I'd say around nine."

"Did he mention any other plans for the evening?"

Elizabeth shook her head. "No. I assumed he was going home."

"Do you know his wife?"

"Patricia? No, we've never met. I knew his first wife slightly."

"How would you characterize your relationship with Mr. Weston?"

"He and I were old friends. As was my husband."

"Had you seen him since your grad school days?"

"Actually, no — or at least not for many years. We exchanged holiday cards, but I had little occasion to come up this way. I

23

was quite surprised when I heard from him."

One of Marcus's eyebrows went up a fraction of an inch. "He contacted you?"

"Yes, he did, last week. He said he was curious about how I had changed, and he invited me to come visit. Since I hadn't seen my daughter, Meg, since she moved here to Granford, I thought it was an ideal opportunity to kill two birds with one stone. Oh, that's a poor analogy, isn't it? But my husband was away, I wanted to see what Meg had done with the house, and then there was this unexpected call from a long-lost friend in the same area. I had no other commitments, so I drove up."

Without telling me, Meg thought, but she refrained from voicing that. If Elizabeth was telling the truth, Marcus could no doubt verify her story quickly enough.

If? Did she actually doubt her mother's story? Whatever her other faults, Elizabeth Corey was scrupulously honest, with loved ones and strangers alike, sometimes to the point of insulting them. But there was something off about her mother's attitude, not that Detective Marcus would necessarily notice. But Meg had.

"You don't work outside the home, Mrs. Corey?" Marcus pressed.

"I'm somewhat retired." When Marcus looked confused, she said, "I'm a freelance consultant to nonprofit organizations. I do some grant writing, organize direct mail campaigns, that sort of thing, for those organizations that cannot afford full-time staff. As you might guess, things are a bit slow at the moment, and I have no projects right now. So, if you're asking, there was no reason why I couldn't take time off on the spur of the moment."

"But you hadn't made time before to see your daughter, who's been here for, what, most of the year?"

Meg wanted to see how her mother would respond to this question, since she'd asked herself the same thing.

"I should have. I know she was going through a difficult time — losing her job, moving here, and then finding Chandler Hale the way she did. I'm sure you know about that?" Marcus gave a curt nod, and Elizabeth went on, "But, although it may reflect poorly on me, I wasn't sure what comfort I could offer. I had every confidence that Meg could work her way through whatever problems she faced, and I thought I'd just be in the way."

Gee, thanks. Meg didn't know whether to laugh or cry. She'd been suspected of murder, for God's sake! She'd been stuck in a crumbling barn of a house, with no friends and no income — and her mother had been sure she could manage just fine? Which she had, with no help from her mother. But a little sympathy would have gone a long way. Of course, Elizabeth could've argued that Meg hadn't even told her what was going on until after it was resolved, so maybe they could share the blame. And truth be told, she hadn't ever picked up the phone and actually invited her mother to visit. Meg sighed involuntarily.

"Did you have something to add, Margaret?" her mother asked, turning toward her.

"No. But Mother's right, Detective. We aren't overly close, and the fact that she would be in the area without telling me isn't particularly surprising. And she did arrive here last night."

"Huh," Detective Marcus said. He turned back to Elizabeth. "Is there anything else you can tell me about Weston? Did he seem nervous? Worried?"

Elizabeth shrugged. "Not that I could tell. But bear in mind, Detective, I hadn't seen the man for decades. All I can tell you is that we had a very pleasant time together."

Meg realized that they had ignored one important question. "Detective, I take it Daniel wasn't found at home? Where *was* he found? His office?"

Marcus hesitated, as if trying to decide how much to say. "He was found at a farm stand on the south end of Amherst."

Meg couldn't restrain herself. "A farm stand? How did he die?" She was almost afraid to hear the answer.

"An apparent heart attack. There were no signs of violence, but since it was an unattended death, there will be an autopsy to confirm that. Did he mention any health issues, Mrs. Corey? Or say that he was ill?"

Elizabeth cocked her head. "Was he?"

"Not according to his most recent physical, a couple of months ago. He was in good shape for a man of his age."

Elizabeth shook her head. "We did joke about how well preserved we both were, after all these years. Surely his wife would know if he'd had a heart condition, though?"

"We're talking to her. What are your plans now?"

"I thought I'd stay and visit with my daughter. Are you telling me that I shouldn't leave town, if that's the correct phrase?"

"I'd appreciate it if you'd make yourself

available if any further questions arise, but I'm sure your story will be corroborated."

Detective Marcus stood up, and handed Elizabeth a card. "You can reach me here if anything else occurs to you. Thank you for your time. Meg, will you see me out?"

"Sure." Meg stood and sent a confused glance at her mother, who remained in her seat, looking blank. She led the way back to the front door.

On the stoop outside, Marcus turned to her. "Is there anything else I should know?"

"Like what? I had no idea that my mother was anywhere near here until she appeared last night."

"Do you believe her?"

"About Daniel Weston?" Meg hesitated. Marcus might lack sensitivity, but he was an honest policeman, and there was little point in prevaricating with him. And if he sensed any inconsistencies in Elizabeth's story or behavior, there was probably a good reason. "What are you asking? Do you think they were having an affair? I doubt it, but then I would, wouldn't I? She's my mother. She's never mentioned him to me, to the best of my recollection, but I haven't lived at home for years, and I don't know why she would talk to me about old friends that she'd lost touch with. You can't possibly think that my mother had anything to do with this man's death, can you?"

"I'm just taking care of loose ends. You have to admit our finding your mother's name on Weston's phone was a little unexpected."

He had a good point, Meg thought. Her local reputation was getting murkier by the day. Might as well face this head-on. "Detective, do you have any reason to believe that Daniel Weston was murdered?"

"Based on the physical evidence we have? No, but the autopsy's not done yet. He was found in an unlikely place, one that he had no connection to. I wanted to talk to your mother to establish a time line. She was apparently the last person to see or talk to him. Now we know that he died sometime after nine."

Had someone drawn him to that farm stand? "You said he was a college professor? Why would anyone want him dead?"

"Meg, we've known about his death for barely twenty-four hours. We still have a lot of questions. You'll let me know if your mother has anything to add to her story?"

His use of the term "story" made it sound as though he didn't believe Elizabeth. Truthfully, neither did Meg: her mother wouldn't lie, but Meg was sure that she hadn't told

Marcus everything. But for once Meg intended to ask. "Of course."

Meg watched to make sure that his car had left her driveway before turning back and heading for the kitchen. She was interrupted by Bree's disembodied voice. "Is he gone yet?"

Meg looked up the stairwell. "Yes."

Bree rounded the corner and came down the stairs. "I do *not* like that man."

Meg shrugged. "He was reasonably polite. He's just doing his job, you know. How much did you hear?"

"Dead prof in Amherst, lots of mystery. And your mom knew the dead guy."

"Apparently she did. Are you heading up to the orchard?"

"Yeah. Don't take too long — we need all the hands we can get right now."

"I know. I'll just see which way the wind is blowing with my mother. She didn't tell me she was coming, and I have no idea what her plans are."

In the kitchen, Elizabeth was still at the table, her cold coffee sitting unfinished in front of her. She was staring at nothing in particular, but she roused herself when Meg entered the room. "Well, that was interesting."

"I take it you've never talked with the

police before?" Meg asked. She wished she could say the same thing.

"No, I've never had need to. Poor Daniel."

Meg sat down opposite her and struggled to contain her temper. "Mother, are you going to tell me what's going on?"

"Margaret, I don't like your tone of voice."

Meg refused to back down. "Mother, you're not answering my question. You knew Daniel Weston?"

"Yes, I did. So did your father."

"Does Daddy know you're here?"

"No. As I told that detective, your father is out of phone communication — by choice. My trip up here was rather unexpected, and I haven't talked to him recently. And before you ask, no, we're not having any problems. We've taken separate vacations before. I understood why he wanted to go off with his friends, and I'm sure he would have understood why I came up here. He would have been happy to come along, if he'd been around."

Meg wondered whether she'd get a straight answer to anything. She didn't have time for this, not now. The harvest was in full swing, and as Bree had said, not for the first time, Meg needed to be up there picking or hauling or doing any one of the other

31

tasks involved in getting the apples down from the trees to the holding chambers in her barn, and then to the local farmers' markets that were selling them. She did not have the time to tease answers out of her mother, who was trying her best both to evade them and to convey the impression that Meg's questions were offensive. No way was this the time to pick a fight.

"Mother, I'm delighted that you've come to visit. But unfortunately, this is the busiest couple of months of the entire year for me in the orchard, and I won't have a lot of time to entertain you."

"Surely you can pry a *little* time loose?"

"Mother, are you listening? I am a working farmer, and this is my harvest season. I'm lucky if I have time to eat."

"You said you were out last night."

"Yes, but that was a special case, which I'll be happy to tell you about later. Right now I've got to play catch-up, and Bree and the men are already at work up the hill." Meg stood up. "I'm sorry, but as I said before, if you'd given me a little advance warning, I might have been able to arrange things better. For now, you'll just have to entertain yourself. Are you planning to stay here?"

"I've checked out of the hotel, if that's

what you're asking. But if I'm not wel-come . . ."

"Mother, of course you're welcome to stay. But you'll have to fend for yourself for today. We can talk later."

Elizabeth sighed. "I understand. Would you like me to prepare dinner?"

"That would be nice. But make plenty — I don't know what Bree's plans are. Do you need me to tell you where the market is? Because I don't think I have much in the fridge."

"Darling, I have managed quite well since before you were born. I'm sure I can find whatever I need."

"Fine. See you later." Meg left before she managed to say something she would regret. Although, she told herself as she marched up the hill toward the orchard, none of her words had been aimed to hurt; she had simply been stating facts. She was incred-ibly busy, and she was needed in the or-chard. It was her business now, and she couldn't just lay it aside to humor her visi-tor. Elizabeth was just going to have to ac-cept that.

But where did the dead man fit?

3

The sun was high overhead, and Meg was taking a long drink from a water bottle after depositing her most recent load of apples into the bin when she saw Seth heading toward her, weaving his way through the orchard rows. She welcomed a few moments of rest, although none of the other pickers, including Bree, had slowed their pace. Meg wasn't in the kind of shape to keep up with them — yet — but she was now developing arm muscles that she had never seen before. She was still trying to find the rhythm of it. The experienced Jamaican pickers she had hired had been working with apples, and with each other, for years and they handled things quickly and efficiently. She, on the other hand, had to keep asking what to do, but so far she hadn't messed up too badly. At least she was careful with the apples: bruises diminished their value.

"Is the coast clear?" Seth called out when he was in earshot.

"What do you mean? Is my mother lurking behind a tree? I don't think so. Why, did she scare you last night?"

He smiled. "No, but I wanted to give the two of you a chance to talk before I barged in." Seth paused in the shade of a tree. "What did you do with her?"

"I left her parked in the kitchen, and told her I had to get to work."

He studied her expression. "Trouble?"

Meg looked around briefly, then led him over a couple of rows, out of hearing of the rest of the crew. "Last night I just pointed her toward the guest room and went to bed. I figured I'd have time to find out what she was up to this morning, but we were interrupted by Detective Marcus."

"What? What did he want from you?"

"Not from me — from my mother. Turns out he found her phone number in the cell phone of a dead man."

"You've got to be kidding. Who was it?"

"One Daniel Weston. I understand he was a professor at Amherst College, and as it turns out, he was an old college buddy of my parents. My mother snuck up here this weekend to see him."

"What do you mean, 'to see him'?"

Meg sighed. "I really don't know. Before you ask, my father is apparently off yachting with some friends and he's not answering his cell phone. From what I gather, he doesn't know anything at all about this rendezvous."

"Wow," Seth said.

"Yeah, wow. I felt like an idiot admitting to Marcus that my mother hadn't even let me know she was in the area." *Instead she had slipped into town and somehow gotten herself involved in . . . something.*

"Do you really think she was up here for . . ." Seth stopped, at a loss for words.

Meg had to smile at his confusion. "A rendezvous with an old flame? I don't know, and I haven't had time to really talk with her — not that we ever shared anything like this. But if I had to guess, something odd was going on. I think she felt pretty stupid, too — getting caught sneaking around like a teenager."

"Are you speaking from experience?"

"Hardly. I led a blameless life in my younger years. I spent most of my time studying. You?"

"For me it was sports. So what are you going to do now?"

"Pick apples." Meg laughed shortly. "You mean about my mother? Have a heart-to-heart talk, I guess. Welcome to my world, Mom: here's your first body. I have to admit that I have real trouble imagining her mixed up in something nasty, but I'd rather find out before Marcus does."

"What's he calling this?"

"I'd guess a suspicious death. The immediate cause of death was apparently a heart attack, but Weston was found someplace that makes no sense. Where my mother fits in all this, I have no idea."

"You want me to stop by later?" He cocked one eyebrow at her.

Meg considered Seth's offer, looking at him in the dappled light that filtered through the trees. She wasn't used to having someone around to rely on, and it was sweet of him to want to help. But much as she wanted his support, Meg had to believe that her mother would be more forthcoming without an audience. "Thanks for offering, but I think I'd better handle this on my own for now. I think I should talk to my mother about Daniel Weston before I make things any more complicated. Are you okay with that?"

"I am a very patient man. Let me know if you need me for anything." He turned and headed for his office by the barn.

"Yo, Meg — quit lollygagging! We've got

to finish up this row today," Bree called out.

"Yes, boss!" Meg yelled back, and went up the hill. As she settled the straps of her picker's bag on her shoulders once again and trudged back to the line of McIntoshes, she wondered what it was her mother wasn't telling her. The timing was lousy: if she hadn't wanted her mother as a guest, she certainly didn't want her here as a murder suspect. No, that was ridiculous. There was no way on earth her mother could have been party to a murder. Too violent, too messy, too . . . unseemly. Murders did not attach themselves to Nice People, and Elizabeth definitely considered herself — and by extension, her husband and her only child — in that category. It was just a peculiar coincidence. Wasn't it?

It was after five when Meg and Bree came back down the hill from the orchard. They'd shared a quick lunch in the orchard with the other workers, and Meg hadn't seen any sign of her mother, not that she'd paid a lot of attention, and the house was out of sight from much of the orchard. Meg was exhausted, and the thought of not having to cook dinner was appealing — although the other issues she and her mother would have to get into were less so. One step at a time.

"Listen, Bree," Meg began.

"You can have the shower first," Bree said.

"Thanks, but it's not about that. Mother said she'd make dinner, and you should join us, but she and I have got to talk about Marcus and this death, so do you mind clearing out afterward? My mother's a pretty private person, so I don't think she'll say much with you around. Sorry."

"I hear you. Sure, no problem. I can update our records, run payroll — I've got my laptop. So you don't have any idea what's going on?"

"Not at all."

They reached the house, and Meg led the way to the back door. When she pulled it open, she found her mother standing in the middle of the kitchen, wearing an apron Meg didn't remember she had. "Hello, darling," Elizabeth greeted her. "Dinner will be ready shortly. Hello, Bree, is it? You're staying, too, right? I made plenty."

"Yeah, sure," Bree said, then ducked up the back stairs to her room.

"I'm going to grab a shower," Meg told her mother, "and then I think Bree will after, so we'll be back down in a few minutes."

"That's fine, dear. It's not like I made a soufflé."

Meg made her way around to the front stairs, and checked the mailbox outside the front door. Upstairs in her bedroom, she stripped off her dusty work clothes — noting that the hamper was overflowing again and that if she didn't do laundry tonight she'd have to recycle something for picking tomorrow — grabbed a towel, and headed for the shower. She kept it brief, mindful of Bree waiting and the limited supply of hot water, then dressed quickly in jeans and a clean T-shirt, and went back down to the kitchen. In the interval her mother had set the dining room table. "We usually just eat in the kitchen, Mother," Meg said when she walked in.

"I thought we should officially celebrate my visit. And it's such a lovely room, isn't it? That woodwork is amazing — that wainscoting is made up of single boards, isn't it?"

Meg sat down at the table. "Yes, it is — probably original to the house, around 1760. And the trees it's built from most likely came from across the meadow there. What are we eating?"

"You weren't joking that you didn't have much in the house to eat, so I found the market and replenished your bare larder. It's a chicken-and-rice casserole."

"Sounds good. So, how long do you think you're planning to stay?" Meg realized that Marcus had more or less told Elizabeth to keep herself available.

"For a few days, if you don't mind. I'm sorry I didn't consult with you before — that was rude of me. It hadn't occurred to me how busy you might be right now."

That was as close to an apology as she was going to get, Meg realized. It also omitted any mention of Daniel Weston and the real purpose of her mother's trip. "If you'd asked me a few weeks ago, even *I* wouldn't have realized how busy I would be."

"But, darling, aren't you management? Can't you hire people to do the heavy work for you?"

Meg sighed. "This is kind of a shoestring operation right now. Yes, I've hired pickers, but I need to know about all aspects of this business. Besides, I'm enjoying the work."

"You look a little tired. And please take care of your skin, out in the sun all day."

"Yes, Mother." Meg smiled: at least her mother hadn't brought up her haircut, or lack of. Yet.

Meg had heard the water stop running, and Bree came down the stairs soon after, her wet hair slicked back. "Smells great."

"You must be hungry, working all day like

41

that," Elizabeth welcomed her. "Meg tells me you're the orchard manager? What does that mean?"

That question, and others about the orchard, carried them through dinner. At her mother's urging, Meg accepted a glass of wine — but only one, since she wanted to keep her head clear for the conversation she knew was coming. Bree ate quickly, then excused herself, and Meg found herself alone with her mother at the dining room table, in the gathering darkness. Elizabeth had found some candles somewhere, which now provided the only light in the room. Meg fought drowsiness — the exertions of the day, and the food and the wine, were catching up to her. She knew she had better speak up before she fell asleep where she sat.

"Okay, Mother, what's really going on?"

Elizabeth toyed with her fork, turning it over and over in her hands. "I suppose I could pretend that I don't know what you're talking about."

"Sorry, that won't fly. There was a detective here this morning, and I happen to know he's good at what he does. He tracked you down, didn't he? And if there's anything else to find out, he will. What's the story with Daniel Weston?"

Elizabeth sighed. "Maybe we should sit in more comfortable chairs. And I'd like another glass of wine. You?"

Meg shook her head. When her mother stood up, Meg did, too, and they carried their dishes into the kitchen.

"Oh, dear — perhaps I should clean up first," Elizabeth said.

Meg took the plates out of Elizabeth's hands and set them on the counter. "No, Mother. You're stalling. Get your wine and we can sit in the parlor. I really haven't had a chance to talk to you since you arrived."

"That sounds lovely, dear," Elizabeth replied.

Meg snagged the half-empty bottle of wine and refilled her mother's glass, then led the way into the front parlor. On the east side of the house, it remained cool during the day, but Meg spent little time there, especially now during the harvest. The September dusk didn't provide much light, so Meg turned on a lamp. She was acutely aware of the shabby furniture — inherited from past tenants and not yet replaced — and the flaking paint and sooty fireplace. The old clock hanging over the mantelpiece — the one piece she had acquired herself — ticked steadily, but it wasn't enough to make the room even come close to meeting her mother's standards.

They sat. Lolly wandered in, looked cautiously at Elizabeth, then jumped into Meg's lap and curled into a ball. Elizabeth settled herself gingerly in an overstuffed armchair and looked around. "This is a charming space — so much potential. Have you thought about what you want to do with it? You know, your grandmother's wing chair would look lovely in here. Does the fireplace work?"

Another diversion. "Not without a good cleaning, which probably hasn't been done in a century. Mother, look, I'm happy to have you here, even if I'm run off my feet with the harvest. I wish I could spend time planning color schemes for the house, or shopping, or eating lunches with you, but this isn't the best time. Right now I'd like you to explain what's going on."

Elizabeth looked at her hands, folded in her lap. "It's so easy to misinterpret, as I'm sure that detective has done."

Misinterpret what? Having an affair? Being found out? Or was there something worse? And what would be worse? Meg took pity on her mother. "Why don't you tell me about how you knew Daniel, when you first met."

"I told you, your father and I knew Daniel when we were all living in Cambridge," she began. "He and your father were in graduate school, and I was working at a string of temporary jobs while waiting for Phillip to finish. I've told you this before, haven't I?"

"Yes," Meg said cautiously, not wanting to derail the story.

"Daniel was getting his PhD in English literature, and your father was getting his law degree. I forget how we all met — probably some grad-student party, where everybody brought a bottle of cheap wine and a bag of chips. That was all we could afford in those days, but we did have fun. Of course, nobody bothered to talk to me, because I wasn't a student like them. My undergraduate degree didn't count for much, and besides, I was a woman."

Meg couldn't contain herself. "And that made a difference then? What about the whole feminist thing?"

Elizabeth smiled ruefully. "We talked about it a lot, but face it — the men were still in charge. I'm not sure that's changed yet. In any event, I was dating your father, and we met Daniel, and the three of us all hit it off. We spent a lot of time together for a couple of years, before your father and I married. Daniel was unattached for a long

time, although I never understood why —
he was an attractive man, and interesting,
and funny. But no woman ever stuck for
long, and I think he was lonely."

"He's married now?" Meg asked. Or was,
until this past weekend.

"Yes. To his second wife. We went to his
first wedding — that was a few years after
we'd left Cambridge, and we were still in
touch, though we hardly knew the woman
he married. I read in your father's alumni
magazine of his second marriage, but I
never knew her at all."

"So?" Meg prompted.

"We drifted apart. I'm sure you've seen
the same thing in your own life, since college. Your father and I married, we had you,
he changed jobs a few times, moving up the
ladder. A very ordinary story."

Meg looked surreptitiously at the clock —
it was getting late, and she wanted desper-
ately to fall into bed. At the same time, she
hated to interrupt her mother's story.

"So why did Daniel call you?" she
prompted.

Elizabeth looked directly at her daughter
for the first time. "It was out of the blue. I
hadn't had even a card from him since, oh,
I don't remember when. Years. I knew he
was teaching somewhere, but I couldn't

have said where. Your father was away, and I was relishing the freedom — you know, no meals to worry about, and I could stay up half the night reading without bothering him. When Daniel called, he said he wanted to catch up, and could we get together? I asked, when, and he said, how about now?"

It sounded plausible enough to Meg — barely.

"I told him your father was out of town for a few days and perhaps we could defer it until we were both available," Elizabeth went on. "Daniel said he was disappointed, but why didn't I come on my own? He was insistent, and I didn't see why I shouldn't. So I agreed."

Why the urgency, after all these years? Meg wondered. "So you drove up. Why didn't you call me?"

Elizabeth looked away. "I'm not really sure. Daniel and I had left things kind of open-ended, and I didn't know how much time we would want to spend together. So I kept my options open, you could say."

Something wasn't right here. "Did you sleep with him?"

"Margaret!" Her mother stood up and began pacing. "You have no right to ask me — your mother! — a question like that!"

"You haven't answered me."

"No, I did not! Nor did I come up here with the intention of . . . doing that. I just wanted to see an old friend, period."

Was she telling the truth? Meg had no idea. "Mother, listen — Daniel Weston is dead. You were with him shortly before he died. Is there anything — *anything* — that you know that might be a factor in his death?"

"No! We had a delightful time catching up. He was a perfect gentleman. He inquired about your father. There was nothing out of the ordinary, and no, he didn't invite me to his house or follow me to my hotel room, and we did not sleep together. How can you think such a thing?"

"With difficulty," Meg said. She hauled herself to her feet. "Mother, I'm sure we have more to say, but I'm tired and tomorrow will be another long day. But you have to recognize that Detective Marcus is not going to let this go until he figures out what happened, and he's got you in his sights. So if you're hiding something, please don't. I'm going to go to bed, and I'll see you in the morning." Meg turned toward the stairs.

"Meg, there's nothing to tell!" Elizabeth threw at her retreating back.

She stopped and turned back to look at

48

her mother. "Then there's no problem, is there? Good night."

4

Despite the emotional confrontation with her mother, Meg had no trouble sleeping. She had more trouble rousing herself the next morning, but she was determined to pull her weight in the orchard. In a way her mother had been right: technically, she didn't *have* to do the manual work. But she really didn't think she was cut out to sit back and act as overseer, and besides, she wanted to understand all parts of the business, even the sweaty, messy ones. Plus, an extra set of hands was always needed. Oops — she had forgotten to do the laundry. She found a clean T-shirt in a drawer and shook out the dusty jeans she had worn the day before and pulled them on.

When she opened the door to her bedroom, she stopped for a moment, listening. Meg could hear Bree in the bathroom down the hall. The door to the guest room across the hall was open, and the room was empty, so her mother must have gone downstairs already. Elizabeth had always been an early riser. Squaring her shoulders, Meg marched down the stairs, opening the front door to assess the weather and let some cool air into the house, then went to the kitchen. Her mother was seated at the kitchen table with a mug of coffee in front of her. It took Meg a moment to realize that the dirty dishes from the night before had vanished, save for a neat stack gleaming in the dish drainer. In fact, all the counters were clean and clear, more so than they had been for a couple of weeks — since the harvest started.

"Good morning," Meg said cautiously as she helped herself to coffee.

"Good morning, dear."

Meg sat down. "Thank you for cleaning up the kitchen."

"You know I hate a messy kitchen. But I'm sure you haven't had time to pay much attention to such things lately."

Was that a dig? "No, I haven't. I've had a lot to learn in a short time, and I'm still playing catch-up."

Her mother looked out the window, at the blue sky that promised another clear day, ideal for harvesting. "Meg, I thought it over last night, and I'm not sure it's a good idea for me to remain in this house."

"What?" Meg was startled.

"Margaret, I hadn't realized how busy you are. I'm sorry if I didn't appreciate that before. But if you're so distracted, we won't have any real time together. And if your nerves are so frayed, things may be said that will be regretted later."

Meg took a moment to parse that statement. Trust her mother to put it in as oblique a way as humanly possible. And also to put Meg in the wrong — too busy to spend time with her mother, too tactless to hold a civil conversation with her. "I'm sorry if I said things that disturbed you, Mother, but you have to realize that when the police are involved, there is no such thing as privacy. I'm just asking the same kind of questions that the detective will, sooner or later."

Elizabeth looked dismayed. "I thought that detective said that Daniel had a heart attack. That shouldn't be too complicated."

"No, but heart attacks can be brought on by any number of things, not all of them natural."

Elizabeth laid her hand over her heart, as if in sympathy for Daniel. "How terrible. Daniel seemed so vibrant, so excited. I mean, he was just past sixty!" She straightened in her chair. "All the more reason I should remove myself. I don't want to bring any part of this down on you. And I think I need some time to think things through."

Now, what could she mean by that? Meg wondered. "I think that Detective Marcus wanted you to stay around, at least for a few days. Where will you go?"

"Margaret, I'm a grown woman. I'm perfectly capable of finding a place to stay. Although that lovely hotel in Northampton was a bit steep in price."

"Mother, it's prime tourist season around here — the trees are turning, and all the college kids are coming back to school with their parents after the summer break. It might not be as easy as you think." Meg thought for a moment, and was struck by what she felt was a brilliant solution: Seth's sister, Rachel Dickinson. "I have a friend in Amherst who runs a bed-and-breakfast."

"Won't she be booked as well?"

"Let me see if she can squeeze you in. How long should I tell her you'll be staying?"

"I suppose through the rest of the week. Is it a nice place?" Elizabeth asked.

"Very nice — I've stayed there myself. Let me give her a call now."

Meg grabbed the handset from her land line phone and retreated to the front parlor, away from her mother. She checked her watch before dialing: 7:30 a.m. Early, but Rachel had kids to get off to school, not to mention breakfasts to prepare for her guests, so she'd be up. Meg hit the speed-dial button.

Rachel answered on the second ring, sounding breathless. "Hi, Meg. What's up?"

"I won't keep you long — I know things must be crazy. I've got a problem: my mother is in town, and she's in a snit and has decided she doesn't want to stay with me because I'm too busy working to spend time with her. Is there any possible way you can take her for a few days?"

"Oh, Meg — we're kind of packed to the rafters, but so is everyone else in the valley. You can't patch things up?"

"Not quickly. Look, I wouldn't ask if it weren't important. An Amherst professor named Daniel Weston, an old friend of my mother's, was found dead of heart attack. My mother had come up to visit him a couple of days ago."

That bit of news stunned Rachel into silence, if briefly. "Oh, my. Were they . . . ?"

"I don't know, and she won't say. But our friend Detective Marcus has asked her to stay around for a few days, so I can't just send her home to New Jersey."

"I see your problem. Huh. Well, let me check my bookings and see what I can juggle. I'll find a way."

"Bless you. But, um, I haven't exactly told her about me and Seth. I mean, she met him when she arrived, but she doesn't know . . ."

"I get it. So I shouldn't tell her I'm his sister, right? But you know, that could be a good thing. Maybe I can talk about how great he is, and she won't know that I know . . . you know what I mean. But don't worry, I'll keep my mouth shut about the two of you."

"Thanks, Rachel, and I owe you big-time. Can I send her over later today?"

"Let me clear out the breakfast crowd and clean up the rooms. Say, after ten?"

"Great. And let me know if you pick up any interesting tidbits around town about the professor, will you?"

"Daniel Weston, right? Sure. I'll see if anyone in Amherst is buzzing. See you soon!" Rachel hung up.

Meg returned triumphantly to the kitchen. "All set. You can go over after ten."

Bree came bounding down the back stairs and started to fill a carry-mug with coffee. "Morning, Mrs. Corey. Meg, you about ready? We need to use all the good weather we can."

"Do you actually pick all the apples by hand?" Elizabeth asked.

"We do," Bree responded promptly. "This place really isn't big enough to justify a mechanical harvester, and besides, they're harder on the apples. So we handpick, then take them down to the barn and sort them, then deliver them to markets or hold them for a few days."

"My word, I had no idea," Elizabeth replied.

"Most people don't," Bree said. "They just go to the store and buy them. Meg, I'm going to go on up the hill. Join me as soon as you can, okay? Bye, Mrs. Corey." Bree grabbed a couple of store-bought donuts and her mug and went out the back door, the screen slamming behind her.

"Then I'd better let you go," Elizabeth said.

"Mother, at least let me show you around, tell you what I've done since I got here," Meg protested.

"If you're sure you can spare the time, I would be happy to see the property."

Meg drained her coffee mug. "Let's go." When her mother arose, and carefully placed her mug in the kitchen sink, Meg led the way to the front of the house.

"How much do you remember, from the times you've been here before?" Meg began.

"Very little, I'm afraid. I certainly wasn't looking at the architecture at the time. My general impression was that it was a nice, typical colonial house, and that back up the line somewhere an ancestor had build it, or bought it, and his descendants had lived in it ever since."

"Yes, the last two of the family were Lula and Nettie Warren, the ones who left it to you. Did you ever explore our genealogy?"

Elizabeth shook her head. "Not really. I wasn't particularly interested. It's too bad — I suppose I should have asked the sisters more about their past, and now it's too late. I was certainly surprised when I heard from their attorney."

"And you weren't curious enough to come up and see the house then?"

"That was, what, twenty years ago? It was a busy time. The attorney — I can't even remember his name, although his firm was still handling the rentals until you moved in — offered to find tenants, and I just said yes. Until you needed a place to go."

Another minefield that Meg didn't want to explore at the moment. The circumstances under which she'd lost her job still smarted, even now. "Well, luckily for us, nobody messed with the place much. Most of what I've had to do has been basic maintenance, and some systems needed replacing. Like the plumbing — that was kind of urgent. The furnace is pretty shaky, and I don't know if it will make it through another winter, but I want to see what kind of income I can get from the orchard before I lay out a big chunk for that."

"Can you actually support yourself this way, Meg?"

Meg checked quickly to see if her mother was being sarcastic, but she appeared to be honestly interested. "To tell the truth, I don't know. On paper, if everything goes right, after expenses — the short answer is yes. But that's going to take some luck and a lot of hard work. Talk to me in a few months and I'll have a better idea."

"I must say I'm surprised to see you doing something so, um, physical."

"You mean, rather than using my well-trained financial mind? Mother, I need every skill I've got to make this work. It's a business, and it involves cost estimates and marketing plans and personnel issues. Sure, I get my hands dirty, but it's a time-honored profession. I know — sometimes I have trouble believing I'm a farmer. If I'd known I was going to end up doing this, I'd have planned my life a bit differently. But I love the challenge, and I'm getting very fond of the town, and the people here. They've been great to me." She hoped having helped to birth the much-needed restaurant went some way toward repaying Granford for welcoming her.

Elizabeth studied her face but didn't comment. Finally she said, "Walk me through the place, then. When was it built?"

"Around 1760, as far as I can tell. I've been going through documents from the Historical Society here . . ." The building tour took another half hour. Meg was pleasantly surprised when Elizabeth was willing to visit the barn and outbuildings. She felt a small spurt of pride as she described the construction of the temperature-controlled compartments where she stored her apples.

"How large is the property again?" Elizabeth asked, shading her eyes as she admired the view.

"Fifteen acres in apples, and a few more for the house lot. It was a lot bigger once — over a hundred acres — but parts were sold off over time. I'm also the proud owner of the Great Meadow there — that's a fancy name for wetlands, but at least no one will build on it."

"And these are your goats." Elizabeth approached their enclosure cautiously. Dorcas and Isabel crowded against the fence, intrigued by the newcomer. "Do they smell?"

"Males do, but these are females."

Elizabeth turned around to scan the sweep of hill and house and barn. "I had no idea . . ."

"Neither did I when you sent me out here."

"Poor dear. If I had known what I was getting you into, I probably would have told that lawyer just to sell the place and be done with it."

"I'm glad you didn't," Meg replied, surprising herself. "Maybe I won't be doing this forever, but I'm enjoying it for now. You're sure you don't want to stay, Mother?"

"No, dear. I'd just be in the way here, and frankly, I'd like some time alone. When you're married, that's a rare treat. If you can spare some time, maybe we can have lunch or dinner together. At that restaurant you mentioned, perhaps?"

"That would be lovely. I'm sorry I'm not being more hospitable, but I do want to spend some time with you." *And I do want to know more about Daniel Weston and whatever it is you're not saying.*

"I'm sure we'll manage something, dear. Now, if you'll just sketch out directions to get to this B and B, I'll be on my way, and you can go pick your apples."

Instructions conveyed, Meg helped her mother load her suitcase — already packed and waiting — into her car and waved her off. She felt both relieved and guilty. Weren't there any mothers and daughters who could carry on an adult relationship without dancing around innuendos and old hurts? She loved her mother, really she did, but that didn't mean they got along well. This current mess just underscored the underlying distance between them, and Meg was having real trouble wrapping her mind around the idea of her mother with Daniel Weston. Elizabeth still had not told the whole truth, which would usually have been fine with Meg — except that Daniel was dead and Detective Marcus was sniffing around. That shifted the priorities.

Meg had one more thing to do before she started picking today. She found her cell phone and called Seth.

"Hi, Meg," he answered in his usual cheery tone. "What's up?"

"I just packed my mother off to Rachel's to stay. It was her idea to go somewhere

61

else — she said staying here made her feel guilty that she was taking up my time, and besides, she wanted some space. But I didn't tell her Rachel was your sister. Does that make me an evil person?"

Seth laughed. "You want Rachel to pump her for information?"

"Look, Rachel is a whole lot better at getting people to open up than I am."

"Meg, she's your mother — you've got too much history together to be open with each other."

Meg felt a stab of relief. "You understand! How do you manage with your mother?"

"Easy. She thinks I'm wonderful, end of story. And I think she's a pretty great lady. Hey, at least your mother is staying in the area for a bit, right? You'll have a chance to work things out."

"I'm glad you think so. Talk to you later — the apples are calling me."

"Go!"

5

If Meg had had time, she would have felt guilty. Had she driven her mother out of the house? Or was it her mother who wanted to escape from her daughter's prying questions? Normally they would have trodden carefully, avoiding any conflicts. Unfortunately this time that wasn't possible. Meg could only hope that Detective Marcus would sort things out quickly and that she and her mother could go back to their usual "don't ask, don't tell" policy of ignoring any important issues.

But right now she had the demanding physical work of apple picking to distract her. Whatever idyllic fantasies she had harbored about the dignity of the Noble Farmer had evaporated fast when she actually started working. Still, as she had told her mother, it was honest work, and it needed doing, even if it was nothing more than removing apples from a tree — carefully, of course, to avoid damaging both the apples and the branches — and taking them down the hill to the barn, and then from the barn to the market. It was also sweaty and boring much of the time. On the plus side, it left her time to think while her hands (and legs and back and every muscle she could name) were busy. On the minus side, most of her thoughts kept veering toward her mother.

She and her mother had always had a distant relationship, and Meg had never really understood why. She knew her parents loved her; she had never been neglected or ignored, and her parents had made sure she'd had every opportunity she could wish for. Meg had attended dance classes, art lessons, horseback riding, martial arts classes, and more. She had tried out more than one instrument in the school orchestra, and then in the marching band — and her parents had been in the audience every time she performed. They had taken family vacations, even to Europe. She had had their attention and their affection.

So why the distance? Why did she and her mother dance around each other like polite strangers most of the time? Meg didn't want a best friend, but she did want some true connection. Meg allowed herself a small

64

spurt of resentment: she had always done what they asked, always been who her parents wanted her to be — performed well in school, had a nice group of appropriate friends. She had never gotten into trouble, never done drugs, never even stayed out past her curfew, for God's sake! So why was her mother so formal with her? And why, Meg asked herself, had she never tried to break through, now that she was an adult?

"Hey, Meg, watch it — you don't have to rip the apples off the tree!" Bree's voice interrupted her internal debate.

"Oh, sorry. I wasn't paying attention. How're we doing overall?"

"The Gravensteins are about done, and Raynard and I think we should wait a couple of days for the Paulareds. So we're good."

"Does that mean maybe I could take a few hours off?"

"To visit with your mother? Sure, no problem. Maybe I'm overstepping here, but that's one uptight lady."

"She is that," Meg admitted. "There's something going on, but she won't tell me what. I keep trying to explain that Detective Marcus is going to ask the same questions. 'How did you know Daniel Weston? What was your relationship with him?' But she

65

just brushes me off."

Bree looked up at Meg, perched on her low ladder. "You think there was something going on?"

Meg shook her head. "I don't even want to go there. But the more she stonewalls Marcus, the worse it will be."

"So does Marcus think . . . ?" Bree asked.

"That it was murder? I don't know. I don't *want* to know. But the fact that a respected professor turned up dead in a remote farmers' market just doesn't seem right, and I'm willing to bet that we'll be hearing from Marcus again. Does Michael have any news contacts in Amherst?"

Bree snorted. "There is no news in Amherst. Haven't you noticed? There are hardly any newspapers anymore. But I'll ask, in case he knows somebody who knows somebody, or something. How about asking Seth?"

"I keep forgetting he went to the college there, although it's been a while."

"He's Seth. He probably has seventeen friends on the staff there."

"True. But I hate to ask him for anything else — he does so much already."

"You got that right. But he seems to like to help, and people talk to him. Marcus hasn't gotten back to your mother?"

"Not that I know of, but she's over at Rachel's now. And he has her cell phone number, so he'll get in touch with her directly if he needs to."

"What about Art Preston?"

"I don't think our local chief of police will be in the loop on this one, since Weston died in Amherst, not Granford." Or had he? Meg didn't recall Marcus saying specifically *where* Weston had actually died. "Maybe I should touch base with Art, just in case. He couldn't know any less than I do."

"Finish this tree, and you can call it a day," Bree said.

Half an hour later Meg deposited the rest of her day's assignment of apples in the large bin nearby and went down the hill to the house. Inside it was pleasantly cool, after a day spent in the sun — September nights did help, even if the days remained hot and sunny. She picked up the phone and dialed the number for the police station, identified herself, and asked for Chief Preston.

"Oh, hi, Meg," the person on the desk replied. "He just walked out of here with Seth Chapin. You want me to buzz him?"

"No, don't bother. I've got Seth's cell number. Thanks."

She tried Seth, who answered quickly. "Art and I were thinking of heading over to your place — we figured you'd want hear what little he knows about this Amherst murder. Are you back at the house?" he said.

"Yes, but give me time to grab a shower before you show up, please!"

"No problem. We'll pick up something to drink along the way."

When he hung up, Meg dashed for the shower.

She was downstairs wearing clean clothes, her hair damp, when Art and Seth pulled in. Despite the matters that had led to her introduction to the local chief of police, she counted Art Preston more as a friend than as an officer these days. He in turn was willing to trust her with information that lay outside of what was released to the public — if and when he had any. As a small-town police chief, he wasn't always included in investigations outside of his jurisdiction, and he and Detective Marcus were not friendly.

"Hey, Meg," he called out when he saw her at the back door. "We didn't know what you had, so we brought beer, wine, and a gallon of iced tea."

"Right now I'm parched, so I'll go with the tea. Are you off-duty, Art?"

"I am. I've got to get home by six or the wife'll skin me alive, but I knew you'd be calling me sooner or later about this Weston death, so I figured I'd beat you to it. And here we are."

"Thank you. I just called your office and they said you'd left with Seth. Sit — I'll get some glasses."

The two men settled themselves in the Adirondack chairs that overlooked the Great Meadow, and Meg ducked inside for some glasses. When she returned, she began, "So, what can you tell me?"

Art sighed. "Unfortunately, not much. Here's what I've got." He pulled a small notebook out of his shirt pocket. "Weston, Daniel. Age sixty-two. Full professor in the English department at Amherst College. Tenured. Lives in Amherst, on the fringes of town. Married, second wife — they've been together about ten years now. A couple of grown sons from his first marriage, living in different places around the country. Well liked by his colleagues, happy with his wife. Financially secure, or as secure as you get these days. No known evil habits, vices, scandals — doesn't mess with students of either gender, or anyone else, as far as anybody knows."

"He sounds like a sterling character," Meg commented. "Our friend Detective Marcus told me he died of a heart attack, but in a rather unlikely location. Has Marcus shared anything with you, Art?"

"He hasn't, and last I heard the medical examiner hadn't issued any information."

"How long does an autopsy take?" Meg asked.

"It's probably done, but that doesn't mean they broadcast the results. Anyway, I can tell you that Weston was found in the cider house adjacent to Dickinson's Farm Stand, maybe five miles from here. It's just over the ridge north of Granford. You've probably been by it without paying any attention."

"On the contrary, I know it pretty well — they sell my apples. Nice old-timey place, right? The cider house is that little building off to the right?"

Art leaned back in his seat and studied the ceiling. "That's the one. The stand stays open late, until about eight, to catch the tourists these days. But Weston apparently paid a visit to the farm stand sometime after that."

"Alone?" Meg asked.

"Hard to say. His car was sitting in the lot there. Weston was found on the floor of the cider room. Just crumpled up like he'd fallen."

Meg and Seth exchanged bewildered

glances. "Why there?"

Art shook his head. "Don't know. Not much to work with, is it? Maybe he was just driving by and needed to take a leak — sorry — and that was the first place he passed."

"Was it locked?"

"Are you asking, did he have to break in? No. What's to steal?"

"So no physical assault. Poison?"

Seth laughed. "Somebody lured the professor to an empty cider house in order to inject him with an undetectable poison? Kind of far-fetched, don't you think?"

"Humor me — I'm desperate." Meg smiled at him. "Does the place have a ghost? Maybe he was scared to death."

"Don't mention that idea to Detective Marcus."

"Not likely." Meg went on, "Did he have a cell phone? Oh, that's right — that's how they found Mother. So he could have called for help if he thought he was having a heart attack, but didn't. Was he robbed?"

"His wallet was in his pocket, along with his car keys," Art replied.

"This is ridiculous!" Meg stood up and began pacing. "There's no reason for Daniel Weston to have been there, and no way to find out why he was. Or whether my mother was with him." Meg turned to Seth. "Seth, you went to Amherst College. Did you ever run into Professor Weston?"

"I've been trying to remember — I'd have to check, but I may have taken a class with him. If I did, he doesn't stand out in my memory. Probably just as well. I could do without Marcus asking me about him."

"Where does that leave the investigation, Art?" Meg asked.

Art sighed. "The state police are going through the usual routine — talking to his wife, his colleagues, et cetera. The only wild card, unfortunately, is your mother, Meg. I'm sure it's all quite innocent, but an old, uh, friend shows up out of nowhere, after thirty-something years, and bingo, a day later the guy's dead? You have to admit it looks kind of odd."

"I know, but I refuse to believe that my mother had anything to do with his death. It's just a strange coincidence. Or maybe Weston knew he had a terminal illness and wanted to tie up loose ends, say good-bye?"

"Maybe. But we don't know about anything like that. If that's true, the ME should find it, or his wife would know. I'll keep my ear to the ground and see what turns up. Your mother's going to be around for a few days?"

"I think so. But she's not here — she's staying at Seth's sister Rachel's B and B."

Art looked troubled. "Did you have a fight or something?"

"Nothing like that, Art. There's something going on with Mother, but I don't know if it has anything to do with Daniel Weston. I'll see what I can find out, if she'll talk to me."

Art hauled himself out of his chair. "I'd better get home — some back-to-school thing going on tonight. I'll let you know if I hear anything new. Seth, I'll see you."

Meg watched him go. Seth stood up, then walked around behind her, and she felt his hands on her shoulders, kneading. She bent her head forward, stretched the kinks out of her neck. "God, that feels good."

"I guess you've figured out by now that apple picking is hard work."

"Isn't that the truth? There was so much I didn't know when I decided to get into this. But Bree says I can take some time off — something about the next batch of apples not being quite ripe. I'd better go over to Rachel's tomorrow and see if I can smooth ruffled feathers." Meg fell silent, enjoying the feel of Seth's hands — until she realized she was nodding off. "Thanks for bringing Art by. It's kind of weird, being part of whatever is going on but not in it, if you know what I mean."

"Let's hope it can all be explained and you and your mother can stay out of it. Listen, I'll get out of your hair."

"I'd ask you to stay for supper, but I'm bushed. Maybe we could get together tomorrow night?"

"Works for me. Oh, and are you planning to come to the Harvest Festival on Saturday?"

"Maybe, if I remembered what it was. Fill me in?"

"It's an annual celebration of Granford's founding, timed to coincide with the harvest. It's on the town green, and there's something for everyone — food, rides for the kids, music. It's fun. It's on Saturday. And that's also the official kickoff for Granford Grange."

"Oh, right — you did tell me. I'll see if Bree and Raynard will let me play hooky. I take it you're involved in the planning?"

"Of course." Seth planted a kiss on the back of her neck, and withdrew his hands. "Talk to you tomorrow."

When he left, Meg still hadn't found the energy to get out of her chair.

6

At breakfast Meg sat at the kitchen table savoring a leisurely cup of coffee. "Bree, are you sure you don't need me today? I feel guilty just enjoying myself."

Bree snorted. "Hey, when I need you, I'll let you know. Go out and have some fun. See a movie, go to a spa or something. Or maybe you and your mother can smooth things over?"

Meg sighed. "Easier said than done. Bree, how well do you get along with your parents?"

"Good, mostly because I don't see much of them. They're in Jamaica half the time, and I'm here. But I know what you're getting at. I understand why my parents did what they did, leaving me here with my auntie, and I'm grateful. If I hadn't been a resident here, I wouldn't have gotten the education I did. But my auntie was older than my mother, and she had no kids of her own, so she kept me on a short leash. We get on better now than we did when I was in high school, but there were a few rough patches. Doesn't sound like that's your problem with your mother."

Meg wondered just how to explain her problem, either to Bree or to herself. It seemed kind of silly to complain that her parents had been too distant with her. She had had everything she ever wanted, except true warmth. Maybe that's why she was attracted to Seth, because he was so warm and open. And maybe that's why she didn't quite trust him, because she didn't really understand that kind of personality. Had her ex-boyfriend Chandler's distance been what had attracted her to him? *No, Meg, don't go there.* Chandler had been a mistake from the beginning, but that didn't make it a pattern.

"I really don't know what our problem is," she said at last. "Growing pains, I suppose. I've been living my own life for a while, and she's not up to speed on that, which is my fault as much as hers. And now I find that she's been . . . well, not hiding things, just failing to mention them. And I definitely think she's hiding something about Daniel Weston, and I'm almost afraid to find out what."

"Like that she killed him? Ha! If that lady wanted someone dead, she'd hire help, she wouldn't get her hands dirty. She'd probably interview six candidates first, to make sure she was getting the right hit man."

"Bree!" Meg was horrified at the snap judgment of her mother, but couldn't suppress a giggle. Bree was right: Elizabeth was efficient, decisive, and dispassionate. But not a killer, even secondhand. "Okay, I'll go over to Amherst and talk to her. Maybe we can do a girly lunch and some sightseeing."

"Good luck! I'm going to check on our supplies and make a few deliveries. I'll call if anything comes up."

After Bree bustled out, Meg poured another cup of coffee and watched her cat, Lolly, take an intense and thorough bath in the middle of the kitchen floor. It was still too early to head for Amherst, and if she admitted it, she was willing to put off seeing her mother as long as possible, even while admitting that it was the right thing to do. She was interrupted by a knock at the back door: Seth. She stood up to let him in. "Hi," she said. "You're up early. You want coffee?"

"Nope, can't stay. But I was thinking about Daniel Weston last night, after you asked if I knew him, and I realized why the

77

name rang a bell. Here." He held out a magazine, folded open to an inside page.

"What is this?" she asked, taking it from him.

"The Amherst alumni mag from this past summer. For one thing, that's a picture of Weston there."

Meg studied the black-and-white photo, which showed a tall, distinguished-looking man, his hair a mix of dark and gray and slightly too long. He was standing in front of a group, lecturing — apparently about something that excited him, if his smile and his expansive gesture, arms flung wide, were any indication. "Good-looking man, isn't he? Is that what you wanted me to see?"

"No, read on. The article was about this symposium he was organizing to entertain the parents who're bringing their kids to school, kind of to ease the separation by providing activities for each over that first weekend, and then bringing them back together now and then, before sending the parents home."

"So?"

"Weston was the keynote speaker and the main coordinator for the event — this year's is taking place this weekend. It's kind of a mix of entertainment and serious scholarly stuff — some kind of face-off between the

Whitmanites and the Dickinsonophiles about who's the best nineteenth-century American poet. But my point is, don't you think it's odd that he'd pick this week of all weeks to renew contact with your mother? He must have been run off his feet, between the symposium and beginning-of-the-year stuff at the college."

Meg looked at the picture again. "Maybe he was really well organized? Still, you're right. He could have gotten together with Mother over the summer, when things were more peaceful. Why now, I wonder?" *Because Daddy was away?* Meg wondered, then squashed the thought. "I'll see if I can find out from her. I mean, it's possible that he'd been trying to set this up for months, and this was the first time Mother agreed, and he didn't want to miss the opportunity?"

"Maybe," Seth replied. "Ask her. You're going to see her?"

"I thought I'd drive over this morning and offer to take her to lunch. If I call first, she might just say no."

"Don't worry. She's probably as eager to patch things up as you are."

Was she? And "patch" seemed to be an appropriate word: slap some goop over the rift and pretend that nothing had happened.

"Well, I promise I'll try to find out. Thanks for the information anyway. I'll let you know how things turn out."

It was nearly ten before Meg headed north to Amherst, after dressing with deliberation. She didn't want to look too grubby, but neither did she want to seem too dressed up. She wanted to send the message that this was a casual event, no big deal, but at the same time she didn't want to provoke Elizabeth's criticism. Whatever she chose, her mother would notice.

As always, Meg admired Rachel Dickinson's ornate Victorian house turned bed-and-breakfast, looking particularly splendid today against a backdrop of vivid autumn foliage, as she approached it. Her mother's car was parked around the side, and Meg pulled up beside it and parked. She took a deep breath before making her way around to the kitchen entrance toward the rear of the house. She rapped on the frame of the screen door. "Anybody home?" she called out.

"Meg, is that you?" Rachel emerged from the back of the house. "I was just showing your mother some guidebooks on Amherst. Come on in."

Meg complied. In a low voice Meg said,

"How's the weather?" nodding toward the front room.

"Partly sunny. Don't worry," Rachel said in a similarly low voice. "We've been having a nice time, but she does seem a bit down. Come on back." Rachel led the way through the kitchen, and Meg followed dutifully.

Elizabeth looked up when she entered the room. Meg was startled to see that her mother seemed to have aged overnight. What had Daniel been to her? More than an old friend, at least once upon a time. But now was not the time to probe. "Meg, darling, are you sure you can spare the time from your orchard?"

Meg refused to look for sarcasm in her mother's comment. "Apparently. Today I'm between ripenings, according to Bree, although that can change daily. I wondered if you'd like to have lunch, and maybe I could show you a bit of Amherst?" If Weston hadn't already shown her the sights.

"That would be delightful, but as it happens, Daniel's memorial service is this morning."

How did she know? Had Rachel told her? "And you're going?" Meg said, trying to keep her tone neutral. She wasn't sure if that was a good or a bad idea, under the circumstances. Elizabeth was neatly dressed in dark pants and a jacket, with a conservative blouse in muted tones; Meg suppressed the irreverent thought that her mother had brought just the right clothes for attending a funeral.

"Of course. He was an old friend."

Was that all he was? Meg thought for a moment. Her mother was still hiding something — that much she would put money on. But if Elizabeth was thinking about going to the service, she must feel sure that her presence wouldn't be ill received. Or maybe she just wanted to send the message that her encounter with Daniel Weston had been completely open and aboveboard — just two old friends getting together. Would Detective Marcus be there? Would Daniel's wife? Children? Members of the college faculty?

"You should go now if you want to make it on time," Rachel said.

Elizabeth stood up quickly. "That's no problem. Just let me find my purse. One minute, I promise."

As Elizabeth disappeared down the front hallway, Meg asked quietly, "Were you the one who told her about the service?"

"Yes. Shouldn't I have? I thought she might want to go, and no one else was going to notify her." Rachel matched Meg's tone.

"No, that's fine. I just wondered how she knew. I figured it was probably you. Did she say anything about . . . anything?"

Rachel shrugged. "Not really. Of course, I don't know what she's usually like, but she's seemed kind of subdued. She spent most of yesterday curled up in the front parlor with a book, but I'm not sure if she even read any of it."

That was troubling. "That's not like her. I'll see how things go today. Did she hear anything from Detective Marcus?"

"Not that I know of. Nothing new on Professor Weston's death?"

"Art shared a few bits and pieces, but they don't make much sense right now. No obvious cause of death, although the autopsy reports aren't in, but no one seems to know what the man was doing where he was found. By the way, Seth showed me a picture of Daniel Weston — definitely an attractive man. I'll fill you in later." Meg could hear the brisk click of her mother's heels approaching.

"All set, dear," Elizabeth said brightly.

"Well, you two should get going or you'll be late. You know where the church is?" When Meg shook her head, Rachel outlined the route.

Meg said good-bye to Rachel and escorted her mother out to her own car. They drove the couple of miles to downtown Amherst with Meg making bland comments about the neighborhood, and her mother making predictable comments about the pretty trees. As the arrived at the church, Meg asked her mother, "Are you okay?"

Elizabeth turned to Meg with an odd expression she didn't recognize. "I suppose. I'm sad, more than anything — this isn't how I expected . . . Poor Daniel. But I thought I should be here."

"Does Daddy know about any of this?"

Elizabeth shook her head. "No, I haven't been able to reach him. Besides, he would probably think he should be here, but I wouldn't want him to interrupt his trip. I'll represent the both of us. Shall we go in?"

The church, another typical plain New England church of the type that Meg was rapidly becoming familiar with, was fairly well filled, and most people looked as though they belonged to the local academic community. Meg checked out the front pew for family members, but she couldn't tell much from the backs of their heads. Daniel's wife, if that's who she was, sat with her back stiff, her head high. She was flanked by a couple of twenty-something young men who wore tailored jackets, a rare sight these days, at least to Meg. Daniel's sons? His wife's by an earlier marriage? Elizabeth slid into a pew halfway down the aisle. Meg sat next to her without speaking, folding her hands in her lap.

The service was short and formal, with no gushing eulogies or histrionics from bereaved family; overall it was simple and dignified. Meg glanced at her mother once and saw that while her face was still and composed, tears were tracing their way down her cheeks. Meg turned away. She could count on the fingers of one hand the times she had seen her mother cry.

When the service ended, Elizabeth sat still, making no move to leave, and the local people, many of whom seemed to know each other, gathered in clots and made their way slowly out of the church. Others moved in the opposite direction, to pay their condolences to the widow. Meg watched as the woman she took to be Daniel's wife stood up and turned to greet people — a small ad hoc receiving line. Several people approached, took her hand, leaned close, and murmured something that Meg was too far away to hear. One figure stood out, a tall black man with silvered hair, wearing a well-tailored tweed jacket. He spent a few minutes talking to her, holding one of her hands in both of his. The woman nodded and produced a smile now and then. The two young men flanked her like guards but said nothing, looking vaguely uncomfortable. The woman didn't look terribly distraught, but Meg couldn't tell whether she was exercising admirable control or was actually numb following her husband's death.

Meg leaned toward her mother and whispered, "You don't know her?"

"Patricia? No, we've never met. She seems to be handling it well."

Meg watched as someone else approached, after a few false starts, as if unsure of her welcome. She was young, likely a student, and even from a distance Meg could see that she was struggling to contain tears. The wife, Patricia, greeted her formally, and stood patiently as the girl twisted her hands together and words tumbled out of her mouth. Eventually she realized that there were others waiting and disentangled herself, stalking down the aisle toward the door without greeting anyone else.

When at least half the crowd had cleared away, Elizabeth stood up and walked slowly to the front, where the woman and young men were still talking with a cluster of people. Meg followed at a distance, uncomfortable yet reluctant to leave her mother unsupported. She hadn't known Daniel — hadn't even known of his existence until the past week — and she had no role to play here.

When the others finally made their farewells, Elizabeth stepped up. "Patricia? I'm Elizabeth Corey. We've never met, but I knew Daniel when he was in grad school. Quite a long time ago. I'm so sorry for your loss."

Patricia studied Elizabeth. She didn't look devastated; she didn't even look upset. "Thank you for coming. I know who you are — Daniel mentioned that he was planning to get together with you. Is Corey your married name?"

"Yes. He knew me originally as Elizabeth Judson."

"Are you staying in the area?" Patricia's eyes flickered toward Meg, standing silently behind her mother. "I'd like a chance to sit down and talk with you, if you'll be around for a while longer."

"Certainly." If Elizabeth was startled by Patricia's request, she didn't show it. "Let me give you my phone number." Elizabeth rummaged through her purse and found a card on which she scribbled her cell phone number. She handed it to Patricia. "I should be around for several more days. Any time that's convenient for you. And if there's anything I can do . . ."

"Thank you. Listen, we need to get back to the house, but I'll call you later."

Elizabeth stepped back politely. "Of course. Don't let me keep you." She turned to leave, with Meg trailing in her wake.

"Are the boys his sons?" Meg asked as she caught up with her mother.

"Yes, from his first marriage. The older one is Daniel Junior, but I forget the younger one's name. They're both a few years younger than you."

"What on earth does she have to talk to you about?"

"Meg, I can't tell you. Maybe she wants to know more about Daniel before she met him. Why don't we just wait and see? Perhaps she was just being polite. She may not follow through."

They had nearly reached the doors when a dark figure stepped forward: Detective Marcus. "Mrs. Corey, may I have a word with you?" he asked formally.

"Now?" Elizabeth said, startled.

"Yes. Let's go outside and find a place to

sit." He led the way out of the church. Elizabeth glanced at Meg, an eyebrow raised, and Meg could only shrug. Conveniently there were several long benches arrayed along the outside wall of the church, and the detective gestured toward one safely away from foot traffic. Meg sat at one end of the bench, leaving the middle for her mother. Marcus waited until they were both settled before sitting at the far end.

There was a cold lump in the pit of Meg's stomach. Part of it was due to her history with Detective Marcus: despite a recent thaw between them, she still felt intimidated — even irrationally guilty — in his presence. That probably made him a good cop, but it didn't make him easy company. How would her mother stand up to his interrogation, if that was what this was?

Marcus was studying Elizabeth's face. Elizabeth met his eyes, but Meg was troubled: normally in a social situation her mother would have filled the silence with light and amusing chitchat, but clearly Elizabeth had recognized, if belatedly, that this was truly serious.

Marcus cleared his throat. "We've received the preliminary autopsy results. Daniel Weston's death was a homicide."

Meg froze, watching her mother. Elizabeth shut her eyes, and when she opened them to look at the detective, they were wet with tears. "How . . . ?" she whispered.

"I can't say," Marcus said.

Elizabeth cleared her throat, and when she spoke again, her voice was level and controlled. "I'm sorry to hear that, but what does that have to do with me?"

Detective Marcus's expression didn't change. "Mrs. Corey, I don't think you were completely frank with me the last time we spoke."

"Why would you say that?" Elizabeth's expression, like his, gave nothing away.

"You came up here without letting anyone know — your husband, your daughter — to meet with someone you said you hadn't seen in, what, thirty-plus years? And then he ends up dead. That's kind of a big coincidence, don't you think?"

"But that's what it is — a coincidence," Elizabeth protested. "I have no knowledge of his death. Haven't you interviewed his wife? His friends?"

"Of course I have. His wife knew next to nothing about you, although she did manage to dig up a few old pictures he'd kept when I asked. I'm guessing they're of you and your husband with Weston." He passed a plastic sleeve with a couple of curling photos across the table toward Elizabeth.

Elizabeth took it and glanced briefly at the photos, then nodded. "Phillip and I were married shortly after those pictures were taken. As I told you before, Patricia is Daniel's second wife, and until the memorial service today, I had never met her."

"Don't you find it curious that he picked this particular time to contact you?"

"Why?"

"It's the beginning of the school term, which is always busy for professors, right? And he was the primary organizer for an important conference. He had to have had plenty to occupy his attention. Why call you now?"

Elizabeth shook her head. "Detective, I have no idea. As I told you, he contacted me, not the other way around. He didn't appear rushed or stressed during the time we spent together."

"What did you talk about?"

"Good heavens! It had been thirty years since we'd seen each other. We talked about our families, our careers. Phillip. Meg. New England. College life."

"He didn't say anything that suggested he was tying up loose ends?"

"No. Mainly we exchanged stories about our children, how their lives have been so different from ours. He was very proud of what his boys had accomplished."

"Hold on, Detective," Meg interrupted. "You aren't telling us everything. What is it that you have that makes you think Daniel Weston didn't die a natural death?"

Marcus regarded her then, his expression an unsettling mixture of anger and speculation. Finally he said carefully, "The preliminary autopsy shows physical evidence. I'm not going to tell you the details, but the evidence was sufficient for us to consider this a homicide."

Meg didn't dare look at her mother, and no one spoke for several long moments. Finally Meg said, "Daniel Weston was murdered? At that farm stand?"

Marcus nodded once. "Yes."

"Do you have any suspects yet?" *Apart from my mother?*

"We're talking to quite a few people — including your mother. The general picture is that Weston was well liked by his colleagues, he had a clean record, he was happy with his wife, his kids are upstanding citizens. Your mother is the only wild card in the bunch."

"What about the people who were here today at the service?" Meg pressed.

"We'll follow up on them, of course."

Elizabeth broke in, her voice steely. "Detective, as I have already explained to you more than once, Daniel called me out of the blue and invited me to come visit. I had no conflicting commitments, so I agreed. I have no idea why he chose this particular time, because we never discussed it. We spent some pleasant time together, but we were effectively strangers these days, despite our past shared history. There's nothing more I can tell you. I very much regret that he's dead, but I had nothing to do with it."

"And you've never visited that farm stand where he was found?"

"Of course not! Why would I? I have no idea where it even is. I came here to see Daniel, not to buy vegetables."

Marcus waited a few beats before responding. "Will you be staying in the area for a while?"

Elizabeth's glance darted at Meg again. "If you wish. I have no current obligations back home."

"What about your husband?"

"I don't know what he could add to what I've already told you, but I will be sure to let you know when I hear from him."

"Thank you." Marcus stood up abruptly. "I'll be in touch."

When he turned to go, Meg followed him,

and when they were out of her mother's hearing, she said, "Detective, what did you hope to find out from her?"

He regarded her gravely. "I don't know, but she's the only thing out of place in this whole scene. I don't trust coincidences. Listen, if she tells you anything she didn't feel like sharing with me, will you let me know?"

Meg wondered how she was supposed to respond to that: he was asking her to rat out her mother. But she had to admit that she couldn't rid herself either of the nagging feeling that Elizabeth hadn't been completely honest. "Yes, I'll tell you. But there's no way she killed anyone, so you'd better look hard at the other people on your list."

Marcus's mouth twitched. "You're the expert."

Before Meg could come up with a response, he was gone. She was annoyed at him, frustrated by her mother's reticence, bewildered by the whole situation, and stressed out by the avalanche of events over the past few days. She made her way back to where her mother was sitting, staring idly at nothing. When Meg sat down next to her again, Elizabeth gave her a grave smile. "That was unpleasant."

94

"Yes, it was. I don't suppose you're in the mood for sightseeing?"

"I think not. Actually I think I'd rather have just a little more time to myself. I hope you understand. Perhaps we could get together again tomorrow, if your schedule permits?"

"I'll see if Bree will give me permission. I'll take you back to Rachel's, if you like."

"That would be fine," Elizabeth replied.

They drove back to the bed-and-breakfast largely in silence. Meg pulled into the driveway to let her mother out. "I'll talk to you in the morning, okay?"

"Certainly. See you tomorrow, darling."

Meg waited as her mother climbed the steps of the house and disappeared inside before pulling away. She felt a bit confused: she'd come over this morning hoping to make peace, but Marcus's unwelcome announcement had only made things worse. On the plus side, though, she had the afternoon free. Bree would be pleased, and would no doubt find something useful for her to do. It would beat stewing over whether her mother might be a murderer.

Back at the house, Meg parked, then went inside to change clothes. When she climbed the hill to the orchard, Bree spotted her immediately. "What are you doing here?" she called out. "I thought you and Mom were doing girly things."

"Turns out Daniel Weston's memorial service was this morning, so I took her over there. And then our friend Detective Marcus showed up."

Bree grimaced. "At the church? Why?"

"The autopsy showed that Daniel was murdered."

"Oh, shoot. That sucks. How'd your mother take the news? I'll assume Marcus didn't arrest her."

"Not yet, but I bet he'd like to. Apparently there's no one else who makes a promising suspect. She seemed sad, I guess. I took her back to Rachel's — she said she wanted a bit more time on her own. I'll call her tomorrow morning. So, you need me here?"

"Of course. Grab a bag and let's get to work."

7

Even after putting in her fair share of picking the day before, Meg still felt guilty about taking time from the orchard. She was sitting in the kitchen when Bree came down on Friday morning. "Look, is it really okay for me to take today off? I can come back later in the afternoon."

Bree waved a dismissive hand. "Don't worry about it. You need time with your mom, and it won't hurt the apples to wait a day."

"You aren't just saying that?"

"Hey, you don't trust me? I know what I'm doing. It'll be fine, and we've got it covered. Will your mom be coming back here?"

Meg shrugged. "I don't know. I hope so. She's been so odd these last few days, I really don't know what she's thinking. I'll ask her again today — after we've done some of those girly things you were talking about."

Bree flashed her a grin. "You do that. See you later!" Meg hurried out the door.

Meg found she was in a strange mood as she drove the familiar route to Rachel's. Did she want her mother to stay with her? She should, she knew. But as she'd told Bree, Elizabeth was not herself at the moment, and until Marcus found out who had killed Daniel Weston, Elizabeth would be under a cloud. Combine that with the erratic pressures of the harvest, and it was a recipe for friction. Still, she was going to ask.

She arrived at the bed-and-breakfast just after eleven, and parked by her mother's car. There were no others parked there — were all of Rachel's other guests out admiring leaves or installing offspring in dorm rooms? Meg made her way to the front door and rang the old-fashioned bell; footsteps followed, and then her mother opened the door.

"Oh, Meg. I wondered if it might be you, but I thought you would call first."

"Sorry." Great — already she was defensive. "I thought you might like to go to lunch. There's a very nice bistro in the middle of town, and after we eat, we could walk around a little, maybe see Emily

Dickinson's house?" Meg laid her peace offering at her mother's feet.

"Sounds perfect." Elizabeth smiled tentatively. Olive branch accepted apparently.

When they arrived at the town center, though, Meg realized that the place was crawling with mid-forties couples, all of whom looked disoriented: she had forgotten about the impact of the multiple school openings in the area. She snagged a parking space just as someone else was leaving and counted herself lucky. As they climbed out of the car, Meg asked her mother, "Have you already seen much of Amherst?"

Her mother shrugged. "Not really." She didn't add anything more.

All right, if that's the way she was going to play it. "Well, Amherst College is over there," Meg began, pointing. "UMass is that way." She pointed in the opposite direction. "Emily Dickinson's house is a block or so that way, and the restaurant I mentioned is right there across the street."

"It looks charming, dear," her mother said.

Meg fed the parking meter and escorted her mother across the street. She was dismayed to find the tiny vestibule crowded with people, all of whom had apparently had the same thought about lunch. She was about to turn away when she heard her name called.

"Meg?"

She peered past the group to see her friend and orchard mentor Christopher Ramsdell at a table at the rear — with Frances Clark, her real estate agent from Granford. *Interesting.* Meg recalled that the two of them had also shared a table at the restaurant opening earlier in the week.

"Won't you join us?" Christopher beckoned. Several people in front of her in line turned to glare. Meg ignored them.

"We'd love to." Before Elizabeth could protest, she dragged her mother over to the table. "Mother, this is Frances Clark and Christopher Ramsdell, a professor at UMass who used to oversee the orchard. Christopher, Frances, this is my mother, Elizabeth Corey. She's visiting for a few days. Are you sure there's room at the table?"

"We shall make room. Albert won't mind — I come here often." Christopher gestured toward the maître d' with a smile; the maître d' quickly found two spare chairs and arranged them around the table. It was a close fit, but it worked. Meg and her mother sat down, and Christopher beamed at them. "There we go! Would you care for something to drink? A glass of wine, perhaps? Is this a special occasion?"

Not the way you'd imagine, Meg thought. "Maybe one glass," she replied, looking at her mother, who appeared absorbed by the list of specials posted on the chalkboard above the small bar. "Mother?"

"Oh, that would be fine," Elizabeth answered absently.

"We were thinking of doing some sightseeing later," Meg said. "Mother hasn't spent much time around here."

Frances cocked her head at Elizabeth. "So you and Meg own the Granford property jointly?"

Meg turned to Elizabeth. "Frances is a real estate agent, Mother. She was going to sell the house, before I decided to stay."

"Ah." Elizabeth nodded. "This would not be a good time to think about selling, would it, Frances?"

"That's the truth. But if you're looking for a condo or something, so you can visit with your daughter, I could find you something nice."

Meg's mother laughed briefly. "I don't think that's necessary at the moment. Christopher, what do you recommend from the menu?"

Meg noted her mother's adroit diversion as she studied the menu herself. A waiter

101

approached and took their orders.

Talk drifted to the orchard. "And how is your picking going, Meg?" Christopher asked. "I'm a bit surprised to see you here today."

"Bree gave me the day off — I gather we're waiting for the next batch to ripen. Hurry up and wait, isn't it?" When Elizabeth looked quizzical, Meg reminded her, "Christopher managed the orchard for years. Bree was one of his students."

"One of my best, in fact. Are the pickers working out?" Christopher turned to Elizabeth. "I don't know if you're aware of it, but there is a long tradition of Jamaican pickers around here. I had hoped that Meg's transition would be smooth. Has it been, my dear?"

"I think so. Raynard is very good at keeping things moving, and nobody has yelled at me yet, even though I've made a couple of bloopers. Thank goodness it's a good crop."

"It is. And you were lucky that the hailstorm missed you. Perhaps the gods are smiling on your endeavors. Mrs. Corey, what do you think of your daughter's new profession?"

"Elizabeth, please. I think she's quite brave to jump into something new with so little experience. I believe she's mentioned how glad she is to have you as a resource."

Christopher looked pleased. "I've been more than happy to help. After all, I've been involved with her — your — orchard for a long time, and I feel quite attached to it. She has some wonderful old varieties there."

As their meal arrived, Meg asked, "Christopher, Frances, what did you think of Gran's?"

"I for one am thrilled," Frances said. "There's finally a place I can take potential buyers. Nothing like feeding people a good meal to put them in a spending mood."

"I thought the food was excellent," Christopher agreed. "I will be happy to return when time permits. Perhaps we could arrange a special event associated with the launch of the new building? That's still several months off, so that will allow your young chefs time to settle in."

"I'm sure they'd love it, Christopher. That's a wonderful idea. By the way, how's the construction project going?" Meg said. "Mother, Christopher is overseeing the construction of a new research facility on campus, which will explore alternative strategies for pest control. He's going to be the director when it's completed."

"Quite well, all things considered. The building should be ready by the end of the year, assuming the weather cooperates. Are you familiar with the practice of integrated pest management, Elizabeth?"

Elizabeth shook her head, looking amused. "I'm not. Tell me why I should be."

Genial conversation carried them through the rest of the meal. Elizabeth appeared interested in what Christopher had to say, although Meg wasn't sure whether her interest was genuine or she was merely being polite. The meal wound down with coffee and individual ramekins of crème brûlée. Christopher checked his watch. "Gracious, I must be getting back. Let this meal be my treat, in honor of your visit, Elizabeth. Frances, it was lovely to see you, and I'll call soon. Good-bye, ladies!" He rose, had a word with the maître d', then departed.

Frances rose, too. "Well, I'd better get back to the office, in case anyone happens to call. And if you're wondering, there are plenty of people who are looking for a bargain these days, and some of them can even get mortgages. I keep busy! Good to see you, Meg, Elizabeth. Maybe we can get together before you go?" Frances looked directly at Elizabeth.

"I'd like that, but I'm not sure what my plans are. Meg knows where to reach you, I assume?"

"Of course. Bye now."

Meg and her mother were left alone at the table. "I guess we should go. There are plenty of people waiting for a table," Meg ventured. She looked at her mother. "Do you feel like seeing Emily Dickinson's house?"

"If we can walk. That was a delightful meal, but I should let it settle just a bit. You said it wasn't far?"

"Just down that street. Are you a fan?"

"Of Emily Dickinson? Actually I'm not sure. I know her more well-circulated poems, and her general reputation, but I'm afraid that's the extent of my knowledge. I would enjoy seeing her home. Is that the ladies' room over there?"

"It is. I'll wait outside for you, if you don't mind."

As Elizabeth went toward the back of the restaurant, Meg headed out the door and intercepted Frances, who was still near the entrance. "So, twice in one week? Are you and Christopher . . . ?"

Frances smiled. "Maybe. He's such a lovely man, if a wee bit older than I am. And you and Seth looked pretty cozy yourselves the other night."

"I guess. Oh, if you happen to get together with my mother again, I haven't managed

105

to tell her about Seth."

"Why ever not? He's unattached, owns his own business, and he's an all-around great guy. What's not to like?"

"I know, I know, but I'd like to explain it to her in my own time. Okay?"

"No problem. Ah, here she is. Good-bye again, Elizabeth." Frances turned and strode down the street toward her car.

"You ready, Mother? I should just feed the meter before we go — I wouldn't want to rush."

"That's fine, dear. No hurry."

Easy for her to say, Meg thought. She didn't have an orchard to run.

8

"You didn't have a chance to see Emily Dickinson's house . . . before?" Meg asked as they followed Main Street toward the large painted brick house down the way, ignoring the other pedestrians who jostled their way past them on the sidewalk. Might as well confront this now.

"You mean, did I see it with Daniel?" her mother countered.

"Yes, I guess I do. I understand Daniel Weston was a well-known Dickinson scholar."

"So he said," Elizabeth replied in a neutral tone. "I'm not particularly familiar with the contemporary academic environment, and I took his statement at face value. Although we did spend some time talking about Emily, and what she meant to the town of Amherst."

"He was hosting a symposium on Dickinson and Whitman this weekend. Did he

107

mention that?"

"No, we didn't talk about specifics of what he was working on at the moment. We had a lot of catching up to do. In fact, we talked about *you* quite a bit."

"Me?" Meg was surprised. "He'd never even met me."

Elizabeth was silent for a moment, studying her daughter's face. "Meg, can we wait for a bit to talk about all this?"

Meg straightened her shoulders. "Mother, I would be happy to, but the fact that Detective Marcus has talked to you twice now makes me nervous."

"Are you accusing me of having something to do with Daniel Weston's death? That's ridiculous."

"I agree, but Detective Marcus doesn't know you as well as I do. And your presence here at this particular moment is one suspicious fact that sticks out like a sore thumb, as he keeps reminding us."

"I suppose." Elizabeth shook her head as if to clear it. "Please, Meg — can't we just do something pleasant for a little while? It's a beautiful day, and a charming town, and I'd like to do something nice with my daughter. Please?"

More evasion, but Meg didn't have the heart to press. "For now, all right. But you're going to have to tell me the whole story sooner or later, and it would help me to help you if it was sooner."

Elizabeth smiled sadly. "All right, dear, I promise."

"When?"

"Maybe tomorrow. I need a little more time to get my thoughts in order. And to grieve for Daniel."

Meg was nonplussed by the last remark. Grieve for someone she hadn't seen in decades? Or grieve for a past now lost, for things that might have been? What had Daniel been to her, and had he been looking to rekindle it? Had she? "All right, deal."

"Now, may we please go pay homage to the Belle of Amherst?"

"See, you do know something about Emily," Meg replied as they continued along the sidewalk. After a minute or so they came to the front of the house. Sitting on a small rise, it was a solidly built brick building, its windows flanked by wooden shutters, its front door guarded by a columned portico, the roof crowned by a windowed cupola.

"A handsome place, although it looks a little bare," Elizabeth said, studying it.

"The town had to cut down the trees in front — some of them were diseased. It's not like Emily or her family had planted them originally — they were twentieth-century additions. In fact, the land across the street" — Meg pointed — "was open farmland when the Dickinsons lived here, and of course they would have had a very different view. Shall we go in? They have guided tours."

"Certainly. Have you been here before?"

"Just once. I keep meaning to come back, and to read a little more about Emily, but I never seem to have the time."

"I can understand that," her mother said.

Can you? Meg wondered, but decided to hold her tongue. She didn't want to disrupt their fragile peace.

They went around to the back of the house, where they paid for tickets and were admitted. "The next tour starts in ten minutes. Please enjoy the gift shop while you're waiting," the cheerful desk attendant said.

Elizabeth wandered into a small adjoining room. "Good heavens, was this the kitchen?" she said. "It's so . . . primitive!"

"It was a simpler time, Mother. And Emily seemed to manage — there are even some of her recipes that survive, although I'm sure she had hired help."

"I should hope so. It's so hard to imagine the work it took, a century and more ago, just to keep a family fed and clean. I definitely prefer the modern era. What is there to see in the house?"

"Emily's bedroom, a few pieces of her clothing, a view of the cemetery. Then there's her brother's house next door. That's open for tours as well." The last time Meg had visited, she'd found the docent well informed and very enthusiastic about the poet, but she would let her mother find that out for herself.

It was close to an hour later when the tour concluded in the small side garden, complete with a couple of young apple trees — Baldwins, Meg guessed. As the docent and the other people on the tour scattered, Meg and her mother drifted toward a bench. The afternoon sun was warm, the air crisp; they had eaten well, virtuously exercised both their bodies and their minds, and Meg was as well pleased as she could hope to be, given the looming harvest and Detective Marcus — who, as she thought about it, also loomed. They sat.

"It's lovely here, isn't it? How very strange that this one frail and frightened woman could have had such a lasting impact on our literary culture," Elizabeth said slowly.

"I suppose it is, come to think of it," Meg answered. "Although as you heard, Emily didn't set out to change the world. She didn't even let many people see her work, and it wasn't until after her death that most of it was published. She wrote for herself mainly, and that was enough."

Elizabeth sighed quietly, her eyes on the house across the street. "I've never felt I had that kind of talent, I'm afraid. Nor the compulsion to make my voice heard. It's not for me to live an inspired life. Wasn't it Thoreau who talked about 'lives of quiet desperation'?"

Meg nodded. "Another Massachusetts writer, although far less self-effacing than Emily. And here we are visiting her house, and you can see where Thoreau's cabin was on Walden Pond in Concord. They still influence our lives. It may sound strange, but I think I've tapped into that kind of historic continuity. I'm living in a house that one of our great-greats built two hundred and fifty years ago. That's something I never expected."

"Maybe you didn't, but I would guess that great-great assumed his family would remain there forever. It would have been far easier for him to envision that than to foresee the reality. How different is what you do in your orchard from what he would have known?"

A question about the orchard? Whether it was simply polite conversation or her mother was actually interested, Meg rushed to answer. "Surprisingly little, actually. The techniques for propagating fruit trees have been around for millennia, and there may be descendants of some of the apples our ancestors planted in the orchard even now. Spraying? Pesticides have come a long way, but more and more we're finding that they create as many problems as they solve — just ask Christopher. So sometimes we have to fall back on the old ways, which were simpler and cheaper. Harvesting? Apples are still fairly delicate, so you mostly have to pick them by hand. I think Thoreau would have recognized most of what we're doing — well, except maybe the Jamaican pickers," Meg joked.

"That's an interesting twist — I wasn't aware that Jamaicans were so numerous around here. Mainly we hear about Hispanic migrant workers when people talk about harvesting crops."

"According to Christopher and Bree, the Jamaicans have been working around here for decades — they come back to the same places year after year. Bree is second generation, although she's a lot more than a picker. And she grew up around here."

"I'm still surprised that you hired her. Given your own lack of expertise, I would have thought you would go for someone more experienced."

Meg tried to stifle her impatience at her mother's naïveté. "I couldn't afford anyone more experienced, Mother. But Bree came highly recommended by Christopher, whom I trust completely. And he's available for backup if she gets in over her head. She knows the pickers and she's been great at handling them so far. I don't regret giving her a chance."

"You don't need to take my head off, Meg. I was just curious."

"Sorry. You're not the first person to wonder, but it seems to be working out. Next year will be easier."

"You'll be here next year?"

It was a question Meg really hadn't answered for herself, but her mother's surprise rankled. She turned on the bench to look directly at Elizabeth. "Why wouldn't I? Look, this is not just a little hobby to keep me busy while I find the next desk job. For one thing, it's a lot of work, and if I'm going to put this much sweat into it, I'm damn well going to stick to it, at least for a while. I don't pretend I can learn everything about orchard management in a year or even two, but I'm going to learn as much as I can. And believe it or not, I like it here. I've made friends. People know who I am. That's more than I could say when I was working in Boston."

"But don't you miss things like restaurants, culture?"

Meg laughed. "I'll have to take you over to Northampton again. You may not have noticed, but they've got just about everything there — restaurants for all and any tastes, from vegan to snob; theaters; music venues. And that doesn't even count the local colleges, which are some of the best in the country, and they bring in terrific lecturers. So I'm not exactly stranded in a cultural desert, you know. And I never had time to do anything of that kind of stuff back when I was in Boston anyway — we were all too busy trying to prove to each other how ambitious we were."

"But how can you hope to meet anyone?" Elizabeth asked.

So that was the subtext. By "anyone," Meg knew her mother meant a potential husband. An "anyone" that Meg had never felt compelled to pursue with any great enthusiasm. But things might be changing: Should she tell her mother now about Seth? Would it make things more complicated if she waited? As Meg opened her mouth, her phone, deep in a pocket, rang. She struggled to fish it out and checked the number: not one she recognized. "Hello?"

"Hello, Meg? This is Raynard. You need to come home. There's been some trouble."

"Trouble? What's happened?"

"Just come, quick." He hung up abruptly, leaving Meg staring at the phone.

"Is something wrong, dear?" her mother asked.

"I think so, but I don't know what. I've got to go. Damn, I need to take you back to Rachel's, but I don't know if I can spare the time right now. Do you mind coming with me, at least for now?"

"Of course not. Let's go."

They walked swiftly but silently back to the parking lot while Meg turned over alternative scenarios in her head. Had the pickers found a new pest and they wanted to know what to do about it? Had the goats gotten loose? What was the worst case? She didn't even want to go there — she could think of too many possibilities. Somehow, from Raynard's tone, Meg guessed it was serious, but he would have told her if the house had burned down. Or the barn. Wouldn't he? Back at the car they climbed in, buckled up, and Meg took off, back

toward Granford and whatever awaited her
there.

9

Meg drove the speed limit back to her house — barely. The twisting two-lane local roads didn't permit speeding anyway. She focused on the road, trying to avoid thinking about what she was going to find, and her mother tactfully didn't interrupt her thoughts.

As she neared her house from the north, she was relieved to see that it was still standing, as was the barn behind it. No fire, then; no natural disasters. But as she passed the orchard, she could see the pickers standing aimlessly in a loose group, not picking. She pulled into the driveway, stopped the car, and jumped out, heading straight up the hill. When she reached the orchard, she followed the sounds of angry voices: Raynard and Bree, engaged in a furious argument. Bree was holding one arm across her chest, and as she approached, Meg thought that Bree looked near tears.

They didn't notice her until she was only

a few feet away. "All right, what's going on?" Meg demanded.

Both turned to her and started talking at once. Meg held up a hand. "One at a time. Bree?" While part of her wanted to let the older — and apparently cooler-headed — man talk, she didn't want to undercut Bree's authority.

"It's nothing. My ladder slipped, and I fell on my wrist. It'll be fine — I just need to wrap it up good."

Raynard cut in. "It is not fine, it is broken, and you need to see a doctor. I have seen plenty of broken bones in my day, and you do not fool with them. Are you an expert, that you can tell all will be fine?"

"Let me see," Meg ordered. Not that she had any medical knowledge, but if something was seriously wrong, wouldn't it be obvious?

Bree glared at her, and extended her injured arm. The wrist was clearly red and swollen. "Can you move it?" Meg asked.

"Not well. Hurts too much," Bree added reluctantly. It obviously hurt more to admit that in front of her crew.

"Okay, then we're going to the emergency room," Meg said firmly.

"It'll cost too much!!" Bree protested. "I'll be okay."

Meg was beginning to lose patience. "Bree, I made sure you had insurance. And if that doesn't cover everything, I'll take care of it. But it's important to make sure it's all right. If it's just a sprain, fine. But if it's broken, doing nothing will just make it worse. Go get into the car."

Bree looked like a sulky child, and Meg was reminded just how young her orchard manager was, despite her tough exterior. Meg looked over at Raynard, who nodded his approval. The other pickers looked relieved, or avoided Meg's eyes entirely.

"Raynard, you're in charge for now. We should be back in a few hours." Meg hoped. Her experience with emergency rooms, and hospitals in general, was limited. But right now, it seemed more important to act decisively.

"Right, ma'am." Raynard turned back to the workers, calling out orders and pointing, while Meg guided Bree down the hill. At the car Meg realized her mother was still there, leaning against it, watching them approach.

"What's wrong?" Elizabeth asked.

"I think Bree's got a broken wrist. I'm going to take her over to the ER at the hospital in Holyoke."

"I'll come with you. Bree, get in the front

seat — you'll be more comfortable. I'll take the back." Elizabeth opened the front door and waited until Bree had settled herself before sitting in the back.

Meg got in and started the car, then headed for the highway and Holyoke's hospital. "I thought you said we weren't picking today?"

"Not much, and we had enough guys to cover it. I thought you could use some time with your mother."

"Thank you, Bree — I appreciate that," came Elizabeth's voice from the backseat.

Great, now Meg had another reason to feel guilty. Bree had been trying to help her out, and look where things had ended up — not that her being there, rather than enjoying a fine luncheon in Amherst, would have prevented the fall. If it was a fall. "Bree, was that the whole story?" she asked as they drove. "I know you're careful."

"What're you asking?"

Meg wasn't sure. "Did someone do something to the ladder? Or maybe stumble over it and make you fall?"

Bree didn't answer immediately. "I don't think so," she muttered, looking at the road.

Meg had known there might be problems — a young and untried woman bossing around more experienced, older, mostly

121

male workers. But she had counted on Raynard to keep them in line, and Bree hadn't complained. "Have you had other problems?"

"No! Nothing serious — just some joking around. It's been fine. I was just clumsy, all right?"

"All right." For now. She'd have to probe later, when they had taken care of the immediate problem. Insurance rarely covered all costs. The hospital took credit cards, didn't they? Meg couldn't remember. Not that it mattered — if Bree had been injured while working for her, Meg would see that she was taken care of. She knew that the pickers, as her subcontractors, were covered under a state-offered program, but Bree was a different case. She'd have to check when she got home again.

The ride took no more than ten minutes. Meg parked in the hospital lot, but by the time she had reached the other side of the car, Bree had already extricated herself and was stalking toward the entrance, and Meg and her mother had to hurry to catch up. Inside Bree made a beeline for the front desk, with Meg close behind her.

"What's the problem?" the nurse-receptionist asked.

"I think I've broken my wrist," Bree said,

her voice tight. She ignored Meg, hovering behind her.

The nurse slid a clipboard across the counter. "Fill these out and bring them back. Take a seat in the waiting area and we'll call you."

Meg led Bree to the waiting area, filled with stiff plastic chairs in rows bolted to the floor. They found three seats together, and Meg scanned the room. Even though it was the middle of the day, there were quite a few people waiting; but nobody looked seriously ill or hurt — or at least, there was no evident bleeding. Maybe this wouldn't take too long?

It was half an hour before they called Bree's name. Meg handed over the forms that she had helped Bree fill out, and an orderly guided Bree off to x-ray.

Meg realized that she and her mother hadn't exchanged more than a few words since they had arrived. "Sorry about dragging you here."

"Meg, you don't need to apologize. I hope I'm not in the way, but I thought maybe you could use some company. These things can often drag on for a while. I'm glad you insisted — she's stubborn, isn't she?"

"She is, but she's trying to look like she's in control. You've had a lot of experience with waiting around emergency rooms?" Meg couldn't think of any time in her youth that she had had an injury that required an emergency room visit.

"Enough."

"Not with me."

"No." Elizabeth paused, as if weighing her words. "Your father had a scare, a while ago."

Meg turned in her seat. "What? You never told me anything about that. When was this?"

Elizabeth nodded. "It was last winter. But it turned out to be nothing. Well, perhaps not nothing — hypertension combined with stress. But of course, Phillip thought he was having a heart attack. It's controlled with medication now. I didn't want to worry you — you were going through a rather difficult patch then."

Meg bit back an angry response. She wanted to say that her mother should have told her, before they knew how serious it might be, but another part of her was relieved that she hadn't had to deal with one more problem, not at a time when everything else had seemed to be falling apart — and that relief made her feel guilty. Yet another part was hurt that her mother hadn't asked for her help, or at least her comfort. In the end she said nothing.

An hour passed, and a big chunk of the next one. Finally Bree emerged from a door, her lower arm now encased in a brightly colored fiberglass cast. Meg and her mother stood up. "So it *was* broken?" Meg asked.

"Yeah, I guess. Not too bad, just a simple fracture, except I've got to wear this thing" — Bree waved her fluorescent arm — "for at least six weeks, and I'm not supposed to do any heavy lifting. I told the guy I needed to pick apples and he laughed at me."

"Bree, you're going to follow his instructions if I have to chain you to the barn. Did he give you any prescriptions?"

Bree fished a bottle out of her pocket. "He gave me some pain pills, not a lot, and a prescription if I think I need more. Can we get out of here now?"

"If there's no more paperwork to do." Meg checked with the harried nurse at the desk and was waved away.

Back in the car, Bree slumped in her seat. Without looking at Meg, she said, "I'm sorry."

Meg concentrated on avoiding Holyoke's rush-hour drivers. "Why? Did you do something stupid?"

"No. At least I don't think so. Maybe I reached too far for one last apple. The ladder tipped."

Her heart sank when she realized there was one more complication: Bree's injury left them one hand short, literally. Was it possible to manage without her, or would Meg need to find another body to fill in? This was the peak of the picking season, and it was likely that everyone was already committed. How much would Bree be able to do? No heavy lifting: that eliminated most of the direct apple handling. Making deliveries? Obviously not. What about driving the tractor to haul the apples down the hill? Meg's worries kept her silent for the full trip home. It was getting dark when they finally pulled into the driveway.

The pickers had vanished, but Raynard was waiting in the drive, leaning against his battered pickup truck. He straightened up politely and removed his well-worn baseball cap when the three women clambered out of Meg's car. Bree was the first to confront him. "Yes, it was broken — does that make you happy?"

"Ah, Briona, don't be mad at me. You have a problem, you fix it. You don't just pretend it's going to go away. You hear me?"

"Yeah, I hear you," Bree said sullenly.

"And don't you be trying to do too much either. We'll get things done."

Meg spoke up. "I'm glad to hear that, Raynard. I can help out if you need me."

"It will be fine, you'll see. Guess I'll be going — just wanted to be sure our Bree was all right. Night, ladies."

Meg turned to unlock the kitchen door, and let her mother and Bree pass through before her. Lolly greeted them loudly, complaining about the disruption of her routine. "All right, I know — it's dinnertime. We've been kind of busy." Meg turned to her mother. "Let me feed Lolly and I can take you back to Rachel's. Bree, why don't you go lie down for a while? I'll put dinner together when I get back."

Meg could have sworn she saw a brief flash of disappointment cross her mother's face before she replied, "No rush, dear. Whenever you're ready."

Bree said, "I'll just grab something and crash. Don't worry about me."

"Well, if you're all right."

"I'm fine, Meg," Bree snapped. "My wrist hurts, I'm tired, and I feel stupid. I just want to go to bed."

Meg looked steadily at Bree, who returned her look. "All right. Mother, you ready to go?"

Her mother nodded. "Bree, you take care of yourself. I'll be back tomorrow — if that's okay?" Her eyes flickered toward Meg.

"Of course," Meg responded, more sharply than she'd intended. She was tired, and she wasn't looking forward to driving back and forth to Amherst yet again. "Let's go."

They drove the first few miles in silence. "She's an interesting girl," Elizabeth volunteered finally.

"She is. It can't be easy for her — she's taken on a lot. And I'm grateful."

"This accident comes at a difficult time for you, doesn't it?"

"I won't say no. I'm sure she was being careful, but things happen — like I needed a reminder. I hope there wasn't any malicious intent involved. From what I've seen, the workers are pretty decent guys, and I'm paying them the going rate. Unfortunately, though, this means we're going to be stretched pretty thin for a bit, until we get the rest of the harvest in. Sorry, Mother, but I guess that means I'll have even less time to spend with you."

"Meg, as you've pointed out, you've got a business to run. I have no intention of getting in the way of that. But it's possible I can help you, you know. Shop for food, cook some meals. If you'll let me come back?"

In the growing dusk Meg negotiated the

country roads that led to Rachel's house. "I'd be happy to have you back, Mother, and I'd really appreciate the help. As long as you understand if I'm busy and tired."

"I do. And thank you for not shutting me out. Ah, here we are. Are you coming in?"

It was tempting. Too tempting. Meg knew that Rachel could be counted on to offer sympathy, and maybe some excellent pastry. If she went in, it would be a while before she came out, and she still had to get herself home and think about the ramifications of what had happened and how to cope now that Bree was sidelined. "I don't think so. Say hi to Rachel for me, though. I'll see you in the morning. But don't skip breakfast."

Elizabeth laughed. "Don't worry, I wouldn't pass up Rachel's breakfast. Around ten? Good night, dear, and don't worry too much, please?"

"I'll try not to." Meg summoned up a smile and watched as her mother went into the brightly lit house. With a sigh she turned her car around and headed back to her own house.

When Meg pulled in, she recognized Bree's boyfriend Michael's car in the driveway. Good — Bree had reached out to someone. Entering the kitchen, she found Michael coming down the back stairs from Bree's room. "How's she doing?"

"I think she's out. I stopped by to make sure she was all right, but I think the pain pills did a number on her — she's not used to them. You think she'll be okay?" Michael asked.

Meg shrugged. "I think so. She said they told her it was a simple fracture, nothing to worry about. The worst part is that she won't be able to take an active role in the harvest, and that will annoy her — she'll think she's losing face with the crew. Can you help persuade her to take it easy?"

"Bree? Yeah, right," Michael snorted. "But I'll try. Tell her I'll talk to her tomorrow?" He disappeared out the back door into the night, and Meg heard his car start up.

She slumped in a seat at the table in the kitchen, too tired to think about eating. At least she'd had a good lunch today. Lolly peered around the doorway from the dining room, as if checking to see if the coast was clear. Seeing no strangers, she sauntered in and jumped up on the table.

"Mother is *not* going to tolerate that, Ms. Cat," Meg said. Lolly ignored her and began to wash her tail. "Fine. You'll find out," Meg added. Her mind drifted, and she was jerked out of her reverie by a knock at the back door, still open save for the screen to catch the evening breeze.

"Hard day?" Seth asked, walking in.

"I've had better. Bree's down for the count, according to Michael, who just left. Wait — how did you hear? Is the village grapevine at work?" Meg smiled but couldn't bring herself to move.

"Your mother told Rachel, Rachel called me. She thought you might need some company. Or a shoulder to cry on."

Meg snorted. "Who said that, my mother or Rachel? I'm betting on your sister."

Seth nodded. "Rachel. But your mother did seem honestly concerned about you. Listen, have you eaten?"

"Not since lunch. Which was very nice, by the way, and neither of us said anything regrettable."

"Good. How about I make you some eggs?"

"Anything I don't have to cook myself would be wonderful."

"Eggs it is, then." Seth headed for the refrigerator, knuckling Lolly's head as he passed.

Ten minutes later he had produced a plate of food that looked good and smelled better. Meg dug in, and felt happier with each bite. "You are a lifesaver. I didn't know how hungry I was." She wiped up the last of the scrambled eggs with a piece of bread.

"I try. Are you going to be shorthanded?"

Meg pushed away from the table and sat back in her chair. "I honestly don't know. I think we can manage if I do more of the actual picking than I have been. I'll have to ask Raynard what the forward schedule looks like, but it's kind of unpredictable. Were you planning to volunteer to pick in between all your other activities?"

"I would if you asked, but I am kind of booked up right now. All those people who've been putting off their home repairs over the summer have suddenly decided they want to get them finished before winter. Of course, a lot of it is niggling small jobs, like beefing up insulation or replacing windows. But it pays the rent."

Meg looked down at the table. She was tired, frustrated, and uncertain about what was going to happen tomorrow, or next week. And her mother was going to be around for who knew how long, with Detective Marcus sniffing at her heels. Oh, yes, it was going to be just lovely.

"Uh, Seth, are you busy tonight? Because my mother's going to be moving back here tomorrow . . ."

Seth cocked his head and looked at her

with a smile. "I'm yours for the evening. As long as you don't mind that I have to leave early in the morning?"

"Not at all," Meg said. She struggled out of her chair and carried her plate to the sink. "The dishes can wait — I'm going up."

"Right behind you," Seth answered.

At the top of the stairs, Meg tiptoed first toward Bree's room at the back of the house. Carefully she opened the door, enough to see Bree lying asleep on her bed, breathing deeply, her casted arm resting on a pillow. She looked ridiculously young and vulnerable. Meg pulled the door closed behind her, and headed for her bedroom.

10

Seth was gone when Meg woke up at six thirty; she hadn't even heard him leave. She ran into Bree in the bathroom and backed out again quickly: Bree was struggling to manage with one good arm, and she didn't look any too happy as she tried to maneuver toothpaste onto her toothbrush. Meg waited until she heard her clomp down the stairs and start rattling things in the kitchen before she ventured back to the bathroom.

When Meg made it downstairs, she found chaos. Bree was banging through cabinets and cursing under her breath every time she knocked into something, which was often. Last night's dishes were still stacked in the sink. Lolly was sitting on top of the refrigerator, out of harm's way, but reluctant to vacate the scene because she apparently hadn't been fed yet. Meg set about silently assembling a clean dish and cat food: at least she knew she could make one member of the household happy. When she set the dish on the floor, Lolly scarfed down her meal and retreated toward the front of the house.

"Coffee?" Meg asked.

"Yeah, whatever," Bree replied, still surly. Then she stopped herself. "Sorry. I keep knocking things over, and I hate it."

Meg filled the kettle at the sink and set it on the stove. "Does your arm hurt?"

"I guess. But I hate to take pills because they make me dopey."

"Bree, you've got a broken wrist, and it just happened yesterday. You've got to give it time to heal."

"We don't have time! There's too much to do! But I can't do my job like this!" Bree waved her cast-clad arm.

"Well, *you* aren't going to be doing it!" Meg replied tartly. "I can't be responsible for you doing more damage to yourself. We can hire more labor."

"No, we can't! Everyone around here's been booked since last year."

Meg wasn't going to back down. "Then you can tell me what to do, and I'll do the heavy stuff. There's no reason why I can't pick apples and load crates and such. What you provide is direction and knowledge, and you can do that with or without both arms."

Meg took a breath. "Now, do you want breakfast? I'll get it. You sit, and make a list of what jobs we need to divvy up."

Breakfast was finished and so was Bree's list by the time Raynard came knocking at the kitchen door. Meg beckoned him inside. "You want coffee, Ray?"

"No, ma'am, I'm good. Just came to see how our girl's doing, and plan out our day."

"I'm nobody's 'girl,' Raynard. I'm your boss," Bree said, but she tempered her bite with a half smile.

"So you say, missy," Raynard countered, "so long as you take care of that arm there."

"Yeah, yeah," Bree snapped back. "Can we get to work here? Ray, have you checked the orchard this morning? What's ready to pick?"

Meg listened intently. She had fifteen acres, and the tree density was on average about 300 trees per acre. She knew she had at least twenty varieties of apple, and they all ripened at different times. The early Gravensteins were about done, but the Cortlands, Spartans, Empires, and McIntoshes were following hard on their heels. And she knew she had a few scattered trees of heirloom varieties — not enough to call a crop, but enough to place in some of the local farmers' markets and restaurants, to pique interest. But most of those ripened later; now, in September, they would be harvesting most of the bread-and-butter apples, the ones that made up the bulk of the orchard's crop. From what Raynard and Bree had told her, it had been a good growing year for apples — plenty of rain and sun, in the right proportions. Good news and bad: Meg was likely to make money on her first crop, but she was going to have to work her butt off until the end of the season.

Raynard was obviously ready to get to work. "Are you going to need me right away, Ray?" she asked.

"What say I walk you through the orchard and show you what's coming along? That'll tell us how many hands we'll need today. Briona, you coming?"

"Of course," Bree snapped. "My legs work just fine."

Meg pulled on a sweatshirt against the early morning chill, and grabbed her keys and cell phone. "I'm ready."

After following Ray through the rows of apple trees laden with heavy clusters of ripe apples, Meg felt relieved. The pickers were already hard at work, and Ray didn't think they'd have to look for any additional help, at least not right away — as long as Meg stepped into Bree's shoes. Bree seemed resigned to her standby role, and Meg thanked the stars that she'd hired Raynard this year — even though he put her to work immediately. When Meg finally looked at her watch hours later, she was startled to find it was late afternoon — and no sign or word from her mother. "Are we all set here, Ray?"

"That we are, I think."

"Good, because I need to find out where my mother is — she said she'd be back this morning and she's late. I'll be down at the house if you need me."

Ray waved a sketchy salute as Meg left, and turned back to Bree. Meg ambled down the hill from the orchard, admiring the view of the deep grass rippling in the Great Meadow, and the turning trees beyond. Still too early for the brightest colors, or maybe the trees needed a cold snap to burst into their full autumn glory. At the bottom of the hill she decided it was too nice to go back into the house, and instead stopped to say hello to Dorcas and Isabel, then settled herself in one of the Adirondack chairs overlooking the meadow. She pulled out her phone to call her mother, but at that moment her mother's car pulled into the drive.

Elizabeth climbed out, looking more cheerful than she had the day before. "Sorry

I'm so late, but Rachel and I got to talking. She's quite a ball of energy, isn't she? Not only does she run the bed-and-breakfast, she's got children to deal with."

"Yes, she's a real fireball." Meg wondered briefly just what they might have been talking about, but she lacked the energy to worry about it now. "Have a seat," she said, gesturing at the other chair.

"My, this is lovely," Elizabeth said. "What a wonderful view!"

"I told you, that's the Great Meadow. That's the name they gave it when the town was first laid out, back in sixteen-whatever. It does provide a buffer zone for the property, so we keep the view."

"Nice."

They sat in companionable silence for several minutes. Then Elizabeth roused herself. "If I'm going to be making dinner, I'd better get started. Are you keeping farmers' hours?"

"You mean, do I want to eat early? Yes, that would be great."

Elizabeth stood up. "Then I'll go in. You stay where you are."

Meg didn't argue. After a few more minutes, Bree came down the hill and flopped into the seat Elizabeth had vacated. "Everything cool?"

Meg nodded. "I think so. She's going to make dinner, and then she'll be staying. Can you handle that?"

"No problem. There's some stuff I need to go over with you before we pick the next batch tomorrow. Before you jump all over me, I didn't overdo today — Ray made sure of that."

"Well, good for him. So, what do we need to look at?"

"Let's take this inside — I need room to spread out."

"The dining room, then." Meg spent a productive half hour reviewing schedules and staffing with Bree, vaguely aware of good smells issuing from the kitchen. "Did the doctor say you couldn't drive? Because if that's the case, I'll need to run some of the apples to our vendors. And you shouldn't be doing any lifting, you know."

"Yeah, yeah, I get it, as if Ray hadn't reminded me like sixteen times. You're right — you'll have to make the deliveries, at least for a bit. You can handle the truck, right? The shift's kind of rough." When Meg nodded, Bree added, "At least it's still early — next month we'll be swamped, but I should be back in shape by then."

"We'll see. Okay, you give me a list of

deliveries for tomorrow, and I'll take care of it."

"Great. And I'll duck out after dinner and give you a chance to talk to your mother."

"Bree," Meg protested, "I don't want you to feel you have to hide out in your room all the time she's here. This is your home, too."

"No biggie. I'm kind of tired anyway."

Bree was gathering up her lists when Elizabeth poked her head in. "Dinner's ready. Do you want to eat in the kitchen?"

Meg stood up. "Sure. That's easiest."

They managed to get through dinner without bringing up anything remotely controversial. Elizabeth asked intelligent questions about the pros and cons of organic farming. Meg had dredged up another bottle of wine and made sure that her mother's glass was filled. Elizabeth wasn't a heavy drinker by any means, but Meg figured it might help to loosen her mother's tongue.

Bree was the first to finish her meal. "Want me to do the dishes, Mrs. C.?"

"With that cast on? Nonsense. We'll take care of things."

"Okay, thanks." Bree glanced at Meg. "I guess I'll go upstairs now, so I'll be out of the bathroom when you need it. Night, all."

Meg carried her dishes to the sink. She was wondering how to frame her first question when there was a knock at the back door: Seth. "Hi. What's up? You want to come in?"

Seth took in the scene: her mother still at the table, the uncleared dishes. "Hi, Mrs. Corey. No, I just wanted to remind you about the Harvest Festival tomorrow. You coming?"

Meg felt a pang of guilt. This was the second time Seth had asked about it, so clearly it was important to him. Of course, it was not just the annual Granford Harvest Festival but also the grand opening of Granford Grange, the new commercial strip on the highway, the construction of which Seth had been overseeing for months now. It had slipped her mind when she was planning the day with Bree, but she couldn't let him down. "Of course. I'd love to come, if Ray and Bree will let me — apples wait for no man, or woman. And Bree tells me we have some deliveries scheduled. I don't have to volunteer for anything, do I?"

Seth smiled. "I'll let you off the hook for this year, since it's your first. Your mother might enjoy it, too."

"That sounds charming," Elizabeth called out.

142

"So I'll see you both there. It opens at nine." He turned to leave, and Meg followed him out the door. "Problems?" he asked quietly.

Meg kept walking, drawing him away from the door — and her mother's earshot. "No, I think we're good. I was hoping to have a heart-to-heart talk with her tonight, if I can stay awake."

"Well, I'll leave you to it. Sorry this has all landed on your head at once. You'll let me know if there's anything I can do?"

"Of course." Well, maybe. "And thanks." Meg leaned in for a quick kiss, then withdrew before it could grow into anything more. "See you tomorrow."

She watched as he headed over the hill, then turned back to the kitchen. Time to get some answers.

11

By the time Meg came back into the kitchen, her ever-efficient mother had taken care of the dishes.

"Mother, we have to talk," Meg began.

"Oh, dear, that sounds ominous," Elizabeth said, striving for a light tone.

"I'm sorry to keep hounding you about this, but I still feel that you haven't told me, or Detective Marcus, everything about what went on with Daniel Weston. I happen to know that Marcus can be very persistent. And he can also be wrong, but he does need all the facts. And so do I, if I'm going to help you at all."

"And I apologize, dear." There was a minuscule pause before Elizabeth said, "As you may have guessed, I did not intend this to be a visit with you." She stared at the empty table. "How odd that sounds. You've been involved in murder investigations, and now I am."

"That's not an answer, Mother." Meg decided to emulate Detective Marcus's approach, and waited silently.

Finally, Elizabeth said, "You're right. I haven't told him everything. Oh, not because I had anything to do with Daniel's death — surely you can't think that. But I'm embarrassed — the story doesn't put me in a very good light."

"Tell me."

"May I have another glass of wine?" Elizabeth parried, holding out her glass. Meg filled it wordlessly. Elizabeth settled herself back in her chair and sipped.

"I've given you the basic story," she began. "It's true that Daniel called quite unexpectedly. I hadn't had any contact with him in years, and I was intrigued. Your father was away, I had no projects lined up, and I thought, why not? I hadn't done something spontaneous, on my own, for quite a while, and I liked the idea. Had your father been around, I would certainly have told him — although he might have wanted to come with me, and that wouldn't have been the same at all, would it?" She appealed to Meg.

"I don't know." Meg realized she wasn't just stalling: she really had no idea.

"Trust me, it wouldn't." Elizabeth stopped again.

This wasn't coming easily. After a few seconds, Meg said, "Tell me about Daniel, back then."

Her mother smiled, more to herself than to Meg. "We were so young then, and there was so much ahead of us. You don't know it at the time. You don't realize that the possibilities will keep closing down, one by one, over the years. You make your choices, and you don't see that you'll have to live with them forever." She took another sip of her wine. "I'm sorry — you wanted the facts. I've told you, and I told that policeman, that we all knew each other in Cambridge, back in the early seventies. I was involved with your father, but he was very focused on getting his law degree and getting on with his life — our life. I admired that. But Daniel was a lot more fun to spend time with, and I guess his degree program wasn't as demanding. Or maybe he didn't take it as seriously, I don't know. Though it worked out for him in the end, since he held a tenured position at an outstanding college, right? He was always the smart one, fast with words. Your father was more of a plodder."

"Were you ever . . . involved with Daniel, back in those days?" Meg asked.

"You mean, was I sleeping with him? Yes."

Meg squirmed inwardly. This was far beyond any conversations they'd had in Meg's younger years, and she certainly had never wanted to ask, nor had her mother volunteered. But now it was important. "Before Daddy? Or at the same time?"

Elizabeth looked at her with something like pity. "Meg, before you judge me, you have to understand the time and the place. It was a different environment, and people viewed things differently. I was pretty straitlaced by standards then, and I knew I wanted a conventional life, no matter what our friends were doing. I felt that I had to make a choice. I loved your father, but in a way I loved Daniel, too. They were very different people. I have to say, your father loved me more than Daniel ever did. I slept with Daniel a few times, to see . . . I don't know what. If it would change what I felt, or what he felt. If it would make any difference. I don't think your father ever knew — I certainly didn't tell him, and I doubt Daniel did. Phillip might have sensed something, but he didn't press. And then he proposed."

"Who proposed? Daddy, or Daniel?"

"Your father."

"And that was the end of it between you and Daniel?"

"Not immediately. I didn't accept your

father's proposal right away. I guess I wanted to give Daniel one last chance. Maybe I hoped he would see what he would be losing and fight for me. But he didn't. Maybe he valued Phillip's friendship more that he cared about me."

An awful thought hit Meg, and she couldn't stop herself from asking, "You're not going to tell me that Daniel is my father?"

Elizabeth turned abruptly toward her, her eyes glittering in the half-light. "Margaret Elizabeth Corey, how can you ask me that? Of course not. I wasn't stupid or careless, and I wouldn't have done that to your father. And you, young woman — you work with numbers. Do the math. You were born two years after I married Phillip."

Meg was embarrassed, but also relieved. "I'm sorry. And I guess I'm sorry we've never talked about those days. Maybe it would have helped me with my own relationships. I don't have a lot to be proud of there."

"You mean Chandler?"

"In part. I know you liked him."

Her mother sighed deeply. "Darling, I thought he was a self-centered ass. But I wasn't about to meddle — that's never a good idea."

Meg sat up straighter, incredulous. "You didn't like Chandler?"

"Not at all. But you seemed happy."

"I tried to be, but I can see now that the whole thing was a mistake. He never really cared about me — I was just a placeholder until someone better came along." How much of Meg's image of a "good" relationship was based on what she'd seen of her parents' relationship when she was growing up? Which, when she thought about it, was pretty distant. "Mother, have you and Daddy been happy together?"

"Yes, I'd say so. It hasn't been a mad, passionate relationship, if that's what you're asking. But we've always supported each other, always respected each other, trusted each other. I would call it a successful marriage."

"Was there passion with Daniel?"

For a moment her mother didn't answer, and then she said softly, "Yes."

Meg waited before framing her next question. "And did you miss that, with Daddy?"

"Oh, Meg . . ." Her mother shook her head sadly. "To be honest, yes, occasionally. But please don't cling to any romantic notions about soul mates or the idea that love conquers all. I mentioned choices earlier. I made a considered, rational choice to marry

149

your father, because I believed we would have a better life together, over time. And I think I was right."

"Then why were you here with Daniel now?"

"Curiosity. It had been a long time."

"Mother, I know you said you didn't sleep with him, and I believe you. But did you plan to?"

After another long pause, Elizabeth whispered, "I would have. If he'd asked."

The single lamp in the room cast shadows in the corners. Meg was conscious of Lolly's purring warmth in her lap, and she felt the weight of the silence in the room. She needed to think carefully. Her respectable mother had come up here for what she probably had hoped would be a romantic tryst with a former lover — but he hadn't been interested. And he had ended up dead.

"Mother, I hate to keep poking at this, but I think it's important. Did you believe that Daniel invited you up here for a . . ."

"An affair? A quickie? A last gasp at youth, now that we're all old and gray?" Elizabeth's tone was strained. "No, I don't think so."

What had so upset her mother? "I know you didn't have a lot of time together, but he didn't, uh, make overtures? He didn't meet you at your hotel room and fling you

150

on the bed?" Meg couldn't believe she was saying this to her mother.

Her mother gave an uncharacteristic snort of laughter. "No. Nothing like that. He talked about his wife and his children. All very proper. We never even got near a bed."

Which, Meg realized, potentially gave her mother a motive for murder. She had come up here with expectations, which Daniel had squashed. Elizabeth had risked her marriage and her dignity and he had rejected her. She could see a prosecutor outlining for a jury the classic story of a woman scorned, a woman with a fading marriage, past her youth, grasping at straws — and pushed over the edge when Daniel had said no, or worse, had said nothing, trashing all of Elizabeth's fantasies.

"Was this what you weren't telling the police?"

Elizabeth smiled ruefully. "I know, it seems silly. I was embarrassed, and I didn't think they needed to know. After all, nothing happened. My expectations had nothing to do with Daniel's death. Are you seriously thinking that I would have killed him because he didn't want to sleep with me?"

"I guess not," Meg said, suppressing an inappropriate grin. Now that her fears had been voiced, they appeared ridiculous. "But it's possible that the police would see this as a motive for killing him, and if they find out you've lied to them, they're going to be even more suspicious."

"Meg, there's nothing to find. We were two old friends meeting in public places. That's all there was."

"But he's dead. Somebody killed him. Are you sure he didn't say something, anything, that would suggest he was in danger, or was afraid of something?"

Elizabeth shook her head. "Not that I can recall."

"Maybe if we go over exactly what he did say, we might find something," Meg said stubbornly. Surely a man who had been murdered could not have been the paragon of virtue that Detective Marcus had outlined. He must have left some small hint, embedded somewhere.

"Meg, are you sure this is going to help? I'm tired, and I'd like to remember the positive things Daniel and I shared."

"Mother, he was murdered, and you're the best suspect the police have. This is not just going to go away. Trust me on that." When Elizabeth didn't answer, Meg pressed on, "Look, the man must have been busy, with classes and this conference. Why did he pick this particular time to ask you up here? Surely there would have been more convenient times. Was his wife away?"

"No. Or if she was, he didn't mention it. He didn't invite me to his home."

"Did he take you to the campus?"

"Not exactly. We drove around it, but we didn't visit his office. We never even got out of the car."

"Did he take you out anywhere in Amherst?"

"No. He said the choices in Northampton were more interesting, and that's where I was staying anyway, so it was convenient."

No doubt someone at the restaurants would remember seeing them, or there would be a credit card trail, to corroborate her story. Tracking that down was a job for the police. "So no one in Amherst — not his family or his colleagues — knew you were in town?"

"No, but I didn't give it any thought. It's not like he made me duck down or put a blanket over my head when we drove through town, as though he were ashamed to be seen with me. Does it really matter?"

"To be honest, I don't know. I'm just looking for something out of place. He didn't introduce you to anyone in Amherst. Maybe he didn't want to be seen in public with you there. Why?"

153

"Meg, I think you're making too much of this. We didn't spend that much time together — less than forty-eight hours."

"All right. What did you talk about?"

"I've already told you. We caught up on the past. We talked about our spouses and our children. He asked about you, and told me what his sons were doing, where they'd gone to college, their jobs."

Meg thought furiously. Weston had asked her mother to meet him here without Phillip, but not for romantic purposes. Yet he'd more or less concealed her presence from anyone who knew him. They'd shared information about their respective spouses and children, which was perfectly normal. On the surface, everything seemed quite innocent. Why didn't it feel right?

Meg was startled when her mother stood up abruptly. So was Lolly, who launched herself off Meg's lap; Meg winced at the dig of sharp claws.

"Meg, I know you mean well, but I don't want to talk about this anymore right now. If you don't mind, I'm going to go to bed."

"Of course. I'll see you in the morning." Meg didn't even have time to get to her feet before her mother left — or more accurately, fled. Meg had struck a nerve, no doubt, but that had been her intention.

Knowing her mother, she could understand why she had withheld certain details from the police. Unfortunately those were details whose concealment did not put her in a good light. Had Elizabeth finally realized that?

What now? Accepting that her mother was not a killer — not that Meg had any such suspicion — why would anyone else have wanted Daniel Weston dead? It made no sense to her. But, Meg admitted, she was exhausted, both physically and mentally, and tomorrow promised to be as demanding as today had been. Reluctantly she dragged herself out of the chair and trudged up the stairs to her bedroom. Her mother's door across the hall was firmly closed.

12

When Meg awoke the next morning, feeling sluggish, she lay in bed listening to the distant sounds of voices. Bree and her mother were early risers and were chatting up a storm in the kitchen, and they sounded so normal. Meg sighed: what Elizabeth had told her the night before did nothing to eliminate her as a suspect in Daniel Weston's death. Ignoring that was not going to make it go away. Did Marcus have any other suspects? Not that he'd share them with her, but clearly he would be annoyed at Elizabeth's ongoing evasiveness. As was Meg. She could understand why her mother had been reluctant to tell the detective everything, but stalling had only aggravated the situation.

So what was she supposed to do? Harvesting her apples was at the top of the list. She had to ask Raynard if he could spare her long enough to put in an appearance at the

Harvest Festival; if she didn't, Seth's feelings would be hurt, even if he didn't say so, since he had done a lot of the planning for the event *and* specifically asked her to attend. Thinking of Seth made her wonder: Why hadn't her mother ever told her that she thought Chandler was wrong for her? And what would she have done if she had? Had she gotten involved with Chandler because in the back of her mind she thought her mother would approve of him? And worse, was she putting off introducing Seth as her . . . whatever, because she was afraid her mother would disapprove of her dating a plumber? *Grow up, Meg!*

To avoid any more unsettling thoughts, Meg hauled herself out of bed. When she made it to the kitchen, Bree and Elizabeth were seated next to each other at the table, and Bree was sketching on a piece of scrap paper and pointing with her pencil. "This area here was replanted a couple of years ago, so they won't be bearing for another couple of years. Over at this end, we've got a bunch of heirlooms. Christopher Ramsdell — that's the professor who's kept the orchard going for years — he's been trying to collect as many of the old varieties as he can, so we don't lose them from the genome forever."

"That's fascinating. And I met Christopher yesterday at lunch in Amherst — he's charming," Elizabeth said.

"Hi, guys," Meg said as she headed for the coffeepot. "Bree, what's on the agenda for today?"

"Well, duh. Picking apples." Bree grinned at her. "There are lots of Macs left."

"I need to sneak off for a couple of hours — I promised Seth I'd stop by the Harvest Festival."

"I think we can spare you. You know, you should have some T-shirts made up with your crate label on them — you could advertise that way."

Was there anyone in town who didn't know who Meg was already? Still, it was a cute idea. "I'll think about it. Mother, did you see the label that Bree designed?" Meg rummaged through a stack of papers until she found a color computer image. "We used a historic example for the background but plugged in our orchard name."

"Very nice. Eye-catching," Elizabeth replied. "I never thought about how many details there are to growing and selling apples."

Meg sat down at the table with her coffee. "Neither did I. But with Bree and Christopher helping, I've learned a lot since I arrived. Mother, you still want to go to the festival?"

Elizabeth nodded at Meg. "Certainly, if I wouldn't be imposing on you."

Bree burst out laughing. "Man, the two of you! You sound like something out of a Victorian novel. Meg, you gonna write an invitation? I can deliver it, if I can find a pair of white gloves."

Meg smiled. "You're right. Mother, you'd be more than welcome. Bree, I'm going to go up and check in with Raynard about what deliveries I need to make. I'll come back and Mother and I can head over to the festival."

Once outside, Bree asked as they climbed the hill, "You two working things out?"

"Sort of." Meg hesitated for a moment, wondering how much of her mother's confidences she could share with Bree. "Let's say that the reason she's been ducking Detective Marcus is embarrassing rather than criminal."

"I couldn't exactly see your mother whacking someone. How did the guy die again?"

"Marcus didn't share, but he knows it wasn't natural, which makes it a murder investigation now."

"Ouch. Just what we need."

Raynard was waiting at the top of the hill, and Meg could see pickers already dispersed through the orchard. "Hi, Ray," she said. "Listen, do you think you could spare me for a bit today? I'd like to take my mother to see the Harvest Festival."

"I think that would be fine — if Briona agrees," he said with a sly smile and a nod toward Bree.

"I'll let you go, Meg, if you'll take care of today's deliveries later. I'm not supposed to do stuff like that with this arm, remember."

"Deal!" Meg responded. "You just let me know who gets what. We should have plenty of time."

"Six crates of apples to deliver to Amherst," Bree said promptly. "They're in the cooler, and they're all labeled. You'll be okay with the truck?"

"I'll manage. If I can handle a tractor, I'm sure I can handle an old pickup. You don't want to go to the festival?"

"I'm going to meet Michael later and we're going to hit up some of the bigger festivals in Amherst and Belchertown. It's a pain that they all seem to happen on the same weekend."

"Then I'll be back in a couple of hours to pick up the apples."

Back at the house, Meg found her mother

160

in her once-again spotless kitchen, wearing practical shoes and a light sweater draped over her shoulders. "So tell me, what goes on at this fair of yours?" Elizabeth asked.

"I have no idea — this is my first one. But it's also the official opening of the new strip mall on the highway — it's called Granford Grange — and I'd like to stop by. I'm going to make the wild assumption that there will be various food products at the festival today, so we'll have plenty of opportunity to eat later. Are you ready?"

"I am."

Meg led her mother out to the car. When they were settled, Elizabeth asked, "What sort of mall is this Grange?"

Meg started the car and headed out the driveway. "That's probably kind of a grand term for it — it's a row of shops along the highway, but it *is* new, and sorely needed in Granford. The original plan was to put it where the orchard is now, but luckily the design was cut back and the whole thing got shifted closer to town." She realized once again she had omitted to mention Seth's role, which had been crucial in that process.

"From what little I've seen of the town, there isn't much commercial development here. Downtown Granford looks just like I remembered it, even after all these years."

"Yes, Granford doesn't change much. Mostly because it can't — no income, dwindling population, and so on. Though that keeps the tourists happy." Meg laughed. "There's the general store in town, and of course, the restaurant now, and some feed stores along the highway, but most people have to leave town to do any shopping. It does take getting used to."

"So what does this little mall offer?"

"A sandwich shop, breakfast and lunch only. My veterinarian, Andrea Bedortha. A card-and-gift shop, and I think an accountant. Plus a couple of others — I haven't kept up lately. The town tried to avoid chain stores, not that we were really big enough to interest them, and stick to those that will benefit the local community. Anything exotic you can find somewhere else around here, like Northampton."

"I will say that the area seems relatively unspoiled, by contemporary standards."

"It is," Meg agreed, "but not because of any sort of agreement or long-range plan. People around here just haven't had much money for a long time, so it's pretty much no-frills. And I think that rural character is probably a plus — we get a lot of tourists passing through, and quite a few stop to take a picture of the church. It's what everybody wants to think New England looks like. Now there'll be a place for them to stop and get a good meal, too, at least."

"This looks festive," Elizabeth said as Meg guided her car into the crowded parking lot at Granford Grange. Not crowded with cars, but overflowing with tables filled with food and other products. Brightly colored balloons billowed, tied in clusters to every possible point, and Meg spied a pony ride in one corner, with a waiting line of small children. The mall's launch certainly appeared to be a rousing success.

"Oh, my," Elizabeth said. "Is this what was going to go into the orchard?"

"Sort of," Meg replied, scanning the crowd. "Only that version was going to be a lot bigger — they were planning to raze the orchard for a parking lot."

"Well, I'm glad that didn't happen."

"Amen." Meg hesitated a moment. "But Seth had to give up a chunk of his family's land for this one." There, she'd said his name. "He lives on the adjoining property, although you can't see it from our house. And I think I told you how he's using part of the barn, or rather, what used to be a carpenter's shop next to the barn in the

163

nineteenth century, as his office, and storing his renovation salvage in the barn." Meg was blathering on, and she knew it. Why couldn't she just tell her mother that she was dating him? Involved with him? She was, after all. Meg searched the crowd and finally spied him — deep in conversation with veterinarian Andrea Bedortha. While she watched, Andrea leaned closer and laughed, laying a hand on Seth's arm. He didn't back away. In fact, he looked as though he was enjoying their conversation. Meg felt an unexpected wash of jealousy, which was immediately followed by annoyance — at herself. Seth had every right to chat with Andrea: he'd known her for years, and he was the one who had persuaded her to set up her own practice here in Granford. He was just being . . . welcoming, right?

"Come on, Mother, and I'll introduce you around." Meg grabbed her startled mother's arm and waded through the crowd to where Seth and Andrea stood. "Hi, Seth, Andrea. Mother, this is Andrea Bedortha — she's the veterinarian I mentioned, and she's checked out Lolly and the goats. And you've met Seth Chapin." She met Seth's eyes squarely.

"Nice to see you again, Mrs. Corey," Seth

said politely.

Elizabeth smiled. "Elizabeth, please. 'Mrs. Corey' makes me feel old. Although longevity apparently runs in our family. I was reminding Meg that we knew the Warren sisters years ago, and they were close to ninety then."

"Did Meg mention Ruth Ferry?" Seth asked. "She knew the sisters, too, when she was a child."

"How interesting. I hope I'll have a chance to meet her while I'm here."

Meg watched the exchange silently, very aware that Andrea's hand still lay on Seth's arm. Did they have a history? She had never asked.

"I'll tell Rachel. She sees more of her than I do. Did you enjoy the bed-and-breakfast?"

"I did. You know Rachel?"

"She's my sister." Seth glanced quizzically at Meg, who shrugged — now was not the time to try to explain.

"Oh. Meg didn't mention that. What a lovely home she has! And her breakfasts were outstanding. So, Meg tells me you're a near neighbor?"

"I am, right over the hill from you. In fact, you're standing on what used to be a piece of our property. My father had a plumbing shop here."

"Excuse me, Seth," Andrea broke in, "but I should be drumming up business with the local small-pet owners. Good to see you again, Meg, and nice to meet you, Mrs. Corey." She smiled and left quickly.

If Elizabeth had picked up any unusual undercurrents, she didn't comment. "So, what shall we see here, Meg? It looks as though there are some nice homemade items over there."

"There'll be more at the Harvest Festival — that's on the green in town," Meg said, her voice tight. "I just wanted you to get a sense of the place. We can come back later when it's not so busy. Seth, it looks like you've got a great turnout here. Let's hope they come back often."

"Are you two headed for the green?"

Meg nodded. "I think so. I've got some deliveries to make later this afternoon, but I wanted Mother to see Granford at its best."

"You picked a good time to visit, Mrs. Cor— Elizabeth. Lots going on in Granford at the moment."

A man Meg didn't recognize bustled up and tapped Seth on the arm. "Seth, we need to run another extension cord for the coffeemaker. Can you help out?"

"No problem. See you later, Meg?"

"Okay," Meg said noncommittally. "We

166

should be back at the house by five or so, but the festival runs into the evening, doesn't it?"

"Yeah, it does, and then there are fireworks after dark, and the cleanup after, so I'll be tied up tonight. Elizabeth, will you be around a bit longer?"

"That's my plan. I'll look forward to talking to you again."

Seth headed off to deal with the latest crisis, leaving Meg feeling out of sorts. Well, what had she expected? That he would plant a wet kiss on her, here and now? That was silly. He had probably picked up on Meg's ambivalence and was letting her call the shots. Or else he had been distracted by Andrea — smart, attractive Andrea, who was obviously interested in Seth Chapin. Why shouldn't she be?

"Meg?" Elizabeth tugged at her sleeve.

"What?" she snapped. "I'm sorry, I was distracted. Did you have a question?"

"I just wondered if we were heading back toward your car? Because we're walking the other direction at the moment, and I don't have any particular interest in hay bales."

"Oh, sorry. Yes, let's go back to the car. It might take a little while to find parking in the center of town. I hope you don't mind doing some walking, but we should be hungry by the time we get to the festival."

Back in the car for the short drive to the town center, Elizabeth said mildly, "Seth Chapin seems very nice."

"Uh, he is. He's been a lot of help with the house and the barn, and he's introduced me to a lot of people around here."

"Really. He seems to keep popping up every time I turn around."

Meg sighed, waiting for a woman with a stroller to cross in front of her. "Well, he lives close by, and his office is in my back-yard, and he's involved in about every community activity there is in Granford." She could feel Elizabeth's glance on her. Why was she so reluctant to talk about Seth? Because she was afraid of what her mother would think of him? Or because she wasn't sure what she thought?

Finally Elizabeth turned her eyes back to the busy road in front of them. "I hope we'll have a chance to get together again while I'm here."

Meg felt an odd mixture of relief and regret. She wanted to explain, but this was not the right time or place to do it. Still, putting it off did not make it any easier.

They entered the town from the west end, and the single main street was mobbed with people. She saw Police Chief Art Preston standing in the middle of the highway, directing traffic, with a big smile on his face. When Meg pulled closer, she yelled out the window, "You look like you're having fun. Where should we park?"

"Amherst?" Art grinned. "Go on past Town Hall — they've opened up the field on the right."

"Thanks, Art." Meg resumed her careful approach. At the field Art had mentioned, she found a volunteer motioning them in, and finally found a space at the back end. "Wow! This is quite a turnout. I wonder if it's always this busy."

They clambered out of the car and made their way back to the two-lane highway and across. Meg pitied the hapless tourists out for a drive, for it would probably take them ten minutes to navigate the half mile through town. But maybe they would decide to stop and boost the local economy? She and her mother stopped at the higher end of the green, across the street from the restaurant, to take in the scene. Meg could make out crafts booths, an array of impressively large pumpkins, a cluster of antique cars in the church parking lot, a tent with what looked like a petting zoo, and a table laden with pies. "Are you ready for this, Mother?"

"It looks charming. I'm so glad you have good weather for it." Her mother was smiling. "Something smells good," Elizabeth said. "Lead on!"

Meg discovered immediately that the chef-owners of the newly opened Gran's, Nicky and Brian Czarnecki, had set up a booth at the end closest to their restaurant and were doling out samples of food. Nicky greeted Meg with a squeal of glee. "Meg, isn't this wonderful? I'm having so much fun! Is this your mother? I'm Nicky and this is my husband, Brian, and we run the restaurant over there. Ooh, I love saying that!"

"Yes, I'm Elizabeth Corey. Meg's told me a bit about your place. I'm looking forward to trying it."

"Of course! Meg, call me and we can set up a night, and we'll plan something really special. Mrs. Corey, we wouldn't be here without Meg's help, you know, and we're just so grateful!"

"I'm just happy to have some great food in town, Nicky," Meg said. "Good to see you, but we'd better check out the rest of the booths."

"Not without tasting this first," Nicky said, handing them each a plate with something that Meg couldn't identify.

Meg and Elizabeth helped themselves.

"That's terrific. What is it?" Meg asked.

Nicky giggled. "It's a secret. A recipe I'm testing. Maybe it'll be on the menu the night you come to dinner. Bye now!"

As they walked away, Elizabeth said, "My, she's a bundle of energy. And she can cook!"

"That she can, and she's a real asset to the town. What else looks good?"

They strolled and ogled, and Elizabeth collected a number of craft items and jars of jelly, which in turn necessitated buying an attractive quilted bag to carry them all in. They feasted on hamburgers and surprisingly good french fries, followed by three kinds of pie, accompanied by fresh local cider. Meg wondered if any of her apples had found their way into the batch. Luckily they had located seats on a bench under one of the old maples that ringed the green.

"You know, I think I'm beginning to understand the appeal of New England," Elizabeth commented. "This is so charming, so timeless." Then she stiffened to attention. "Didn't we see that man at Daniel's service? Is he from town?"

Meg followed the direction of her gaze. "The tall black man in the nice jacket? I don't know him, but then, I still don't know a lot of people in town. He does look a bit overdressed to be local. I think you're right, though, that he was at the service. Did you want to talk to him?"

"I'm not sure what excuse I could give . . . Oh, why not?" Elizabeth quickly gathered up the remains of their lunch, deposited them in the nearest trash can, then walked over to where the man was standing, apparently admiring odds and ends on a white elephant table. Meg trailed behind.

"Excuse me," Elizabeth began, "but were you a friend of Daniel Weston?"

The man regarded her gravely. "I was a colleague, yes. Why do you ask?"

"I thought so." Elizabeth flashed what Meg recognized as her social smile. "I saw you at the service on Wednesday. Are you from the college?"

"No, I'm here for the symposium — which, as it happens, is going forward, this afternoon. In fact, I should be headed there now, Mrs. . . . ?"

"Corey. Elizabeth Corey. I was an old friend of Daniel's. This is my daughter, Meg — she lives here in Granford."

"Ah. Nice to meet you. I'm Kenneth Henderson." He looked at his watch. "I'm sorry, I don't have time to talk right now — I was so carried away with the day and this delightful event that I lost track of time, and I really must run. Perhaps we could get together at another time and talk about Daniel?"

"I'd like that. Are you staying in Amherst?"

"Yes, at a charming bed-and-breakfast. Dickinson's."

"I was just there myself!" Elizabeth said with delight. "How is it that I didn't see you there?"

"I treated myself to a bit of a ramble, doing some sightseeing, since I didn't need to be at the college until today. It was only by accident that I learned of Daniel's death, and the service, and I felt I should come back for it. Why don't we try to get together, say, tomorrow?"

"Fine," Elizabeth said promptly, before glancing at Meg, who nodded with bewilderment. "Let me give you my cell phone number, and you can let me know what time would be convenient." She found a piece of paper in her bag and scribbled the number on it. "I'll look forward to seeing you tomorrow, then."

"As will I. A pleasure to meet you, Mrs. Corey, Meg." He turned and headed for the end of the green nearest the parking area.

Elizabeth turned to Meg. "I hope you don't mind. You don't have to come along."

"Mother, I wouldn't miss it." Then Meg

173

spied Gail Selden standing in the doorway of the Historical Society. She waved, and Gail waved back.

"Mother? I'd like you to meet Gail, and see the Historical Society. She's the one who roped me into cataloging part of their documents collection in my so-called spare time."

"I'd be delighted."

They crossed the drive to the small, one-story Historical Society building near the church. "Hi, Meg," Gail called out at they approached. "Is this your mother?"

"My, news travels fast in a small town," Elizabeth responded. "Yes, I'm Elizabeth Corey. Meg was just telling me about working with you. She thinks I should start putting together a family tree."

"Great idea. I'd love to help, but maybe later? You going to be around a bit longer?"

"Yes, at least through next week. Of course you must be busy at the moment. What a wonderful event!"

"We enjoy it. And it's one of the few days that the Society is open to the public, so I encourage people to come in and see what we've got, even though it's only the tip of the iceberg. Come on, I'll give you the nickel tour."

Meg had to swallow a smile at her mother's first reaction to the cluttered interior, particularly the stuffed birds and animals that nestled in the unlikeliest places. She tried to remember if she had ever seen the interior with all the blinds open. The bright September sunshine streaming through the tall windows was a mixed blessing: it was easy to see the collections, but it was even easier to see the thick layer of dust that lay over everything, as well as all the patches and darns and frays. But Gail made no apologies, pointing out the local treasures, and Elizabeth made appropriate admiring noises.

Half an hour later they emerged from the building, blinking at the bright light. It was a double shock, stepping from the quiet detritus of Granford's past into the vibrant reality of its present. "Goodness," Elizabeth said. "That was interesting. And your festival seems to be a great success."

"That it does. Was there anything else you wanted to see? Or revisit? I could see you eyeing the white elephant table."

"Maybe we could take one more look? Or are you in a hurry? You mentioned you had deliveries to make this afternoon."

"I do, so I've got to get back to the house and pick up the apples, but I can spare a few more minutes. Then I can drop you off back at the house."

"Would you like company?"

"What, you want to come along on the apple deliveries?"

"Sure. We can at least chat in the car. I might even carry a crate or two, if you'll let me."

Will wonders never cease? Meg thought to herself. Her mother volunteering to do manual labor? It was too good an opportunity to pass up. "Sure, I'd love to have you. But it's not a car, it's a pickup truck, and the shocks aren't in very good shape. Still game?"

"I am."

13

Sated with sun and baked goods, Meg drove home with her mother. Bree was nowhere in sight, but as she had promised, she had left the crates of apples stacked just inside the first holding chamber, with a list on top. Only three stops, and all toward Amherst. One of those scheduled deliveries was at Dickinson's Farm Stand — the place where Daniel Weston had died. Was it ghoulish to want to see it?

Meg started up her new old truck — yet another of Seth's finds, through a friend of a friend — and backed it up toward the entrance of the barn so she could load the apples.

Elizabeth approached and eyed the elderly pickup incredulously. "This is yours?"

"Sure is," Meg replied. "A 1996 F150 with two-hundred-thousand-some miles on her. How else did you think we delivered crates of apples?"

"Of course, of course. Give me a moment to get used to the idea of my MBA daughter driving a pickup truck. It boggles the mind."

"Hey, if you like, I'll give you a demonstration of the tractor."

"One shock at a time, please. Those are the apples you're delivering?" Meg had led her mother into the dark barn and opened the nearer temperature-controlled chamber.

"They are. Bree usually does this, but she can't with her broken wrist. Anyway, I've met the people at the markets before, and it's good to touch base with them."

When Elizabeth reached for a box of apples, Meg stopped her. "You don't have to do that. I can handle them."

"Meg, my love, I'm not ancient, nor am I frail. I'm perfectly capable of picking up a box. Let me help." Three boxes later, Elizabeth asked, "How many of these are we delivering?"

"Just the six today — three stops, two boxes each. If we want them to be fresh, they have to be recently picked. If they sit out for too long, they can get mealy."

"But not everything ripens on a tidy schedule, right?"

"Nope. That's why we built the holding chambers — we can stockpile apples and keep them at the right temperature until the vendor is ready for them. Up to a point, at least. Some apples hold better and longer than others. In fact, some actually improve if you keep them for a while."

"So much to learn!" Elizabeth shook her head and shoved the crate toward the back. "And who are these going to?"

"Some farmers' markets in Amherst. This is peak season for them, and for us, so I'll be making this run quite a few times this week." And until Bree was cleared by her doctor to resume lifting. Meg knew how much this first harvest meant to Bree, but it was up to her to prevent Bree from doing anything foolish.

"How did you find vendors?" Elizabeth asked.

"I got lists from the local organic groups, and Christopher — although when he was managing this, he just turned them all over to a local co-op to sell and didn't pay much attention. I put together a list of vendors and then I went and talked to them, one at a time. Some were pretty well fixed with apples, but there were enough who were interested in giving a new grower a chance. We've got some unusual varieties in the orchard, which helps. There's increased interest in heirloom varieties these days."

"And the restaurant in town buys some?"

"They do. Remind me to call them about booking dinner one night, when we get back."

"They're that busy?"

"I hope so. Of course, this is their first week, so they're still a novelty. But they picked a good time to open, between the parents bringing their kids back to the local colleges, and all the leaf-peepers passing through." It hadn't been easy, meeting the September opening deadline, but it had definitely been worth it financially.

"You mentioned something about cider?"

"Oh, right. I don't make it, but I sell the less-than-perfect apples to some of the places that do. Including Dickinson's, where we're going now, but I've got only the good apples today."

"My, there are certainly a lot of Dickinsons around here. Are they all related, do you think?"

"Maybe. I haven't had time to check."

Elizabeth frowned, "Isn't that where . . . ?"

"Yes," Meg said. Where Daniel Weston's body had been found.

"Did you plan to ask about . . . Daniel?"

"Probably, if it's not too awkward. Would you rather not go?" She wondered if the location would dampen her mother's interest in accompanying her.

Apparently not.

Elizabeth settled herself in the passenger seat and buckled her seat belt. "No, I want to see it. Look, Meg, you don't have to tiptoe around the subject of Daniel and his death. Whatever I felt for him once, it was over long ago. And I rather resent being considered a suspect in his murder, so I welcome the opportunity to see where it happened, and I would encourage you to find out anything you can. Maybe someone can tell us why Daniel was there."

"One can but hope." The absurdity of the situation struck Meg suddenly, and she had to suppress a giggle. She and her mother were sleuthing together? How weird was that? "Well, you can take a look at Dickinson's, and then we can drive up to the town center, so you can see how far it was. It couldn't have been more than a ten-minute drive, especially at night without traffic."

From the house the ride to Dickinson's Farm Stand took less than fifteen minutes, and Meg pulled into the busy parking lot. "Farmers' market" seemed inadequate as a description, as the complex sprawled over perhaps a hundred feet of frontage. The public portions were cobbled together out of multiple small, ramshackle structures of indeterminate age. Somewhere in the midst was what appeared to be an old colonial house, long since swallowed up by its later additions. The business was highly successful, if the number of cars in the lot was any indication. Hand-lettered signs advertised a wealth of products, both natural and processed: the usual late-season tomatoes and zucchini; pumpkins, squash, and exotic gourds; local honey; baked goods, primarily pies; firewood; and of course, cider. In fact, the cider operation occupied its own small building, off to the right of the rest of the hodgepodge. It, too, was doing a thriving business.

"I assume it's a bit less crowded at night?" Elizabeth ventured.

"No doubt. Well, it's right on the main road, but I'd bet security is a joke. Nobody expects someone to break in and steal pumpkins or pies. There's a certain amount of trust around here. I hope that doesn't change now. Well, I'd better go hand the apples over. Are you coming?"

"Of course."

Meg hauled one crate of apples out of the back of the truck and her mother grabbed a second one. Meg led the way into the main building. At the cash register, she asked the young girl working, "Is Joe around?"

"He's out back," she said, nodding to the rear before turning to the next customer.

Meg went out the back door and set her crate down just outside the door — she wasn't sure what Bree's usual practice was. "Joe?" she called out.

A lanky man in faded jeans and a plaid shirt, its sleeves rolled up, answered, "Right here. You Meg Corey? Your manager called, said you'd be making the delivery. Two crates of the Gravensteins, right?"

"Yes. This is the last of them. And the Spartans should be ready by next week."

"Good, good. You've got a nice place there in Granford."

"You know it?"

"Sure do. Grew up a couple of miles from there. You're next door to Seth Chapin's place, right?"

Did everybody in the local universe know Seth? "That's the one. You're taking some of our heirloom varieties, right?"

"Oh yeah. People are snapping up all kinds of heirloom fruits and vegetables these days. The heirloom tomatoes went really well this year, and we had maybe twenty to thirty of the old kinds."

"That's good to hear. I understand some of the orchards have cut down their heirloom trees, just because nobody was inter-

183

ested and it didn't make economic sense to keep them."

Joe shrugged. "I can sell 'em. Here, let me give you a hand." He reached for the crate that Elizabeth had set down.

"Oh, sorry, Mother. Joe, this is my mother, Elizabeth Corey, who's visiting this week. She knew the Warren sisters years ago."

"Is that so? They were a pair! I think my grandparents mentioned them. We've been buying apples from you folk for years."

"How long have you been running this stand?" Elizabeth asked.

"Heck, I think my grandparents started it back in the thirties maybe? I've been doing this all my life, and I took over from my father. The land's been in the family for generations back of that."

"Dickinsons?"

"Yup. Plenty of 'em around here."

"Any relations to Emily?"

"Got me. I'm not into all that family history stuff. Well, I've got to get back to work. You coming by next week, too?"

"Probably. Bree broke her wrist so she's not supposed to lift anything for a while."

"She's a spitfire, that one. Smart kid, though, and a great haggler. She got me to go up on the price for the heirlooms."

Meg turned to go, but then stopped. "Oh,

Joe — we supply some of the apples for your cider operation, right?"

"Yeah. Why?"

"I've never seen cider being made. Can I take a look at your shed?"

A look of discomfort flashed over Joe's face. "You know about . . . ?"

"The death?" Was it public knowledge yet that it was a murder? "Yes, I do. That was an awful thing. Who found him?"

"My daughter, Jennifer. Nasty thing for anyone to see, and she was real upset."

"Well, of course she would be," Meg said soothingly, wondering if there was any way she could talk to the daughter. She had to tread lightly: she wanted to keep Joe's business, and pumping his daughter about finding a body was not likely to endear her to him. "But I would like to know how cider is made."

"It's okay. The cops cleared the site, and the place is open to the public. They don't know what happened here. Just wander over and take a look. See you next week." Joe turned away, effectively ending the conversation.

"Shall we?" Meg asked her mother.

"I suppose. He wasn't very friendly at the end there, was he?"

"Well, he's busy. And I didn't want to

make too much of the murder." Meg led her mother out through the store, smiling at the teenage girl at the register — the daughter Joe had mentioned? — and then around to the stand-alone building. Meg could hear machinery. She stepped into the interior and waited for her eyes to adjust.

The smell of apples was like a blow to the face; it was so thick you could taste it. A mechanical crusher reduced the apples to chunks, and a conveyer belt moved them along to the press itself, where pressure forced the juice from the pieces. Then the pulp was scraped from the press and the process began all over again. Three people were busy managing the machinery, and from their smooth and economical movements they looked like they had been doing it for a long time.

Elizabeth was studying the process with curiosity. She leaned toward Meg and whispered, "Where . . . ?"

Meg tore her eyes from the hypnotic machinery and scanned the rest of the space. There weren't many options, because most the floor was cluttered with boxes of clean bottles, caps, and labels, among other things. She whispered back, "I'd guess we're standing on it."

One of the cider makers — a high school

or college kid, from the looks of him —
sidled toward them. "This is where that guy
died, you know," he said, his tone conspira-
torial. The tourists watching the cider
process didn't notice.

"Wasn't that a terrible thing?" Elizabeth
said brightly. "You must have been horrified! You weren't the one who found the
body, were you?"

The boy shook his head regretfully. "No,
but Jen was having hysterics all over the
place when she opened up, and then the
police came and everything. I kind of hung
back and listened, you know?"

"Well, a healthy curiosity is understand-
able. But he wasn't found . . . in the press?"

"Oh, no. Jen said she kind of tripped over
him in the dark when she came in. He was
just laying there. But she knew he was dead,
'cause he was a funny gray color."

"What did the police say?"

The boy shrugged. "Not much. They
didn't know what to make of it. They looked
around — the cider works were shut down
for a day, which pissed off a lot of tourists
— but they didn't find much. Then they
said we could go back to business."

"And nobody had seen the man here before?"

The boy shrugged. "I hear he was some

professor type from the college. 'Sides, we get lots of people through here this time of year — nobody would have noticed just one random guy."

Another dead end, or maybe an open end with no resolution in sight. Daniel's presence here was odd; his death even odder. What had he been doing at Dickinson's Farm Stand? And who had been with him?

Meg and her mother stayed around long enough to be polite, watching the mesmerizing flow of apples into the machinery, emerging as cider. They each sampled a small paper cup's worth. "Well, we've got more deliveries to make, so we should be going," Meg said. "Seen enough?"

Elizabeth shrugged. "I suppose, given that I have no idea what I'm looking for. Smells wonderful, though, doesn't it?"

"It does. You want to get some to take home?"

"That would be nice. Funny to think that some of your apples are mixed in here somewhere. You sure you don't want to think about making cider?"

Meg laughed. "Not for a long time. Let me get through one season and see where things are."

"Goodness," Elizabeth replied. "Then we'd better get moving with these deliveries, right?"

"Right."

After their deliveries, they returned to the house, and Meg went to take a quick shower, then joined her mother in the kitchen, where she was already cooking. Bree had left a note on the table saying she wouldn't be back for dinner. It felt odd to sit at the table and watch someone else work, but at least Elizabeth was trying to make herself useful, and Meg didn't want to discourage her.

"How do you decide your day-to-day schedule?" Elizabeth asked as she whisked something into something else on the stove.

"At this point it depends on how the apples ripen," Meg replied. "Ray does the scheduling."

"Not Bree?"

"Well, they do it together. But Bree is kind of like middle management: she hires the workers, but Raynard is the boss of the pickers and plans the day-to-day routine. He's got far more experience than Bree and I put together, and he's been working the orchard for years."

"Well, that's a blessing. Can I get you a glass of wine while dinner's cooking?"

"I can get it," Meg said, pushing her chair back.

"No, no, don't get up. You've had a hard day, and this is the least I can do."

Meg stayed put. "You did the same things I did today! You know, you sound like a classic wife. 'How was your day, dear?' 'Can I get you a drink?' "

"In case you haven't noticed, that's what I've been for nearly forty years." Elizabeth filled a glass with white wine and handed it to Meg.

"Oh, come on — you were more than that. You always worked — outside the home, I mean."

Elizabeth poked at something in a pan, then set a lid on it. She filled a glass for herself and sat down at the table. "Yes, I did, thank you for noticing. But believe it or not, your father is a bit of a sexist. He applauded my working, but he did expect to find food on the table and a clean house when he came home. You never noticed?"

"I suppose, not that I thought about it much. But I guess I should apologize — I should have pitched in and helped."

"I never asked you to, dear. I wanted you to enjoy your growing up, and you'll have plenty of time for housework in your life."

Meg shuddered. "Don't look around. I'm

not going to win any prizes for neatness."

"And why should you? You're working hard. And if I'm not mistaken, you've been doing a bit of the structural work here. Didn't you mention you'd refinished the floor in here?"

Meg felt a spurt of pride. "I did, and I loved doing it. But it's hard to keep up with old buildings — something's always falling apart. Like the plumbing." Meg hesitated: she'd just given herself yet another perfect opportunity to introduce Seth into the conversation. Seth's office was on the property, a hundred yards away. *Meg, you're chicken!*

"I'm sorry I can't be around more, now that you're here. But I may have an idea to keep you busy," Meg finally said.

Elizabeth dished up dinner, setting plates in front of them and then sat down. "What did you have in mind?"

"Well, you have to know more about the Warren family that lived here than I do — wouldn't be hard, since I know next to nothing. Maybe you could write it down? And fill in some of the details from online sources? Are you comfortable with a laptop? You are computer-literate, right?"

"Yes, Margaret," Elizabeth said patiently. "I've been using a computer for years. Do you have dial-up or broadband, dear?"

"I splurged on broadband, not that I get much time to use it. It came bundled with my cable package, not that I have any time to watch television either. I could set you up in the dining room, because the light's better in there."

"I'd be delighted. I do feel rather badly now that I never came up here for all those years, at least to look the place over and make sure it was being taken care of. I hope most of the . . . detritus dates to tenants?"

"What, you don't think I picked the tasty overstuffed chairs in the parlor?"

"Oh, I hope not!"

"Don't worry, they weren't my idea. But redecorating has been low on my priority list. Did you say something about Grandmother's wing chair?"

"We'll see. So, about this genealogy project . . . can you get me started?"

"Sure, at least for the basics. Why don't I show you now, and you can get an early start in the morning?"

"Can we finish eating first?" Elizabeth asked plaintively.

Meg laughed. "Of course!"

Fifteen minutes later they finished dinner, and moved into the dining room. Meg pulled out her laptop, plugged it in, and logged on. "Okay — it's pretty self-explanatory: word processing here, spreadsheets here, Internet log-on here. Once you go online, the primary genealogy sources are Ancestry-dot-com and FamilySearch-dot-org. Or you can just search on keywords. I think some of the nineteenth-century histories of the town are available online, but I have paper copies of those anyway. Questions?"

"Dozens, Meg darling, but you don't have time to answer them right now. I'm sure I can muddle along. I think you made a good suggestion, to write down what I know first and use that as a starting point."

"Great. I'm going to go up now, but I'll see you in the morning."

"Good night, dear," Elizabeth said absently, her eyes on the computer screen.

14

When Meg came down the next morning, she found Elizabeth seated exactly where she had left her the night before. Meg went to the kitchen and helped herself to coffee, then came back to the dining room. "You did go to bed last night, didn't you?"

"Of course I did, dear. But this is certainly absorbing."

"Don't I know it! Anything interesting?"

"Very interesting actually. It's amazing how many of the old families are still here, more than three hundred years after they settled in Granford."

"Does that include the Warrens?"

"I believe so. I'm just beginning to make sense of it, so I won't bother you with details now. What do you remember about visiting the sisters?"

"Not much. They seemed so old!"

"My dear, they were! They were both close to ninety at the time. Tough stock, that. And they seemed to have outlived most of their family — I think they were the youngest of their siblings."

"So they inherited by default, having outlived everyone else. Remind me to call Ruth Ferry, and maybe you two can get together. I think you'd enjoy her."

"She can't be young herself."

"No, but she's still sharp as a tack. Rachel introduced us."

Elizabeth sat back in her chair. "Hardy Yankees. Which means we are, too, you know. I'm sure they'd all be proud."

Meg pulled a chair up to the table. "Why don't you start by explaining how we're connected to the people who lived in this house?"

"All right. So, I started with Lula and Nettie and worked backward . . ." Elizabeth began. And continued.

Half an hour later Meg was getting itchy to head up to the orchard, and her mother showed no signs of slowing. "I had no idea! So how was it you ended up with this house?"

"If I've got it right, Lula and Nettie were my first cousins three times removed. Or to put it another way, my great-grandmother was their first cousin. But I guess a lot of the relatives kind of drifted away and lost touch, particularly in the later twentieth century."

"How on earth did you know about them, and this place?"

"My grandmother used to visit here when she was a child, and she'd tell me stories. Come to think of it, she probably mentioned the orchard — I just never put two and two together. The visit you remember was in the 1980s, but I'd seen them a couple of times before that. They were amazing women, in their own limited way. They lived more or less the way they always had. Visiting them was like entering a different world."

"Did Daddy ever meet them?"

Elizabeth shook her head. "No, he wasn't interested, and he was busy."

"So they remembered that you'd been nice to them, and they left you the house."

"I don't know if there were any other relatives left, or at least, none that they knew about."

"Why didn't you come up here when you inherited?" Meg had wondered about this more than once, as she wrestled with decades of tenant neglect.

"I meant to, but somehow I never found the time — out of sight, out of mind. The rental income went into its own account, and I drew on it occasionally, but it wasn't as though I needed it, or not often — as I recall, a chunk of it went toward your college tuition. But I feel badly that I never even came to the funeral — by the time they'd found the will and contacted me, the sisters were long in the ground. I suppose I should pay my respects in the cemetery here. Have you?"

"I have, actually. I'll show you, maybe tomorrow. There are plenty of Warrens in that cemetery, and it's not far from here."

"I'm sure. What a narrow life it must have been. Or am I being judgmental? It was a farming community, and our ancestors were no better than anyone else here."

"Still is, Mother. In case you haven't noticed, I'm a farmer."

"So you are." Elizabeth looked at her daughter fondly. "Who would have imagined?"

"Not me, that's for sure. So, have you got all this information input into something simple?"

"Not yet. Mostly I've been scribbling things down — and erasing a lot of it. But to tell you the truth, I've enjoyed it. And it's certainly interesting to be doing this on the spot where it all took place."

"Great. Look, I've really got to go now, but it sounds as though you've got plenty to keep you busy. I'll be up the hill, and I'll probably eat lunch up there. I'm not sure when we'll be done for the day — we're at the mercy of the apples. If you need me, you can come get me."

"Meg!" Bree's voice came from the kitchen. "Get your butt in gear! Time's wasting!"

"Gotta run!" Meg went back to the kitchen to grab a bottle of water, then followed Bree out.

They were swept up in the flow of the harvest activities, and the next time Meg had a chance to breathe, it was well past lunchtime. She hadn't even noticed there was an unfamiliar car in her driveway. How long had it been there? "Bree, looks like we've got company again."

"You want to go check it out? I think we're good here," Bree said after scanning the activity around her.

"Yes, thanks. I'll see you later. Good work today!"

Hard work, at least, Meg acknowledged as she felt every muscle on her way down the hill. She debated briefly about ducking in the back door and showering off the dust and leaves before confronting whoever was waiting, but she didn't want to leave her mother alone with the mysterious caller.

As she came in the front door, she called out, "Mother?"

"In here, dear," came her mother's voice from the front parlor.

Meg pulled down her wrinkled shirt and followed the sound, to find her mother seated in the front parlor across from . . . Patricia Weston? "Hi. Patricia, isn't it? What brings you our way?" Meg took in the teacups and teapot on the scarred end table between the chairs — it looked like the two women had been settled there for a while.

"Meg, darling, please sit down and have a cup of tea. I was telling Patricia how you've taken over the orchard in the last few months."

"I admire you," Patricia addressed Meg. "I can't imagine taking on a project like that, with no experience."

"It has been interesting," Meg replied, accepting the cup of tea her mother held out to her. "And unexpected. But I'm enjoying it. As long as the weather holds for another month or two, I should have a good crop this year, due more to luck than to anything I've done."

Meg took a sip of her tea, wondering again why Patricia was here. She noted that Mrs. Weston hadn't answered her question. How much did Patricia know about her late husband's history with Elizabeth?

Patricia apparently possessed the ability to read minds, for she said, "I'm not here to beat up your mother over her relationship with Daniel, you know. That happened long before we met, and I think I can say Daniel and I had a decent marriage. I thought I'd ask Elizabeth what he was like as a young man, before I knew him. I wish I had known him then — from what your mother has told me, it sounds as though he was a lot more relaxed. Or do I mean 'laid-back'?"

"Had he been tense lately?" Meg asked.

Patricia shrugged. "Not tense exactly. And he hadn't changed much recently. But I hate to say it, I think he was feeling his age, past sixty, though his doctor told him he was perfectly healthy. Not that he was thinking of retirement. Heavens, I wouldn't have known what to do with him if he was underfoot all the time. But I think he wanted to make sure he'd made his mark in his field, that he'd left something that would be remembered. And he felt that time was running out."

Elizabeth was staring over Meg's shoulder, lost in her own memories. "Funny, but he was one of the least ambitious men I knew, back in the day. He didn't care about awards, or prestige, or even about making a lot of money. But he did love what he was studying."

"That never changed." Patricia and Elizabeth exchanged a complicit glance. "He was a good teacher, and the students loved him. He could really reach them. Maybe Emily Dickinson's poetry appeals to a generation of young people raised on short tweets."

"Was that his specialty?" Meg asked.

"Technically, it was American poetry, specifically nineteenth century. But it seemed a waste not to study Emily when you live in Amherst. Can you believe it? The 'other woman' in our lives was a dead poet. How do you compete with that?" Patricia's eyes glinted with sudden tears. She shut them for a moment, regaining control. "I can't believe he's gone. You never met him, did you?"

"Me?" Meg replied, surprised. "Not that I recall. I've spent time on the UMass campus, taking some ag classes, but I don't think I've set foot on the Amherst College side."

"He would have enjoyed meeting you, I'm sure. In fact, that was one reason I came over today." Patricia reached into her bag and pulled out a piece of paper, which she offered to Meg. "I found that in the desk in his office."

Meg took it and read it. It was a clipping from a local newspaper with a brief report on the death of a local organic activist; attached to it was a piece of a paper with Meg's name and address. "Is this his handwriting?" Meg asked.

"Yes. Maybe he recognized the surname and was planning to look you up. I didn't think it was important, but I was curious . . . I didn't want to keep sitting around the house . . ." Patricia's composure was crumbling fast.

Elizabeth reached out a hand and laid it on Patricia's arm. "We understand. I can only imagine how hard it must be to come to terms with your loss. Are his sons still home?"

Patricia rummaged in her pockets until she came up with a tissue. She blotted her eyes and blew her nose. "Sorry. I still have these weepy spells. No, they haven't lived at home for a few years, so when they're here, they kind of wander around, looking lost, which only makes things worse."

Meg was torn: obviously the woman in front of her was grieving, but she wasn't sure when or if she'd get another chance to talk with her. "I'm sorry to bring this up, but your husband's death has put my mother in a rather awkward situation."

"Meg," Elizabeth said sharply. "I don't think now is the time to —"

"No, it's okay," Patricia interrupted. "You're talking about why that lumpish detective seems to think Elizabeth might have killed him?"

Meg tried to read her expression and found no malice there. "Exactly. I don't know what you think, but I certainly don't believe it. But if Marcus is right, and it wasn't just a heart attack, that means that someone else killed him. Was there anyone you could think of that might have wanted your husband dead?"

Elizabeth silently poured fresh tea into Patricia's cup, and Patricia swallowed some before answering. "The detective asked the same thing, and I couldn't come up with anyone. We were happy together. We had enough money. He loved his work, and was respected in his field. His students loved him. I couldn't think of anyone I know who would do this."

"Do you know the farm stand where he died?"

"I've been there. After all, we've lived here for years, and we both liked to support local produce. But we had no special attachment to it, and I'm sure we've patronized all the local stands at one time or another.

Are you asking if he had a midnight craving for fresh carrots? Very unlikely — he went out occasionally in the evening for college events, but otherwise he was rather settled in his ways. I told the police all of this." She stood up abruptly, almost toppling the table with the teapot. "I should go."

Elizabeth stood as well. "You don't have to. Or maybe you'd like to get together another day? I'll be in town for a bit longer."

Patricia managed a weak smile. "I'll think about it. And thank you for sharing your memories. Meg, it was nice to meet you." She all but fled out of the room, then the front door.

Meg followed and watched her leave before turning back to her mother. "What was that all about?"

"Oh, Meg, don't be insensitive. She's just lost her husband, whom she obviously cared for, and now she's been told that he was murdered. She wants to keep the good memories alive a little longer. She's still trying to process the fact that he's dead, and she's not ready to deal with the idea that somebody helped him to die. Poor woman." Elizabeth turned and began gathering up the tea things.

No sooner had Patricia pulled out of the driveway than Meg's cell phone rang. She was surprised to see an unfamiliar number. "Hello?"

"Is this Meg? It's Kenneth Henderson. We met yesterday at the festival?"

"Oh, yes, of course. What can I do for you?"

"You said you and your mother might like to get together to talk about Daniel Weston. Would now be a good time? I know it's short notice, but my plans for the rest of the week are somewhat uncertain."

"Now?" Meg checked her watch: it was already four. "I think we could be there in twenty minutes or so. Are you still at Rachel's?"

"I am, and she's promised to make you a high tea. She thought that might convince you."

Meg laughed. "She's right. We'll be right over."

Meg went to the kitchen. "Uh, Mother? That was Kenneth Henderson, the professor who knew Daniel. He wants to talk with us, and Rachel will provide tea."

"Now? But we've just finished one tea," Elizabeth protested.

"I know. But he offered, and I'm not sure how long he'll be around. Can you handle it?"

"I suppose I can manage another cup. Do

you think there'll be pastries?"

"At Rachel's? I guarantee it."

15

When Meg and Elizabeth arrived at the bed-and-breakfast, Rachel was sitting on the porch in one of the slat-backed rockers, talking with animation to Kenneth, who occupied the adjacent chair. Meg parked, and she and her mother climbed out of the car.

Rachel bounded out of her chair to greet them. "Hi, Meg. Hi, Elizabeth. Glad you could make it on short notice." Kenneth stood more slowly.

"Hi, Rachel," Meg said. "It's so nice of you to do this — you must be as busy as I am. Professor Henderson, it's good to see you again."

"Please call me Kenneth. I have enough students who call me professor. Mrs. Corey, I'm glad you could come."

"Elizabeth, please. And we should thank you for taking time away from your other activities to meet with us."

Kenneth brushed away her comment. "I'd

had enough pomposity for one day, at the symposium. Thank heaven it's over."

"I'll set up the tea," Rachel said, disappearing into the house. "Give me five."

Elizabeth smiled at Kenneth. "I thought as an academic you'd be in your element there."

Kenneth sighed. "I've seen far too many such events, and I thought the concept, pitting Whitman against Dickinson, to be rather contrived. There is little new to be said. Although I suppose the visiting parents enjoyed it." He paused, searching for words. "As I told you, I was shocked to hear about Daniel's death. You said that you knew him, Elizabeth?"

"Many years ago, yes. I hadn't seen him for a long time."

"A tragic thing — a real loss to the academic community."

Rachel called out from inside the house, "Tea's ready! Come in and sit down, so you can talk comfortably."

"An excellent suggestion," Kenneth said. He opened the screen door. "Ladies?"

Elizabeth and Meg formed a small procession, and Kenneth brought up the rear. Inside, in Rachel's elegant Victorian dining room, the table was set for four. Meg saw a profusion of goodies, including one clearly antique multi-tiered tray stand laden with finger sandwiches and tiny, bite-size cookies that Meg couldn't even begin to identify, and her mouth began to water.

They sat. "Kenneth, it was the symposium that brought you to Amherst?" Elizabeth began.

"Yes, initially."

"Don't you have classes to teach this time of year?" Meg asked.

"I'm on the faculty at Princeton, but I'm on sabbatical this year. When Daniel invited me to the symposium, I thought it sounded amusing, and I came up a bit early to do some research and to indulge in a little sightseeing. Like Daniel, I specialize in nineteenth-century American poetry, so this little get-together he had planned sounded like a nice diversion. He asked me to participate in a panel discussion, which promised to be spirited."

"Did you know Daniel well?" Elizabeth asked.

"Yes and no. We'd crossed paths at various academic conferences over the years, and we would get together for drinks or a meal, if we were both free. He always had something interesting to say. But I can't recall that we ever saw each other outside of that setting."

Rachel picked up the teapot and began filling cups. "Please, help yourselves."

Meg bit into a dainty sandwich. Watercress? "Yum. Kenneth, how did you find this place?"

"A friend who had stayed here recommended it." He smiled. "Although I almost passed on it because of the name. After all, I'm the spokesperson for the Whitman side of the debate, and staying at Dickinson's could be seen as treasonous. And you?"

"A friend introduced us, too, when I first moved up here. Actually, Rachel's brother. I had a plumbing crisis and needed a place to stay fast, while it was being repaired, and he asked Rachel to fit me in." Meg was conscious of her mother's gaze — when was she going to come clean about Seth? "And then I sent my mother here."

Rachel had finished pouring. "I hope you don't mind, but we got to talking and I told Kenneth that you were interested in Daniel's death for personal reasons."

Elizabeth helped herself to a plate and some sandwiches, avoiding everyone's eyes. "You might as well say it, Rachel — I came up here to see Daniel, after quite a few years, and now I'm a suspect in his murder. I'd say that's quite personal."

"Good heavens!" Kenneth burst out. "I

can't believe anyone could consider you a likely candidate for murderer. In fact, I couldn't believe it was a murder when Rachel told me. What an unlikely end!"

Meg turned to Rachel. "How did you hear?"

"It was in the local paper. They reported the death one day, and then they had a follow-up article a couple of days later, saying that the police were calling it a homicide. Something about a killer blow? It sounded quite sensational."

Meg hadn't seen the Amherst paper. For that matter, she hadn't had time to look at any newspaper since her mother had arrived. So now everyone knew that Daniel had been murdered. Meg helped herself in turn to some cookies. She wasn't really hungry, but Rachel's cookies were always irresistible. "Kenneth, can you imagine why anyone would want Daniel Weston dead?"

"Not at all. He was a respected scholar, an entertaining raconteur. I never heard him say an unkind word about his colleagues — or his competitors. I suppose I fall in the latter camp, but we were always cordial about it."

"Tell them about the symposium," Rachel said, checking to see that everyone was well supplied with food. "It was such a shame that he put all that work into it and then didn't have a chance to be part of it."

"Perhaps I should begin at the beginning." Balancing his cup and saucer, Kenneth settled himself in his chair. "Daniel enjoyed some renown as an expert on the works of Emily Dickinson, as you no doubt have heard. He'd published a goodly number of definitive articles in respected journals, and he was in demand as a lecturer. This particular event was something of a popular show rather than a scholarly one, although there were elements of both. Amherst College has a reputation for excellence to maintain, so they wouldn't mount anything that was completely trivial. But the symposium was also geared to entertain the parents who were bringing their offspring to the college — sort of an intellectual welcome. For that reason, I think the publicity was couched in rather silly terms, as a competition between Walt Whitman and Emily Dickinson for the title of Best American Poet. Did any of you attend?" When everyone signaled "no," he went on. "The centerpiece was a debate between the opposing sides, represented by an interesting collection of scholars."

"Were you part of this?" Meg asked.

"I was, in fact. As was entirely appropriate, given my standing as one who has studied Whitman in depth. But I wouldn't have missed it in any case — I came along to see the debate, which promised to be entertaining."

Elizabeth asked, "Did it live up to your expectations?"

"I think Daniel's death put something of a damper on the proceedings, at least from the panelists' point of view. I'm sure the general public was unaware of it. But Daniel's personality — dare I say charm? — would have taken it to a different level."

"Did you see him before he died?" Meg asked.

"I did. I told him I'd be in the area for a few days before and after the event, and he suggested we meet for a drink, so we did. More than a week ago — Friday, if I recall. We met, and then I took off to pursue some of my own research at a small library in Maine that owns some of Whitman's papers, and stayed there for the weekend. I returned here this past week to be greeted by the news of Daniel's death."

"How did he seem when you saw him?"

"That's what's so interesting, in light of subsequent events, as I told Rachel. He was in good form — distracted, of course, since the school term was just beginning, and he was responsible for this symposium. But

213

there was a curious undercurrent of . . . I'd have to say excitement. He dropped several hints that he was working on something new, that he thought would have a major impact. He was quite coy about it, but when I pressed for details, he said that I'd have to wait for the symposium. I had the general impression that he planned to make some sort of announcement there."

"Which he never had a chance to do," Meg said. "Mother, did he say anything to you when you saw him?"

Elizabeth shook her head. "No, nothing like that. But I'm not a member of the academic community, so he may have thought it wouldn't interest me. And we had a lot of catching up to do. Tell me, Kenneth, what would constitute an important scholarly announcement? Not his retirement presumably?"

"I doubt that his retirement would be of great interest to the community, except possibly to new PhDs looking for a teaching slot to open up. Nor was he even contemplating leaving academia, as far as I know. He was still at the top of his game intellectually, and I don't think he planned to retire anytime soon. No, I'd say this was more likely to be something else — something that would send ripples through our little pond."

Meg was beginning to get frustrated by Kenneth's arch style. "And what would that be? He was an Emily Dickinson expert, right? Would it have something to do with her?"

"That is a distinct possibility," Kenneth agreed.

"Surely the scholarly community has been over Dickinson's life and work with a fine-tooth comb?" Meg said. Even she knew that much about their local celebrity.

"Of course. But there is always something new to be said. That's how we professors stay in business."

"What would have been the impact of something like that, coming at the symposium?" Elizabeth asked.

"It would have made quite a stir, I'd guess. He'd gathered together many of his colleagues, after all. Trust Daniel to maximize his exposure — he always did have a flair for the dramatic. Sadly we'll never know what, if anything, he might have found."

"Do you think it was just hype?" Then a thought struck Meg. "Who's been through his office on campus?"

"I would expect the police have," Kenneth replied. "Perhaps his wife. I don't suppose the college needs the office space immediately. Shortly, though — prime office space is always much coveted."

"But would the police know what to look for?" Meg pressed.

Kenneth looked thoughtful. "Regrettably, I think they'd see no more than a lot of papers and books. If the police have seized his computer, they might find something relevant there, although they might not know what they were looking for. But I should add, if Daniel had something he believed was important, and that he wished to keep secret, it's unlikely that he would keep it in his office on campus."

"Where, then? At home? And what would be important?"

"I'd have to guess a personal document of some sort, or a reference in someone else's document that might shed new light on Miss Dickinson's life. I would think it would have to be an original source. Of course, the Holy Grail would be an autograph Emily Dickinson document, something in her own handwriting, particularly a poem. As you say, the research on her poetic oeuvre has been exhaustive. You may recall a scandal, oh, a decade ago, when a Dickinson poem surfaced at auction and was bought by a local library. It turned out to be a forgery, but a particularly skilled one that fooled a number of experts, and there was heavy competition when it came up for auction. But my point is, anything new by or about Emily would be highly prized — and coveted."

"Interesting," Meg said. "We're not talking just about dollars, but about prestige?"

"Certainly," Kenneth agreed. "If Daniel had come into possession of a physical object — say a letter, or a poem — as for where he might keep it, I don't know the particulars of his home situation. As I said, we didn't often meet socially. I've never been to his home, and I only met his wife, Patricia, at the funeral."

"May I summarize?" Elizabeth asked. "You're saying that Daniel seemed excited about something, and that he may have planned to make an announcement about it at the symposium. Obviously that didn't happen, but he may have left a trail among his papers or on his computer, which are now the property of his wife? Or possibly the college?"

"I'm no lawyer, but that sounds about right."

Elizabeth tapped her finger on the table, and responded slowly. "As it turns out, Patricia stopped by Meg's house earlier."

"Whatever for?" Kenneth appeared puzzled.

"I'm not sure. I knew of her, but I didn't know her — like you, we met for the first time at the memorial service. You spoke to her there, too, as I recall."

"Ah, yes, I did," Kenneth said. "I was happy to see that the event was well attended — many of the faculty put in an appearance, as well as the symposium panelists. Daniel would have been pleased."

Elizabeth continued, "Patricia said she wanted to talk about my memories of Daniel, and I was happy to share." Elizabeth's mouth twitched. "She did say that she regarded Emily Dickinson as the 'other woman' in Daniel's life — apparently he was borderline obsessive about her. So that much, at least, would fit. And you're guessing he had found something, something that he thought was important."

"Yes. Sad to say, we may never know what it was," Kenneth said softly.

They shared a moment of silence, which Rachel broke. "Elizabeth, don't you think it's a little odd that Daniel's wife came calling? Maybe she thought *you* knew something."

Elizabeth looked at her. "He never said a word to me, but I suppose she wouldn't know that. And I have no way of knowing how much he shared with her. Kenneth, do you know if she is an academic?"

"I think not. I recall Daniel saying that one academic per family was enough."

Meg interrupted. "You know, what's even odder is that she said Daniel had *my* name."

"Why would she know you, Meg?" Rachel raised her eyebrows.

Meg replied, "Patricia found a slip of paper with my name and address on it on Daniel's desk at home. If I had to guess, I'd say he probably made a note because he saw the name 'Corey' in the local papers, and wondered if I was related to his friends, Elizabeth and Phillip Corey."

"Which may be what led to his contacting me at home," Elizabeth followed. "I hadn't heard from him in years, and then suddenly he invited me up here."

"And your husband . . . ?" Kenneth said delicately.

"Has gone fishing. So far he knows nothing about any of this. He knew Daniel, too, when they were in graduate school. That's how we all met. In Cambridge."

"Ah," Kenneth said, and nodded, as though this explained everything. Meg wondered if there was some sort of academic code that she didn't share, but saying the magic word "Cambridge" immediately made Kenneth shift his evaluation of Elizabeth.

Rachel had followed the exchange, but now she interrupted. "So let me get this straight. For whatever reason, Daniel got in touch with Elizabeth and invited her to visit, even though it was one of the busiest times of the year for him, right?" When Kenneth nodded, she went on, "And then, boom, he's dead, under kind of weird circumstances." When Kenneth started to say something, Rachel held up one hand. "Life goes on — the symposium happens, without him. There's the memorial service before, and a day or two later Patricia shows up on Meg's doorstep and chats up Elizabeth. Now you, Kenneth, you say you think Daniel was hatching something, but he didn't tell you what, and hinted he was going to make some surprise announcement at the symposium. So let me ask you this: What would be important enough to kill him for? And why on earth did whoever it was drag him to the far end of Amherst and break into a cider mill? Isn't there some more convenient place to meet him, even if this person wanted complete privacy?"

"That's the sticking point. Why there, of all places?" Meg agreed.

They fell silent. *None of this makes sense,* Meg thought. Daniel was well liked, respected, successful. The police had said they had no evidence of financial wrongdoing — no blackmail money coming in or going out. He wasn't sleeping with any students. He might have planned to sleep with Elizabeth, but he hadn't made any moves on her, and the only person who would have cared was his wife. Or maybe her father, Phillip, but he hadn't known anything about this. Had he? But maybe Patricia didn't know that nothing had happened. Still, why would she have taken him to Dickinson's Farm Stand to have it out with him? Did the place hold any special meaning?

Rachel stood up, interrupting Meg's thoughts. "Sorry, guys, but I've got more people coming in tonight, and I've got to finish prepping the rooms. You're welcome to continue this discussion, but I've got to get moving."

Kenneth had stood when Rachel did — a nice courtly touch. "I quite understand, Rachel. Don't worry about my room — I think I can live with my own mess."

"You're staying on?" Elizabeth asked.

"Yes, I had originally booked for a few more days. And now I'd hate to leave until this is resolved — I feel that I owe Daniel that much. Maybe I can offer some help to the authorities?"

"You might be able to give them some insights into his professional life. Although I'm pretty sure they'll have talked to the faculty and to the other people who came to the service. Have they contacted you?" When Kenneth shook his head, Meg added, "It can't hurt to introduce yourself to them. Get in touch with Detective Marcus at the state police headquarters in Northampton, if you think you know anything that might be relevant."

"You seem quite well informed about the process," Kenneth said.

"I am." Meg didn't elaborate. She turned to Elizabeth. "Mother, we should go and let Rachel do what she has to do. Rachel, thanks so much for the lovely tea. Kenneth, it was a pleasure to talk with you. We should get together again in the next couple of days and see if we come up with anything else, especially if you talk to the police. Sorry I have to run."

Kenneth waved them off. "Go, go. I have your number. And I'm sure if we put our heads together, we can make some progress here."

Let's hope so, Meg thought grimly. *Be-*

cause if it involves dead poets, I don't think the police will.

16

"Kenneth seems nice," Elizabeth said in the car on the way home.

"He does," Meg agreed. "Interesting that he thought Daniel was onto something. But as he pointed out, we may never know what. I wonder where he was last weekend."

"Are you seriously considering Kenneth as a potential murderer? I'm sure any number of people can vouch for his relationship with Daniel over the years. Are you suggesting that Kenneth may have taken out a hit on Daniel out of professional jealousy? That he couldn't stand to be trumped one last time by a long-term rival?"

Meg laughed. "That does sound a bit melodramatic, but anything is possible. Too bad Kenneth doesn't know Patricia — he could've asked to look at Daniel's papers. He might actually know what he's looking for, if he found it. I wonder if the police will think of that. Did Patricia say if she worked outside the home?"

"She didn't mention it," Elizabeth said. "You know, I could probably ask her about Daniel's papers, and whether she would mind someone going through them."

"Not the police?" Meg asked.

"Do you seriously think that they would recognize an academic discovery?"

"No, I think that's beyond them. But are you thinking that might be a motive for killing Daniel?"

Elizabeth sat back in her seat. "It's been a long time since I've been involved in the academic community, but it is a possibility, if remote. Do you have any better ideas? I'd like to be able to hand that detective of yours something to look at, other than me."

Meg sighed. "Mother, Marcus isn't stupid, and I doubt that he sees you as a serious candidate for killer. But he does have to do his job, so you're on the list. Still, I think this angle is worth looking into, and the police aren't the best ones to do that. You have a plan?"

"Let me talk to Patricia tomorrow and see if she'll let me look at Daniel's papers. That's a start. Maybe she has some idea what had Daniel so excited, but no one has asked her yet and she doesn't see a connection."

"Well, I promised Bree that I'd help with picking tomorrow, so you're on your own."

"That's probably for the best, dear. I can speak to Patricia as a peer, and if you came along, she might feel that we were ganging up on her. I think I can handle a simple conversation with a grieving widow."

Meg wondered just how seriously Patricia was grieving. She had seemed relatively composed at the service, but she had almost broken down when she had visited Meg's home. On the other hand, Meg had sensed a certain coolness when she'd spoken about Daniel, and there was that odd crack about Emily Dickinson as the "other woman." "Then go, and come back and tell me all about it."

They drove a couple of miles in silence. Then Meg said, "I know this is an idiotic question after two teas, but have you thought about dinner?"

Elizabeth burst out laughing. "Not exactly So far I've had four meals today. Are you actually hungry?"

"No, but Bree will be. I just thought we should have a plan."

"Well, I'm sure we can figure something out."

An hour later, Bree ambled into the kitchen. A timer went off, and Elizabeth went to the stove to check something.

"Smells good," Bree said, sitting down next to Meg at the table.

"Thank you, dear," Elizabeth said. "What have you been up to?"

"Picking. No, not me — watching the other guys pick. Planning. The usual."

"Who buys your apples?"

"We thought about the pros and cons of doing a farm stand," Meg began, "but we decided we didn't want to deal with staffing that kind of thing — and other people around here do it better and already have a following. We also talked about selling the whole crop to a major vendor, but we don't really produce enough to interest most of the chains. We're still feeling our way along. Right now we're selling mainly to the local farmers' markets like Dickinson's and a couple of local groceries."

"Eat while it's hot," Elizabeth said. "Once again, I hadn't realized how many decisions went into all of this. Good thing you have a business degree, Meg."

"That it is." Meg dug into her food. One plus of farming: she could eat all she wanted, knowing she would burn it off picking. She'd have to be careful come winter, when there was less to do.

An hour after dinner, Bree had long since

vanished, and Meg was trying to read a book, lulled by the consistent tap-tap of her mother at the computer. What had she started? She was reading the same paragraph for the fourth time when her mother said, "Heavens, look at the time! You need your sleep, young lady. And I think I'll take this lovely volume" — Elizabeth held up a heavy book, and Meg could barely make out the title: *History of Hadley,* which she knew to be exhaustively thorough — "and do some background reading."

Meg smiled. "It's better than a sleeping pill — I don't think I've made it past the first couple of chapters. See you in the morning, then."

"Good night, dear."

Meg trudged up the stairs, feeling the weight of the day's exertions. Farming was hard work, no question about it. In earlier centuries, people had had no choice, if they wanted to eat. Now they did have choices — and most people opted out of farming, letting the big corporations take over and manage food production. Maybe it was efficient, but something had been lost along the way. There was something fundamental about watching your crop grow and being able to hold — and eat — the end result. Still, she would never have considered it if she hadn't stumbled into it, driven by an odd set of circumstances. And she was still so new, and there was so much to learn!

Where would she be in another year, or five years? Meg asked herself as she brushed her teeth. She had saved the orchard from destruction, but what kind of obligation did she have to it now? She'd arrived in Granford with every intention of selling the property, and gotten sucked in by it, and by other things. But did she have a long-range plan?

She gave herself a shake. She did not have to decide the future of Warren's Grove right this minute. She had a plan for tomorrow, and a plan for the next few weeks. Once the harvest was in, she could sit back and assess the situation, both financially and personally.

It was only as she was falling asleep that she acknowledged she had once again failed to bring up Seth to her mother. Well, tomorrow would be time enough.

The next morning Meg peeled open one eye: since her bedroom lay on the west side of the house, she didn't get morning sun, but from where she lay she could see the shadow of the house on the hill toward the orchard. When she rolled over to get up, every muscle protested. She flopped back and lay in bed, staring at the ceiling. Apple picking used muscles she hadn't known she had; all that reaching and twisting, over and over again. Picking wasn't on her schedule for today, but hauling crates of apples was — from barn to truck to market, which would use a whole different set of muscles. How had people managed, in the early, pre-mechanized days? Even in the house, how had women handled vast piles of laundry, not to mention carrying the water around? The amount of physical work was staggering, at least by modern standards.

She listened for a moment, and heard voices outside — Bree was apparently already out trying to boss Raynard around. Meg could hear the rumble of his replies, and thought she caught a note of amusement. No sound from the kitchen, or her mother's room. She got herself out of bed, dressed, and ambled downstairs. Elizabeth was sitting at the kitchen table sipping a mug of coffee and reading the newspaper, with Lolly asleep on her lap. She looked up when Meg came in.

"Good morning, dear."

"Hi. You're up early. I see you've made a new friend." She nodded toward the sleepy cat.

"I find as I grow older, I need even less sleep than I used to, and that front bedroom catches the sun. As for Lolly here, we get along fine."

"I didn't think about that, since I don't spend much time there. You're lucky you have curtains at all, although I've been meaning to change them. I can't even guess how old they are."

"I found it rather lovely, waking with the sun. There are so many birds here!"

"You should hear the peepers in the spring — they're as loud as the birds." Meg filled a mug for herself and sat down. "Breakfast?"

"I can find something. Don't trouble yourself."

"I was thinking of something simple, like an English muffin."

"Then I would appreciate that. I won't need to disturb the cat."

"Heaven forbid!" Meg laughed, going to the refrigerator. When she emerged, she asked, "You still want to talk to Patricia today?"

"I already have, and we're all set. You know, strike while the iron is hot and that sort of thing. And Kenneth won't be around too much longer, if we need his opinion on something."

"You can find your way there?"

"I and my trusty GPS system. I'll let you get to work."

Five minutes later Meg watched her mother pull out of the driveway, then she set off up the hill, where Bree was waiting for her.

"You're late."

"Sorry, sorry. What are we picking today?"

"Meg, you've got to pay attention! Cortlands, Spartans, McIntoshes. Oh, and Christopher and his gang planted some Honeycrisps about five or six years ago, before my time, and they're looking really great this year."

"I don't know that variety," Meg said.

"They're kind of new — it's a 1960 cross from Minnesota, and you have to have a license to plant them. But they've sold well." Bree handed her a picker's bag. "Let's go."

It was after six when Bree finally declared the day's picking over. Meg had long since lost count of how many bags' worth of apples she had deposited in the crates, and she knew that more than one of the crates had been shuttled down to the barn. The Honeycrisps were tasty — of course Meg had sampled one — but they were large and heavy. Meg was hot, sweaty, and tired, and wanted nothing more than a shower and some food. She hadn't noticed her mother's car return, but when she saw it in the driveway, she entertained a small hope that Elizabeth had started dinner.

Inside the door it was clear from the good smells that Elizabeth had read her mind. "Mother?" Meg called out, her mouth watering.

"In the kitchen, dear. Dinner in fifteen. You go wash up."

Bree gave Meg a thumbs-up. "Dibs on the shower first."

"Go on, but leave me some hot water."

As Bree bounded up the stairs — where did she get the energy? — Meg made her way to the kitchen. Lolly was perched in her usual place on top of the refrigerator, watching Elizabeth's every move eagerly. "How was Patricia?"

"Let's wait until we're all settled before we get into it. Unless Bree doesn't need to hear all this?" Elizabeth replied, stirring something on the stove.

"That's not a problem. And it might be good to get her perspective on this — she's closer to the academic world than either of us."

"Oh, Detective Marcus called again while I was at Patricia's, so I couldn't pick up. He left a message. I haven't had a chance to return the call. But I will, I promise."

"If you don't, he'll just keep trying, you know."

"I'm sure. Now go clean up and I'll have things ready when you get back."

Upstairs Meg passed Bree in the hallway, and took her own abbreviated shower. She was hungry, not to mention curious about what her mother had found out.

At the table in the kitchen, the first five minutes were devoted to eating rather than conversation. When Meg came up for air, she said, "Bless you — can you stay on as a housekeeper?"

Elizabeth smiled. "I think your father might have something to say about that."

"Speaking of whom, have you talked to him yet?"

"No, but he should be home by the weekend."

"It's cool that you give each other so much space," Bree volunteered.

"We've been together for a long time. Sometimes space is rather nice, now and then. You're seeing someone?"

Bree chewed and swallowed. "Yeah, my boyfriend, Michael, works in Amherst. We're both kind of busy, but that's fine — works for us. For now anyway."

"As long as you're both happy with the arrangement, that's what matters. So, are you ready to hear about Patricia?"

"Was she friendly?" Meg asked.

"Reasonably so. In any event, I told her that we had wondered if there might be something in Daniel's papers that could shed light on his death."

"What did she say?"

"She said she had no idea, but she didn't care if we looked."

"Had the police asked about them?"

"Apparently they looked them over, both the files at the college and at his home office, but didn't see anything that they thought was relevant."

"What, no note that said, 'In the event of my suspicious death, check out Mr. X'?" Bree said, grinning.

"Hardly. Apparently what they saw was a lot of notes and drafts for articles. Nothing that they construed as a clue to murder. And they didn't bother to call in an outside consultant, which I take to mean that they didn't think they were important."

"Did they leave everything where they found it?"

"I have no idea, though Patricia didn't say they'd taken anything. The college hasn't asked her to clear the office yet."

"Did you talk to her about Kenneth Henderson?"

"I mentioned him, and her reaction was interesting. Correct me if I'm wrong, but didn't Kenneth imply that he and Daniel were more or less cordial colleagues?"

"That was my impression," Meg agreed. "Why?"

"Because to hear Patricia's side of it, they were bitter enemies, at least on a professional level. She confirmed that they had never met face-to-face, but she certainly knew *of* him, from various rants of Daniel's. That was the word Patricia used: 'rants.' "

"Interesting." Meg forked up the last of her meal. "Was it like Daniel to rant about things, or people?"

"Not as far as I knew — Daniel was generally quite even-tempered. Although he could have changed over the years."

"So Daniel had some sort of conflict with Kenneth," Meg said slowly, "that Kenneth didn't tell us about. I guess that means she's not going to let Kenneth go through Daniel's papers?"

"Not for love or money, to hear her tell it. But she did have a suggestion. Oh, did you want dessert, you two?"

"Always," Bree said.

"Sure, fine," Meg said absently. "Who?"

"Apparently Daniel had a graduate student who worked closely with him — not

236

from the college but from the university. Is that common, Bree? Going outside your own school?"

"Sure. I know UMass has a pretty good English department, but sometimes students request an outside person for the thesis committee, especially if he or she needs someone with a specialty that UMass doesn't cover. So I'd guess that the student must be working on Emily Dickinson?"

"Yes. Patricia knew about this student, Susan Keeley, mainly because she called Daniel a lot, at home." When Meg raised an eyebrow, Elizabeth went on, "No, nothing like that. No hanky-panky."

Bree snorted.

"Patricia didn't seem concerned about their relationship," Elizabeth insisted. "She saw this Susan person as a nuisance, very insecure and needy, not a threat to the marriage. Apparently Susan needed a lot of reassurance, thus all the phone calls. But she would be well qualified to go through Daniel's work. She might want to, for that matter — there might be information pertaining to her thesis work buried in there somewhere."

"Was Daniel neat or sloppy?" Meg asked.

"Again, I can't say. Years ago, I would have said sloppy. It was quite a contrast to your father, but probably lawyers are more organized than English professors. I wouldn't care to guess now. The materials could be in an incredible mess, or they could be neatly organized and labeled. There is only one way to find out."

"So we've got Patricia's green light to go ahead? Will she call Susan?"

"She will, but she said she wasn't going to babysit her. Patricia has a key to Daniel's office, and if the police are done with it, there's no reason why Susan can't get in there. One of us can go along."

Meg said, "Then it had better be you, Mother, since Bree and I have plenty of work to do here."

Elizabeth dished up dessert, and Bree volunteered to do the dishes. "Why don't we go into the parlor? You know, I have real trouble calling it a living room," Meg suggested to her mother.

"That sounds nice. Do you want coffee? Tea?"

"Whichever you want. These days, nothing keeps me awake anyway."

"I think tea, then," Elizabeth said.

"I'll make it. You two go chat," Bree said, shooing them out of the room as she pulled on a rubber glove to protect her cast.

In the parlor, Elizabeth settled herself in

one of the old chairs. "It would be lovely to have a fire in here, when it cools off a bit more."

"Sure, once I spend a few thousand dollars relining the chimney," Meg replied.

"Ah. Well, that could be a problem, but it's something to think about. And you really should do something about this furniture."

Meg sighed. "I know. But it all costs money."

"Are you having money troubles?"

"To tell the truth, I won't even know until after the harvest. The renovations and improvements, plus the equipment I had to buy, have eaten up most of my severance pay, so I'm counting on selling the apples for income."

"I'd be happy to help you out, you know."

Meg fought down her irrational annoyance. "I appreciate that, Mother, but I'd really rather make it on my own. If this orchard isn't financially viable, I need to know it, and then I may have to rethink things. But not until December probably."

Bree came in with a small tray bearing two mugs, tea bag tags dangling, and sugar and cream. "Microwave," she said tersely.

"Thank you," Meg said. "Bree, are we going to have any break in what's ripening?"

"Can't say. We test daily, you know, for sugar content. So no promises. But I might be able to let you off for a couple of hours — if you work really hard." Bree grinned.

"Oh, thank you, thank you! I'll do my very best!" Meg retorted, tongue in cheek.

"I'll hold you to that. Well, I'm going upstairs. Meg, don't stay up too late — you've got a busy day ahead. Night, Elizabeth."

When Bree had gone, Meg turned to Elizabeth. "Are you going to call Marcus?"

"In the morning. Do you think I should tell him about looking at Daniel's papers?"

Meg sighed. "It's probably better to tell him too much than too little. At least if you mention them, you might get some idea whether they've already looked at them or whether they haven't bothered. That should tell us something."

"It might. You know, I'm not avoiding the detective, Meg. I don't have anything to hide. How odd to be a murder suspect — that's something I never expected. But then, you'd know about that." She paused. "Were you frightened? That they wouldn't get it right, or that they'd make a case against you, just to clear the books?"

Meg sat back in her chair. It had been a difficult time, for more than one reason.

Had she ever believed she would be arrested? "No," she said finally. "I was kind of incredulous at first, like you. But I guess I do still believe in the integrity of the system, and I hoped they'd get it right in the end. Which they did, even if it took a little nudging from me. And I had friends, which helped."

"Like Rachel?" her mother asked.

"Yes, like Rachel. And others around here." Time to mention Seth? No: it was late, she was tired. *Tomorrow,* she promised herself. "I think I'll follow Bree. Are you coming up?"

"I think I'll stay down here and read for a while, if you don't mind. Or maybe do some more research on your computer?"

"Good idea. Don't stay up too late — it's easy to get sucked into following a trail when you're doing that kind of research, and the next thing you know, it's hours later."

"Noted. But all the people I'm looking for have been dead for quite a while, so I'm sure they'll wait. Good night, dear."

"Good night."

17

"You're going to meet this grad student?" Meg asked her mother at the breakfast table. Her muscles still ached from yesterday's efforts, but she knew that Bree wasn't about to let her off the hook today.

"Yes. Patricia called on my cell phone after you went to bed, and said she'd talked to Susan, and we're all set. I said I'd meet Susan on campus tomorrow afternoon — apparently she has classes or something today. Patricia will give her the key to Daniel's office. You'll be picking apples all day?"

"Yes, she will," Bree said firmly before Meg could respond. "And I've got some deliveries to make."

"No, Bree! You're supposed to be taking it easy with that arm," Meg protested.

Bree held up her cast, now rather grimy. "Hey, it feels fine. And somebody usually feels sorry for me when they see this thing, and offers to help. No problem." She stood up. "You about ready?"

"You go ahead. I'll be there in a few minutes."

Bree went out the back door with a spring in her step, leaving Meg again wondering just how she did it. Youth helped, combined with Bree's desire to prove herself up to this job. Meg, on the other hand, felt as though she had been pummeled with baseball bats. She still had a long way to go before she could match the work of even the oldest picker.

"It's hard work, isn't it?" Elizabeth said.

"It is. I have trouble imagining how farm families did it, back before mechanization. And it never ended — cows to be milked, pigs to be slopped, fields to plow or harvest. The longer I do this, the more I respect them."

Meg swallowed the last of her coffee just as she heard a firm knocking at the front door. She peered out the kitchen window to see Detective Marcus's car. "It's Detective Marcus. I take it you still haven't called him?"

"Good heavens, Meg, it's barely eight o'clock. I thought I'd wait until nine, at least."

"Well, he's here now." She made her way through the dining room and parlor to let

243

him in. "Good morning, Detective. Looking for my mother?"

"She's been ignoring my calls — again. Is she taking this investigation seriously?"

"Calls? She's only mentioned one to me. Well, come on back, she's in the kitchen." Meg led him to the back of the house. "Coffee?"

Detective Marcus stood awkwardly for a moment, then took a chair. Meg set a mug of coffee in front of him. "Thank you," he said formally. "Mrs. Corey, I thought we'd talked about returning my calls?"

Elizabeth looked contrite. "I know. I'm sorry I didn't get back to you, but I meant to today. Is there something new?"

"Have you heard from your husband recently?"

"Phillip? No, but he should be back home this week sometime."

"Do you normally communicate this infrequently?"

"Detective, what possible interest could you have in how often my husband and I communicate?"

He didn't back down. "It's relevant to the investigation. So far I have only your word about your relationship and your involvement with Daniel Weston. I'd like to hear his side."

"And Phillip won't be able to help you, other than to corroborate our past friendship," Elizabeth responded tartly. She stood up abruptly and stalked to the kitchen sink, where she turned to face Marcus. "This is ridiculous! I came here to visit an old friend. The last time I saw him he was perfectly fine. I don't know this area, or at least I didn't until Meg started showing me around, so why would I have lured him to an unfamiliar place — after dark, I might add — and killed him? Why would I have wanted Daniel dead at all? It makes no sense. And say I lured him out there. How would I have overpowered him?" Elizabeth spread out her hands. "Look at me — I weigh half of what Daniel did."

Marcus glanced at Meg, then looked at Elizabeth. "Weston was killed by a single well-placed blow. It wouldn't have taken a lot of strength," Marcus said stubbornly. "Maybe he made, uh, advances and you had to fight him off."

"Detective!" Elizabeth's expression wavered between amusement and dismay. "If he'd wanted to make advances, as you put it, he could have done it in the comfort of my hotel. Why choose a deserted farm stand in the middle of nowhere? It's not exactly an ideal place for hanky-panky, you know, especially at our age."

Meg thought Detective Marcus swallowed a smile. "Don't you have any other suspects, Detective?" she said gently.

He sighed. "We're working on it. I'm sorry — I'm just frustrated. Weston's been dead a week now. From all I've heard, the man was a saint. Everybody loved and admired him. Ergo, he shouldn't be dead."

"Did Kenneth Henderson contact you?"

"The professor? Yeah. He's coming in later this morning to talk to us. How do you know about him?"

"We saw him at the memorial service, and then we happened to run into him at the Harvest Festival on Saturday. He's staying at Rachel Dickinson's place, and we all had tea together yesterday. He said —"

Marcus held up one hand. "Don't tell me anything. I want to hear it from him." He swallowed more coffee and turned back to Elizabeth. "Mrs. Corey, when you ignore my calls, it makes me wonder if you have something to hide. Maybe you don't, but I'd prefer that you cooperate with this investigation."

"I apologize, Detective," Elizabeth replied. "You're right. And of course I want to see this cleared up as soon as possible. Is there anything else I can do to help?"

Marcus shook his head. "Just tell the truth. You've told us about your history with the victim, and why you were here. I still want to hear your husband's side of it. And I can't involve civilians in an open investigation — whatever your daughter here may tell you. I'd appreciate it if you'd steer clear of the whole thing and let us do our job." He spoke to Elizabeth, but his eye shifted briefly to Meg.

"Don't look at me, Detective," Meg said. "I have enough to do getting my crop harvested and delivered."

He managed a small smile. "Can you keep an eye on your mother?"

Meg avoided her mother's eyes. "I've sicced her on putting together the family genealogy. Since there are a lot of generations of ancestors around here, that should keep her busy."

"Uh-huh." He didn't look convinced. "Just try to keep out of it, will you?" He stood up.

Elizabeth hadn't budged from her place by the sink. "I promise I'll let you know when I talk to Phillip, Detective."

"Thank you. And tell him to call me. Thanks for the coffee, Meg. See me out?"

Meg led him back to the front door. "You don't really think she had anything to do

247

with this, do you?" she asked in a low voice.

His shoulders sagged. "Not really. It's not personal, Meg. It's a homicide — I have to check out everything."

"I know. Good luck." Meg watched him climb into his car and drive off before she returned to the kitchen, where Elizabeth was washing up the breakfast dishes.

"You didn't mention he had called more than once. Are you really trying to tick him off?" Meg demanded.

Elizabeth didn't look up. "I resent being accused of murder."

"He's not accusing you of anything — he's investigating. He's a good cop, and we'll all be better off if you cooperate."

Elizabeth turned off the water and faced Meg. "I realize that. And perhaps I have misjudged him, which was stupid of me. But I notice you didn't say anything about looking at Daniel's papers. Were you afraid he'd tell me not to?"

Meg smiled reluctantly. "I guess so. I thought I'd let Kenneth mention them. Besides, either Marcus will tell him they've already looked through them, or by the time Marcus does follow up, you'll have seen them."

"Ah, Meg, I didn't know you had such a devious streak in you. Where could that have come from?"

Meg ignored the question. "If I don't get up the hill, Bree will have my hide. Good luck with Daniel's papers. You'll be back for dinner?"

"If I haven't been arrested," her mother replied.

Meg came back down the hill for lunch; she wanted a few minutes to sit and do nothing. Absolutely nothing. Didn't she deserve a break?

And it was only September. Would things get easier or harder as the season went on? At least the crop looked good. There had been no significant pests or blights or scabs, or whatever else they were called. Not that she had had anything to do with that, other than hiring the right people to oversee the trees. But maybe the harvest gods, or goddesses, were smiling on her.

Her lunch options boiled down to a peanut butter and jelly sandwich and a glass of cider. She'd bought a jug at Dickinson's, which reminded her once again: what had Daniel Weston been doing there?

Her peaceful lunch was interrupted by the sound of her goats bleating in unison, combined with the barking of a dog. Dog? Meg hurried to the kitchen door. Yes, there was a dog, a youngish golden retriever, or so she guessed, who appeared fascinated by Dorcas and Isabel. The goats were holding their ground on the other side of the fence, but looked wary.

"Sorry about that." Seth emerged from the barn, leash in hand. "He kind of got away from me."

"He's yours?"

"As of yesterday."

"I didn't know you were looking for a dog." Seth had once told her he'd had a dog years earlier, but he hadn't given her the impression that he was in any hurry to replace him.

"I wasn't, but someone had to give him up for financial reasons, so Andrea thought of me."

"Andrea?"

Seth caught up with the dog and clipped the leash to his collar. "Yes, Andrea Bedortha — the vet?"

"I know who Andrea is, Seth — I just saw her Saturday," Meg reminded him. "She knew you wanted a dog?"

"I'd mentioned it."

Meg remembered that the two of them had looked pretty chummy at the Harvest Festival. "How's she settling in at the new office?"

250

"Great. I've been helping her with some of the plumbing — she wanted another sink in the back."

Of course. Helpful Seth, always doing another good deed. *Meg, stop it!* she chastised herself. Seth had every right to help Andrea out in setting up her new office. He'd known her for years — longer than he'd known Meg. He'd cajoled Andrea into taking on a solo practice in Granford, and since he was so involved with Granford Grange, he'd want the tenants to be happy and successful. So why was Meg upset?

She swallowed her irrational pique. "What's his name?"

"Max. Andrea says he's about six months old. And not very well trained, as you can tell." Max was pulling hard at the leash, far more interested in the goats than in the humans. The goats stood sentinel, watching curiously. Meg felt a pang: she hadn't had much time to talk to them lately. Could goats get lonely? Or bored? At least they had each other.

"Have you eaten? Not that I have much to offer. My mother's off searching Daniel Weston's office. Come on in and I'll tell you about it. Marcus was here this morning — again."

"Can I bring Max inside?"

251

"Does he like cats?"

"Oh, right — Lolly. I don't know. We haven't met any cats since I picked him up."

"How about you tie him up outside here? We can leave the door open so you can keep an eye on him."

"Will do."

Seth joined her in the kitchen after a few minutes. Max whined plaintively, but Seth ignored him. "What's up?" He took a seat at the table.

"Sorry I can't offer you much — Mother's been doing the shopping lately, but I think we've eaten everything. PBJ okay?"

"Fine. How're you two doing?"

"Not bad. I think being a murder suspect has shaken her a bit. And she's trying not to interfere in the investigation."

"The operative word being 'trying'?"

"Well . . . Right now she wants to find out if Daniel left anything in his records that might point to someone in the academic community as his killer."

"Marcus hasn't come up with any suspects?"

Meg shook her head. "He even admitted he's frustrated. Daniel had no obvious enemies. It's ridiculous — if my mother is the best suspect they've got, the state police really are grasping at straws." She set the sandwich on a plate and put it in front of Seth. "Cider?"

"Sure."

She poured a glass for him, then sat down in front of her unfinished sandwich.

Seth ate half his sandwich and washed it down with cider. "Meg," he said suddenly, "are you trying to keep me and your mother apart?"

She was startled by his question, and at a loss for how to answer him. "No, not really. It's just that she and I haven't spent much time together in the last few years, and things got kind of sticky when Daniel died, and . . ." She trailed off, knowing how lame she sounded.

Seth was regarding her steadily. "What have you told her about us?"

What is "us"? They'd never really talked about it. Meg dismissed several flippant answers before ducking the question and saying, "Maybe we should plan a dinner together, just the three of us. I would have before now, except I've been so busy."

"We could go to the restaurant. That's nice, neutral ground. And I can show your mother I clean up real nice."

"Seth!" Meg was hurt by his sarcasm, but she had to admit he had a point. She took a breath. "I'd be delighted to have you spend some time with my mother. And that's an excellent idea. I'll call Nicky right now." Before she could change her mind, she stood up, went to the phone, and punched the speed-dial number for the restaurant.

"Hi, Nicky. How's business?" Meg listened to Nicky burble on: the gist was that everything was great, terrific, and wonderful. "Listen, can you fit in three of us, say, tomorrow night? Me, Seth, and my mother." Nicky was ecstatic, and the deal was done. Meg hung up and turned back to Seth. "There. Tomorrow. That work for you?"

"Great. Look, Meg, I don't want to force anything." He stood up and moved closer, then laid his hands on her shoulders. "If you don't want to tell her."

Meg leaned against him. "I'm sorry. I'm not being fair, to you or to her. You know I care about you, and I'm making unfair assumptions about what she's going to think. Which is dumb. You're a great guy, Seth, and she should see that. And if she doesn't, that's her loss."

"It's okay, Meg. I know I am but a humble plumber . . ."

She swatted his arm, laughing. "Stop that. You're making me feel ashamed of myself. And you're so much more than a plumber — although a plumber is a pretty good thing to be these days."

"Meg, shut up." He leaned in to kiss her, only to be interrupted by Max's barking. "That dog's probably gotten himself tangled up in the leash. He's kind of a klutz."

"He's young. Think of him as a clumsy teenager. Are you going to be leaving him here a lot?"

Seth looked sheepish. "I can't leave him locked up at my house, can I? He can come with me on some jobs, but at least here he can have a little space. Maybe I should set up a dog run for him out back. And I'm sure he'll be a good watchdog."

"Yeah, right," Meg replied. One more thing to take care of; one more thing to worry about. And a constant reminder of Andrea, right in her backyard. "I'm sure we'll manage. Well, Bree will be sending a search party for me if I don't get back up the hill. See you tomorrow?"

"Should I pick you up?"

"Let me get back to you on that."

"I'll call you during the day, then. Thanks for lunch." Seth went out to release Max from bondage and headed off toward his office at the rear of the property, whistling as he went, with Max at his heels. Meg put the dishes in the sink, locked up, and trudged up the hill once again.

18

In the gathering dusk, after another long day of physical labor, Meg stumbled her way down the hill and through the back door. Her mother's car was in the driveway, along with an unfamiliar car, so Meg was prepared for the sounds of voices when she came in the front door. One was clearly her mother's, but whose was the other? She wavered in the hallway, debating about ducking upstairs for a much-needed shower or confronting whoever was in her kitchen. In the end curiosity, combined with the good smells once again wafting from that direction, won out.

"Meg, darling — you look exhausted," her mother greeted her. "Would you like a cup of tea? Or a drink?"

"Tea sounds good. Bree should be joining us shortly. I take it you made dinner again?"

"I did. It's the least I could do." Elizabeth handed her a steaming mug.

"Bless you!" Meg wondered when she would next have a chance to buy food, or clean house, or do laundry, or get her car serviced, or get her hair cut . . . probably December, at the rate things were going. "You must be Susan Keeley?" Meg eyed the rather plain young woman hovering in the corner, a mug of tea clutched in her hands. As Meg gratefully accepted the mug that her mother handed her, she thought she recognized their visitor from Daniel's memorial service.

The woman straightened up and put down the mug to hold out her hand. "Yes, hi. Are you Meg? Your mother and I were so busy this afternoon that we lost track of time, and then she said, why didn't I just come and eat with you here and we could keep talking? I hope you don't mind?"

Meg assessed her unexpected guest. Tall, but with lousy posture; pale, as though she lived under a rock; a bit spotty of skin and chewed of nails. Was this what English lit graduate students looked like these days? But Susan's gaze was unapologetic, as if she was saying, *Take me as I am, and I really don't care.* "Not a problem, Susan. I'm glad to meet you." Meg shook her hand: Susan's handshake was firm and brief. "I'd love to hear what, if anything, you and my mother have found. But first I'm going to grab a quick shower. I'll be back in five." She fled up the stairs.

Lolly was lying curled in a tight ball on her bed, no doubt avoiding the stranger in the kitchen, and Meg scratched her behind her ears. "Have you been fed, silly animal?" When Lolly tucked her nose under her tail and went back to sleep, Meg guessed the answer was yes. She grabbed some clean clothes and headed for the shower.

Mere minutes later Meg was back in the kitchen, where she found Bree talking to Susan about details of UMass life. "It was really hard to get any studying done in the dorm," Bree was saying. "How do you do it? I mean, you have to think about words and ideas — most of what I was working with was facts and figures."

Susan nodded. "It's not always easy. I've found some pretty quiet corners in a couple of the libraries, but sometimes I just had to get out of there, you know? Luckily I have a car, so I could go find quiet places here and there. Summer I could work outdoors — sometimes it was a relief to get away from the Internet and just concentrate on the research and writing."

"How much longer do you have before you get your degree, Susan?" Meg sat down at the table after refilling her mug of tea. Elizabeth was bustling between the stove and the microwave, stirring something.

Susan shrugged. "I should finish by the end of this academic year — next spring. But it's kind of complicated, now that Daniel's out of the picture."

"You were at his memorial service, weren't you?" And had appeared very upset, as Meg recalled.

Susan nodded, and her eyes filled with tears. "That was so hard. I mean, I couldn't believe he was dead. But wasn't it great that so many people came out to honor him?"

"He must have been well respected. How did Daniel Weston become involved in your studies? I mean, he was at the college, and you're at the university, right?" Meg asked. "I'm sorry — I didn't mean that to sound like you weren't entitled to his attention."

"It's okay, I know what you mean. He was really important in his field, and I'm just a state university student. But it's not unusual to have an outside committee member, depending on your area of specialization. I felt really lucky to have him on my committee."

"You're working on Emily Dickinson?"

Susan leaned back in her chair. "She's my main focus, yes, but I'm looking at her in the context of other nineteenth-century American women poets. You know, whether they published and where, how they were reviewed, if at all — that kind of thing. Sort of a socio-politico-feminist slant. Male poets got a lot more pages, and a lot more attention. I'd love to find out if these women were communicating with each other — you know, sort of like a critique group, or maybe just sharing because they knew they weren't going to find a bigger audience. People did a whole lot more letter writing in that century. Too bad most of the correspondence was tossed out as unimportant."

"I thought a lot of Dickinson's work had been preserved?"

"As much as anyone's, I guess. You know, back in those days nobody thought some woman's correspondence was important. In fact, Emily's own family threw a lot of hers away after she died. What survives is scattered through a lot of different collections, although there's a big chunk at the college in Amherst. Anyway, Daniel Weston was the big name around here, and a recommendation from him would mean a lot. Would have, I mean. Guess that's not going to happen." Susan slumped back into her chair.

"Is the job market tough for PhDs these days?" Meg asked.

"When isn't it? That's why knowing the right people matters — they can help. It takes more than a solid dissertation — you need publications, and conference panels, teaching experience. A lot of people give up and don't finish, and a lot more spin it out as long as they can, since they don't have anywhere to go. Of course, most people don't go into English literature in the first place, if they've got any sense."

"Why did you?"

Susan smiled ruefully. "I love language. I love seeing another era filtered through a poet's eyes. And if I may oversimplify, the women poets tend to be more rooted in ordinary life. The men were all busy describing battles and history and grand ideas, but the women talked about a smaller, simpler world. That's why Emily is so interesting — she deliberately shrank her universe, and then studied it very carefully, trying to capture it, which she did with surprising economy. Do you know her work?"

"Not well, I'm afraid, but as much as your average person, I guess. Is it true that she never intended to publish her work?"

"There's some disagreement about that."

"Dinner's ready," Elizabeth said, setting a large bowl on the table. "It's a white chili recipe I've been experimenting with — I thought that was a good compromise for this between-seasons period, neither hot nor cold." She went back to the cupboard and brought out bowls, distributing them around the table.

Fifteen minutes later, Meg felt much more right with the world. A glass of wine helped. More than one and she might fall asleep with her face in the bowl. She noticed that Susan didn't drink much either, but she certainly ate with a healthy appetite.

Meg leaned back and surreptitiously loosened her belt. "So, you two looked at the files in Daniel's office today?"

"We did." Elizabeth glanced at Susan, who nodded for her to continue. "From what we could see, the police had gone through the drawers and shelves, and they took his computer, but not much else that we could identify. So we spent the afternoon sifting and sorting."

"Was Daniel good at keeping records?" Meg asked.

Susan snorted. "Uh, not exactly. I mean, he wasn't a total slob, and besides, this was his campus office, so he had to keep a couple of chairs free for visitors, and a path clear to get to his desk — it couldn't be too much of a pit. But most of the important stuff was in his head. I mean, I could walk in and ask him, say, 'Where's that article that appeared in the *Hampshire Gazette* in 1878?' And he knew exactly what I meant and could put his hand on it like that. He had his own peculiar logic, but it worked for him."

"Did he give you much feedback on your work?" Bree tossed out.

"Quite a bit, actually. I was surprised. He always made time for me, and I could tell he'd read what I'd given him. So I knew he took his role on the committee seriously. Which was great for me. I mean, the man knew everything there was about Emily Dickinson."

"So what did you hope to add to the body of knowledge with your thesis? It has to explore something new, right?" Meg asked.

"Yes," Susan agreed. "Scholars are always reinterpreting, you know? I mean, we can only understand a work of art through the biases of our own culture and time, and those are always changing. There are lots of new avenues to follow, even with someone as well known and well studied as Emily — her physical problems, or her psychological issues. Was she going blind? Was she depressed, or bipolar, or agoraphobic? I've read articles discussing all of these things."

Meg was impressed. "Wow. I hadn't

thought about it like that. Will Daniel's death make things more difficult for you?"

Susan shrugged. "I'd finished most of the research, and now all I've got left is to write the thing. I think he would have been a big help in shaping my arguments. He was great at talking through a lot of things. I'll miss him." Tears welled again, and she looked away.

Meg glanced at her mother. Time to change the subject. "Did Mother tell you what we're looking for? Did you think Daniel was particularly excited lately?"

"He'd been really up, you know? I kind of figured he thought he was onto something new, but he didn't share it with me. I mean, why would he? I'm just a student, and he was the big important scholar. But he was like a kid, and he kept dropping hints."

"Weren't you curious?" Meg prompted.

"Sure, but I figured I'd find out eventually."

"But he hinted to Kenneth Henderson that he had some surprise," Elizabeth said, almost to herself.

Susan laughed briefly. "That doesn't mean much. He and Professor Henderson were always trying to outdo each other — you can see it if you look at the literature. So it was the professor who put you onto this hunt?"

"Yes, he brought it up."

"Maybe Daniel was just yanking Professor Henderson's chain."

"Do you really think so?" Elizabeth said.

Susan shrugged. "I don't know. I know they've been after each other for years now. I heard at a conference once that Professor Henderson thought that Daniel had taken one of his ideas and rushed it into print, and he wasn't too happy about that. It's still 'publish or perish' in academia, but Professor Henderson would have looked like a sore loser if he'd made a public stink. So he just swallowed it, but he was real careful about what he said around Daniel after that."

"My, this all sounds so competitive," Elizabeth observed.

Susan nodded. "It is, pretty much. Even with tenure, professors are vulnerable now. And they know there are plenty of grad students like me who would love to have their jobs, for a lot less pay. I'm sorry Daniel's dead, but to be honest, it's mostly for selfish reasons. I really could have used his recommendation when I start job hunting." Susan turned to Meg and abruptly changed the subject. "Your mother says this house dates to the 1700s. Would you mind showing me the rest of it? I love this time period, you know."

Elizabeth stood up. "Meg, why don't you give her a tour while I clean up? And I'll dish out dessert."

Meg led Susan to the dining room. "From what I've learned, the house was built by Stephen Warren in the 1760s, when he first settled in Granford. Not long after that one of his sons built the house next door. The same family lived here continuously until about twenty years ago, which is kind of remarkable."

"Great woodwork," Susan said, eyeing the wainscoting. "It's all original?"

"That part is, but the door and window moldings were replaced during a remodeling in the mid-nineteenth century. The grandson of the original builder was a carpenter. They actually had a small sawmill out back, between the two houses. And plenty of available lumber — there are still some old-growth trees out there, across the meadow."

"Wow. How'd you learn all this? Your mother said you just moved here this year, right?"

"Gail Selden at the Granford Historical Society has been helping me do the research, and I'm returning the favor by doing some cataloging for her. They've got some wonderful resources for local history, but it's hard for the public to get at them because they're not cataloged."

"I know what you're saying — cataloging's a challenge at any institution, and even if they have the information, sometimes it's next to useless. Like the file will say, 'Documents.' Could be anything, from a copy of the Declaration of Independence to receipts for hay."

"Exactly." Meg laughed. "I'll bet you have a lot more interesting stories than I do, since you must spend a lot more time working with original documents. Now, here in the hallway, I think Eli Warren replaced the stair rail — it's definitely not from the colonial period . . ." Meg continued the tour, and Susan asked some intelligent questions about construction and architectural history, many of which Meg couldn't answer. Susan seemed interested in every nook and cranny, but Meg drew the line at showing her the basement, particularly after dark.

They returned to the kitchen to find warm apple cake and coffee waiting. Bree had disappeared, and Elizabeth was wiping off the countertops.

"Great house!" Susan said. "A real sense

of history, and you can feel the hands of the people who lived here. Do you have a time line for them?"

"Mother's been looking into that," Meg said, taking a forkful of cake. "I really haven't had much time lately, since this is harvest season. I do know they're all in the local cemetery. I visit them now and then. Is that weird?"

Susan shrugged. "Emily spent her life with a view of the cemetery where she'd be buried. I think it's kind of nice that you remember your ancestors."

"Heck, I'm still just getting to know them." Meg stifled a yawn. How could she wrap this evening up and send Susan on her way home without being rude? She decided that being direct was the simplest course. "Susan, do you have any idea who would have wanted Daniel Weston dead? Kenneth Henderson? Someone on the faculty?"

"I've met him once or twice, and I can't see Professor Henderson resorting to actual violence. He might have sniped at Daniel in person or even in print, but they've been going on like that for years."

"By the way, which side won the Dickinson versus Whitman debate at the symposium?"

Susan smiled briefly. "Who do you think? We're talking about Amherst. The deck was stacked from the beginning, even without Daniel. Or maybe as a tribute to him."

"Would that be enough to drive Kenneth to murder?" Meg asked.

"I don't think so," Susan replied. "He must have known what the outcome would be."

"What about Daniel's wife?" Elizabeth said suddenly.

Susan turned to her. "Patricia? Why? She was better off with him alive than dead. And I doubt she felt strongly enough to kill him."

"What do you mean?" Meg said.

"She's the second wife. The kids aren't hers, and they aren't even around. She liked the lifestyle — you know, faculty wife at prestigious college and all that. They had enough money. He hadn't let himself go. But she really wasn't interested in his work."

"Did they have personal problems?"

Susan made a face at Meg. "Like he'd tell me? I only saw them together a couple of times. I wouldn't say they were close exactly, but they weren't throwing crockery at each other or anything. I think they lived in sort of parallel tracks. And they were kind of old — what were they going to do at this point? Why bother splitting up?"

Elizabeth cast an amused glance at Meg; she was, after all, the same age as Daniel and older than Patricia. "I thought she was a few years younger than he was. You didn't hear any rumors about his involvement with any students, did you?"

Susan faced Elizabeth. "Heck, no. He was Mister Squeaky-Clean. Are you asking if he hit on me? No. He didn't try, and I wouldn't have been interested. I wanted his input on my thesis, period, and that worked fine for both of us."

"But he's dead," Elizabeth said softly. "And not from natural causes. Why?"

"I don't know. Anyway, I wish whoever killed him had waited a few months, long enough to review my thesis." She stood up abruptly. "Sorry, that came out wrong. Daniel was a decent person and a good scholar, and I can't see why anyone would have wanted to kill him. Anyway, I should let you go to bed. Thanks for dinner. It was nice meeting you both."

"Thank you for your help today," Elizabeth responded. "Even if we didn't find anything significant, at least we can eliminate one possibility."

"What about his house? Are you going to look there?" Susan asked.

"I'll talk to Patricia again, but she seemed

to think there wasn't much there. Anyway, let me walk you out."

"Good night, Susan," Meg called out to their retreating backs. She tried to summon up the energy to move out of her chair and failed.

"Did you find *anything* useful at Daniel's office?" Meg asked when her mother returned.

Elizabeth shook her head. "His office was a mess. We straightened things up as best we could, and Susan was very helpful there, but there were no secret compartments, no files labeled 'IMPORTANT NEW DISCOVERY.' " Elizabeth made air quotes. "No more than what you'd expect."

"What now?"

Elizabeth sighed. "I don't know. This may be a wild-goose chase. We're looking for something we aren't even sure exists, based on some vague hints from someone who had a history of conflict with Daniel. Maybe Daniel was toying with Kenneth in the first place and there never was anything to announce at the symposium."

"But as you said, Daniel's dead, and there must have been a reason."

"That he is. And I'd like to see justice done for him, not to mention have my name cleared. But I'm running out of ideas.

Maybe the police are better equipped to handle this."

Meg yawned. "I'm fading fast. Maybe in the morning you should do something else, like work on that genealogy for the Warrens. I've often found that shifting gears helps clear my head. Unless you had other plans?"

"That *is* a good idea. And I think I've got the hang of computer searching now. Maybe there is one thing I can finish while I'm here."

Meg stood up and stretched. "From what I understand, genealogy is never finished. Oh, by the way, I made a reservation for dinner at the restaurant in town tomorrow night."

"That sounds lovely. You'll be picking tomorrow?"

"I'll be picking until all the apples are picked." Should she mention that Seth was invited, too? No. Elizabeth could find out tomorrow.

"Good night, dear. Sleep well."

Like she had a choice. Meg was out the minute her head hit the pillow.

19

When was this going to get easier? Meg asked herself as she hauled herself out of bed for another day of picking. The sky was overcast and threatened rain, but she suspected that that wouldn't stop her pickers. They were used to this. Shouldn't she be by now?

Downstairs Elizabeth was in the kitchen, as was Lolly, sitting in her favorite perch on top of the refrigerator and washing her face. Elizabeth wordlessly handed Meg a full mug of coffee. Three minutes later, half the mug gone, Meg ventured to speak. "What're you doing today?"

Elizabeth sat opposite with her own coffee. "I thought it over and decided I'd call Patricia after all and see if she would let me take a look at Daniel's home office. I have a better idea what to look for now, but I'm not holding out a lot of hope of finding anything useful. Maybe Susan was right, and Daniel was just toying with his colleagues."

"Did he have a sense of humor?"

"He liked to poke fun, I guess. But as I remember it, he always took his scholarship seriously, and this falls under that heading. Anyway, I doubt that shuffling through those files will take all day, so I thought I'd follow your suggestion and finish roughing out the family tree." Elizabeth smiled. "We're both working with trees, so to speak. You said something about dinner reservations tonight?"

"Yes. I thought you'd like to see the restaurant. And then you won't have to cook."

"That sounds lovely."

Meg got up and put an English muffin in the toaster.

Elizabeth made a tsking sound. "You need more nourishment than that — you're working hard."

"Tell me about it," Meg replied glumly. "Muscles I never knew I had hurt."

"Will it be like this every year?"

Meg sat back in her chair. "Well, this year we're shorthanded because of Bree's accident. As for the future, who knows? Things happen. We almost got hit by a hailstorm a month or two ago, which could have severely damaged the crop and reduced its value. Heck, for all I know, the barn could fall down tomorrow." Although Seth swore it was structurally sound. "Farming isn't easy, which is probably why not many people do it these days. It's easier just to let the big corporations take over. Except that won't work for orchards, because you can't exactly mass-harvest apples without damaging them — you still need to handpick them and handle them gently. Scientists can breed apples that will stand up to rougher handling, but they taste like cardboard. And that's why so many orchards get paved over. They're just too hard to maintain." Meg shook her head. "Listen to me! I'm lecturing, and I haven't even had my breakfast."

"Why are you farming, then?" Elizabeth asked with what looked like genuine curiosity.

Meg took a moment before answering. "I suppose because it makes me feel connected — to a place, to our past. You're looking at the genealogy — do you know how many generations of our ancestors lived and worked right here? I mean, I'm an only child, you're an only child, and Daddy's got only the one brother. We don't have a lot of family, near or far. But here, we have roots. And that's not all: working with my hands is something I never really considered before, much less tried. I like it, at least some parts of it." Meg ran her fingers through her hair. "Look, I haven't made any final decisions about this place. I thought I should get through one apple season and then take stock, think about it. We can still sell the house if it comes to that. Nothing's final."

Elizabeth looked around the kitchen. "You know, I feel different about the house, now that I've spent some time in it. I think I know what you're saying, about having a history with a place. Nothing woo-woo like talking to our ancestral ghosts, but knowing that their hands made this, that they lived out their lives here — it changes things. I'm glad you're not in any hurry to sell."

Bree chose that moment to walk into the kitchen. "You're selling?"

"No, no," Meg assured her. "Actually Mother was saying she was less inclined to sell, now that she's gotten to know the place."

"It grows on you, huh?" Bree grinned.

"It does. Breakfast, Bree?"

Bree dropped into her seat. "Sure. Sounds good."

Elizabeth turned away toward the stove, but not before smiling and adding, "See,

Meg? Somebody thinks breakfast matters."

Meg rolled her eyes. "Bree, what're we picking today?"

"I'm thinking the Empires and the Cortlands are ready."

"We've got a lot of those, do we?"

"We do," Bree replied. "They've got a long shelf life. You looking to finish early?"

"Mother and I were planning to have dinner at the restaurant tonight. I'd like time to clean up."

"What, and you didn't invite me?" Bree feigned indignation. "Well, as it happens, I made plans with Michael for tonight, so you're off the hook anyway. You two go and do that mother-daughter bonding thing. Good food helps."

"Yes, boss," Meg said.

Elizabeth set full plates in front of Meg and Bree. "There you go!" she said. "All set. Do you think it's too early to call Patricia?"

"It's, what, nine? I think that's safe enough," Meg said.

"Then I'll see if I can run over there sometime today." Elizabeth picked up the handset of the phone and disappeared into the privacy of the dining room.

Bree dug in with a healthy appetite. "You know," she said between mouthfuls, "I could get used to this."

"What, someone fixing you breakfast every day?" Meg said, eating more slowly. "Don't get any ideas, because I'm not volunteering. What we need is a housewife."

Bree gave a snort of laughter. "I hear you. Who could maybe dust and vacuum and do all that stuff, too."

"In your dreams. But it is nice, isn't it?" They both ate in contented silence for a few minutes. Finally Meg said, "How much more picking do we have to go?"

"The last apples should ripen by mid-November, but the peak period will be the next month or so. But this cast should be off long before that."

"You wait until the doctor tells you it can come off," Meg said sternly. "I can handle my end of things. Is it going to rain today? It looks cloudy out there."

"Forecast says no. You won't get off that easy," Bree said.

Elizabeth returned, looking troubled. "Patricia's house was broken into last night."

"Oh, no!" Meg said. "I wonder if it's connected with Daniel's death? Somebody saw the announcement and figured a woman living alone might be vulnerable? What was taken?"

"Not much, she said. A television, some

small electronics, but no jewelry. But Daniel's home office was trashed. The police already had his laptop, but maybe the thief was looking for something else?"

Meg shook her head. "Poor Patricia. That sounds much more troubling. I guess there's no point in your trying to check it out now?"

"I don't think so. Maybe after things have settled down a bit."

"Did she call the cops?" Bree asked.

"Of course."

"When did this happen?"

"Last night sometime. Patricia was out with friends, and didn't get home until midnight, and when she saw the mess, she called them immediately. Poor woman — she must be having a hard time right now, with all this happening at once."

"Is there anything we can do?" Meg asked.

"I doubt it. She must have some people in the area that she can call on for support. Anyway, I guess I'll dig into the genealogy stuff today."

Bree stood up quickly. "Then let's go, Meg, and let your mother get some work done."

Meg stood up more slowly, feeling far more than ten years Bree's senior. "Lead the way."

As Meg was dumping yet another bag's worth of apples — by her estimate, her seventieth — her cell phone rang. It was Seth.

"Hey, we still on for tonight?" he asked.

"If I survive another day of picking, we are. Shall we meet at the restaurant?"

"Sure. Have you told your mother I'd be there?"

Meg swallowed a spurt of guilt. "No."

There was a moment of silence from Seth's end. "Okay. You sure you want me there?"

"Yes. Yes, I do. I'm sorry, Seth, but there just hasn't been a good moment . . ." Her voice trailed off.

"We can work it out at dinner," he replied neutrally.

"Of course. And did you hear that there was a break-in at Daniel Weston's house in Amherst?"

"How did you hear about that?"

"Mother called Daniel's widow to see if they could get together today to look at his home office, and Patricia told her then."

"I see. Why are you interested?"

"Well, doesn't it seem kind of odd that it

should happen now?"

"Not necessarily. Some people prey on the bereaved."

"Yes, but isn't that usually during the funeral, when they know the house will be empty? Patricia could easily have been there last night, but luckily she was out. And she told my mother that not much had been taken, but that Daniel's office was trashed. Doesn't it all seem a little strange to you?"

"Don't read too much into it, Meg. These things happen, even around here. Look, I've got to run. I'll see you at seven . . . unless you change your mind." He hung up before she could respond.

As she approached the next tree, Meg promised herself that she'd do right by Seth tonight. Over a nice, civilized dinner. Finally. This was getting ridiculous.

In the end, Seth scotched her plans by showing up early at her place — with Max on a leash. Meg had come back down the hill from the orchard in time to shower and change, and was in the kitchen chatting with Elizabeth until it was time to leave for dinner when he knocked at the back door.

"Hi, Meg. Hi, Elizabeth. Look, is it all right if I leave Max here for now? Mom's not home or I'd ask her, and I haven't had time to dog-proof my place yet."

Meg wondered briefly — and unkindly — if Seth was just making up an excuse to force the issue. "Sure. You want to leave him in the kitchen here? I can shut Lolly in a different room. What with all that polyurethane, there's not much he can do to the floor. Does he need food or anything?"

"No, he's good. I thought we could drive to the restaurant together."

Seth's words hung in the air while Meg scrambled for an explanation. Elizabeth said, "So you'll be joining us for dinner? Lovely. I've been looking forward to getting to know you. Meg, are we ready to go?"

Blushing, Meg avoided her mother's eyes. "Just let me get a coat. I'll go out the front and meet you by the car. Don't forget to latch all the doors if Max is in the kitchen." She fled.

At Gran's they were greeted at the door by co-owner Brian, looking harried but happy. "Meg, Seth — great to see you."

"Something here smells wonderful!" Elizabeth said appreciatively.

"My wife's the chef — you met her on Saturday at the festival. I just keep doing everything else so she can do what she does best, which is cook. Let me show you to your table."

Brian proudly escorted them to a table in

a quiet corner, and Meg was happy to see that the room was well filled, even though it was a Wednesday night. Better yet, all the diners looked happy. The room glowed with candlelight and discreetly placed indirect lighting, emphasizing the rough (and original) plaster and exposed brick. Meg felt herself begin to relax as Seth pulled out a chair for her mother, and Brian did the same for her.

"Something to drink?" Brian asked.

"A bottle of wine?" Seth looked at Elizabeth and Meg. They both nodded. "What's on the menu tonight, Brian?"

"You're wondering what kind of wine to order? Why don't you let us put together a meal for you and pick the wine to go with it?"

"Sounds good to me," Seth said.

"Just as long as we can taste a variety of dishes, please," Meg added.

"Of course," Brian said. "I'll just be a minute." He retreated toward the kitchen, leaving the three of them alone.

"Well," Meg began tentatively, and then realized that both of her companions were smiling at her. "What?"

"Seth stopped by this afternoon while you were in the orchard," Elizabeth began with a small smile.

Meg shot an angry glance at Seth.

"Margaret, don't blame him. Did you really think I couldn't see what was going on between you? I may be old, but I'm not dead — or stupid."

"Shoot," Meg said. She could feel herself blushing again. "Okay, Seth and I are seeing each other. We have been for a while. I didn't tell you because I wasn't sure what you'd think."

"Why on earth would I disapprove? Seth, you seem like a nice person, you're gainfully employed, and it's obvious that you care for Meg. I'm happy for you both. That is, if you're happy about it, Meg?"

Meg swallowed, and glanced briefly at Seth, who didn't offer any help. "Yes, I am."

Elizabeth smiled. "Well, then, Seth, I really would like to get to know you better, if you're going to be part of Meg's life."

"Thank you. And I hope I will be."

Much to Meg's relief, Brian chose that moment to appear bearing two bottles of wine, white and red, and he and Seth engaged in a mock-serious ritual of tasting. She was glad for the respite, because she needed a moment to sort out her chaotic thoughts. Her mother *liked* Seth. She had been worried for no reason. But was her mother's opinion the main sticking point, or did she herself harbor reservations about her relationship with Seth? And why? Because she didn't trust herself? Or because she had doubts about Seth?

Food appeared, one course following another, and it was all good, and between that and the wine, Meg could feel herself relaxing. Her mother made cheerful small talk and smoothed things over. This was exactly what Meg had imagined and hoped that the restaurant would be — a place with good food and good company. She felt proud that she had had a part in making it happen. The fact that her mother and her boyfriend were getting on like a house afire was just icing on the cake. Hmm . . . better slow up on the wine, since her metaphors were becoming increasingly muddled.

Dessert and coffee appeared. "You've been quiet, Meg. Tired?" her mother asked.

"A bit, but I'm enjoying the moment. I'm so glad that Nicky and Brian are doing well. She really can cook, can't she?"

"Indeed she can. I can't remember when I've enjoyed a meal so much," Elizabeth said. "Oh, by the way — we haven't had a chance to talk about the genealogy, and I found something interesting today."

"What?"

"We're related to Emily Dickinson! Well,

it's not exactly a close relationship. More like distant cousins. But I was tickled to figure that out. Actually, there were quite a few Dickinsons living in Granford in the nineteenth century, and most of them are related to her in some degree, if you go back up the tree a bit. And to us, then, I guess."

"You'll find that happens a lot around here," Seth volunteered. "In fact, I think the Chapins and the Warrens are some kind of distant cousins, too. You look at the road signs in Granford, which were usually named because they led to someone's farm, and most of those names are kin, too. It's a small community — always has been."

"That's so rare these days," Elizabeth said, and Meg thought she could detect a wistful note in her mother's voice. "My generation and our parents' moved around so much, and it's hard to create that kind of connection now. I must say I'm glad that Meg asked me to look into the family history. It has certainly been enlightening. Not to mention addictive."

Nicky emerged from the kitchen, wiping her hands on her apron. She looked tired but happy, her dark curls damp with sweat and springing wildly around her head. "Hi, guys — great to see you here! Did you enjoy dinner?"

"It was delightful," Elizabeth answered. "I can see why Meg was so excited to help you get this started. How has business been since you opened?"

"Booming! Oh, I know it's barely been a week, and there's a lot of curiosity because we're new. But we're trying to keep prices reasonable, and some people from Granford have been back. And we've got plenty of bookings for the next couple of weeks. Your idea of a cooperative was just brilliant, Meg. I don't know how we can ever thank you!"

"Just stay open, so I can keep eating meals like this. But I think you've got a winner here, Nicky."

"I think so, too. Well, I won't keep you, and I've got to get back to the kitchen. Night, all!"

"I wish I had half her energy," Elizabeth murmured at Nicky's retreating back.

"I wish I did, too," Meg agreed.

"What did she mean by a cooperative?" Elizabeth asked.

"She and her husband were running out of money just before the restaurant was about to open. I suggested that the local farmers could become shareholders of sorts — they'd provide the food up front, and they'd receive a share of the profits later.

Everybody loved the idea, and the restaurant opened on time. In fact, a lot of the local growers have already eaten here more than once."

"What a wonderful idea!"

"I'm glad it worked. Ready to head home? I think we've eaten everything on the table except the sugar."

The cool autumn air outside the restaurant felt wonderful, and Meg perked up a bit. One hurdle surmounted: Elizabeth knew about Seth, and everybody seemed happy. It was a relief, and while she was annoyed at Seth for forcing the issue, apparently he had been right to do so. They drove home in peaceful silence, but when Seth pulled into her driveway, he tensed. Meg followed his glance: her back door was hanging open.

Oh, no — had she been robbed as well?

"You two wait here," Seth said, and climbed out of the car before they could say anything. He approached the back door cautiously, and Max came bounding up to him out of the darkness of the backyard. Seth snared him by the collar and kept a tight grip on the dog as he cautiously entered the kitchen.

Meg relaxed slightly. "Maybe Max has learned to open doors? He's smarter than he looks."

They waited for a few moments in tense silence until Seth reappeared. "Did Max let himself out?" Meg asked.

Seth held on to Max, who was eager to greet the women. "I don't think that was Max's doing."

"What? Was it a break-in?"

"That's my guess, but I think Max scared whoever it was away. Nothing seems to be missing anyway."

Meg's warm and fuzzy feeling from dinner evaporated. "So that makes two break-ins in twenty-four hours, here and at Daniel's house. Do you think they're connected?"

"Oh, Meg, why would they be?" Elizabeth objected.

Meg shrugged, suddenly tired. "I don't know. I thought this was a pretty peaceful place, but now I have to wonder. Seth, should we call Art?"

"I think we should talk to him, but maybe off-the-record, since nothing seems to be missing, although you'd better look around to be sure. But I agree with you, Meg — this is kind of an odd coincidence, and it can't hurt to get his take on it. Maybe he knows of other incidents in the neighborhood."

"Can it wait until morning?" Meg asked. "If there's no damage, and nothing's missing, I'd rather just get some sleep. And I'm sure my head will be clearer in the morning."

"Good idea. I'll give him a call when I get home and tell him to swing by on his way to the station in the morning. Does that work for you?"

"That's fine."

"Meg, darling, I think I'll make use of the facilities now so I won't be in your way later. Good night, Seth — it was a lovely evening. I'm sure I'll be seeing you again." Elizabeth vanished into the house, leaving Seth and Meg alone on the stoop.

"Tactful, isn't she?" Meg asked, leaning against him.

"Your mother is a delightful woman, and yes, she is tactful. You had me expecting an ogre."

"Did I? I didn't mean to. I seem to keep misjudging her. And you."

He wrapped his arms around her. "Meg, it's never easy to deal with parents, and I don't think we ever outgrow wanting to please them. Mom and I are close, but sometime I'll have to fill you in on my father and me. Still, it's clear that your mother loves you, and I like her, and I'd say that even if she weren't your mother. I think I should go home now. I'll stop by in the morning."

"Sounds good to me. Oh, one more thing." Meg pulled him closer and kissed him thoroughly, then gave him a small shove. "Now you can go home. See you in the morning." She turned and went inside as Seth called out, "Lock your doors!"

20

Meg found her mother in the kitchen when she came downstairs in the morning. "You're up early," she commented, helping herself to coffee.

"I had some trouble sleeping. Weren't you concerned about the break-in?"

"I'm still not convinced that Max didn't manage to push the door open on his own. In old houses like this, the doors and windows can be pretty loose, and maybe the latch didn't catch."

"Or maybe whoever tried to break in wasn't counting on finding Max waiting for him," Elizabeth responded tartly.

Meg took a harder look at her mother, who appeared a bit drawn. "But nothing was taken. And Max is a sweet puppy, who probably wouldn't scare anyone."

"Maybe." Elizabeth did not seem convinced. "Anyway, I thought since I was awake, I'd work on the family tree a bit more, but I can't seem to find my notes. Have you seen them?"

"Where were you working on them?"

"In the dining room, on the table there. I gathered them up and stowed them with your laptop, but they aren't there now. Maybe I'm just getting old and starting to forget things. Most of the material is in the computer anyway, so I can print it out again. I just don't like feeling stupid."

"They'll turn up. And I wouldn't worry about losing your marbles just yet. We all forget things. I know I do."

Her mother gave her a sidelong glance. "You mean, little details like the fact that you're dating someone?"

Meg felt a curious mix of shame and defensiveness. "I wasn't sure how you'd feel about him."

"Darling, this is your life. I haven't told you what to do since you were about ten. What's the problem? Telling me, or admitting that you care about him?"

"A little of each, I guess. I mean, when I first got here, Chandler had just broken things off, and I felt kind of raw about it. I figured I'd throw myself into fixing this place up, as a distraction. And then a lot more stuff started happening — like finding out about the orchard, and trying to make it work. And Seth was kind of wrapped up in all that, but I wasn't sure if he was just trying to be helpful, which he does a lot, or because of me in particular. I'm still having trouble sorting that out."

They were interrupted by a knock on the kitchen door: Art, followed by Seth. "Morning, Meg, Mrs. Corey," Art said. "Seth tells me you had a little problem last night?"

"Hi, Art," Meg greeted him. "Want some coffee? And I'm still not sure anything actually happened here."

"Coffee's good. And don't worry, this is off-the-record for the moment. I'm on my way to the station, but I just wanted to check in."

Meg's mother stood up. "I'll get the coffee. And it's Elizabeth, please."

"I didn't want Max branded as a criminal," Seth joked. "You didn't notice anything else unusual around the house, Meg?" he asked more seriously.

"Sit down, both of you. No, nothing missing, nothing disturbed, unless you count Mother's genealogy notes, which she can't find. Who on earth would want those? Half the people around here probably know a lot more than we do about local kinship in Granford. She probably just put them down somewhere and forgot where," Meg said.

Elizabeth made a face at her daughter.

"Just walk me through what happened last night, Meg." Art accepted the mug of coffee that Elizabeth held out to him.

"There's not much to tell," Meg said, and gave him the scant details from the night before. "So, as I was just telling my mother, I'm not convinced that Max didn't do it himself."

"No scratches on the door," Seth noted. "Are you saying that Max got the door open on the first try?"

"I guess I'd rather not think that there's been someone prowling around here and breaking in for no apparent reason then leaving without taking anything. Art, have there been any other incidents like that?"

"Nope. Pretty quiet, even with the tourists coming up for all the leaves, not to mention the apples. I just wanted to make sure."

"Art," Meg said slowly, "did you hear that Daniel Weston's house was broken into the night before last?"

"In Amherst? No, I didn't. Hmm. That puts things in a different light. You're connected to both of the break-ins, one way or another. Or your mother is. All the more reason to be careful. You do keep your doors locked, right?"

"Of course I do. And the locks are new

since I moved in."

"Anybody else have keys?"

"I have one. Bree has one. I gave Mother one. And Seth, of course — he's got keys to all the buildings here. That's all that I know about."

"Is there a spare?"

"Sure, somewhere. You want me to dig it up?" Meg paused, vaguely disturbed. "Art, why are you making such a big deal of this? Nothing's missing, nothing's damaged. Maybe I was sloppy and forgot to put the dead bolt on last night when we left." Maybe Seth's unexpected arrival had flustered her, Meg thought. "Look, I do appreciate your concern, but I think this is probably an innocent mistake."

Art smiled. "If it was anybody but you, Meg, I'd probably agree, but you do seem to attract problems. Well, I've got to get to work. Thanks for the coffee, Elizabeth. You enjoying your stay?"

"I am. And I'm beginning to like Granford."

"Always good to hear that. I'll be on my way then."

Art left in a flurry of good-byes. Seth stood hesitating by the door.

"What, you, too?" Meg asked. "I mean, it's nice of you all to worry about me, but can't you save it for something more important?"

"If you're sure it's nothing. Just make sure you lock your doors if you go anywhere. See you later." Seth, too, headed out the door toward his office across the driveway.

When Meg returned to the table, Elizabeth said dryly, "I see what you mean about everybody here knowing everybody's business. But it is nice of them to care, don't you think?"

"I guess." Meg took a deep breath. "Okay, Mother — I've come clean about Seth and me. Why don't you tell me what's really going on with you and Daddy?"

Elizabeth regarded her levelly. "I had to worm it out of you, dear. And as I told you before, nothing is going on with Phillip. We're fine, Meg. Maybe it seems odd to you that he's been out of touch for so long at this particular time, but if you find yourself in a long-term relationship — and I hope you will one day — you'll discover that you both benefit from a little time on your own. Marriage doesn't necessarily mean that you're permanently joined at the hip and have to do everything together. Phillip had planned this trip some time ago."

"But, Mother, shouldn't Daddy be back by now?"

"Any day now, I expect. Darling, please don't worry about us. We understand each other."

There was no point in belaboring the issue, and Elizabeth had already been more honest with her than at any time Meg could remember. "I'm glad. I'll try to stop back here for lunch. Do you have any plans?"

"More genealogy, I suppose. That's more than enough to keep me busy."

"Keep your eyes open, will you? Just in case Art's right and the two break-ins are connected somehow. Please don't take any chances."

"Of course. I'll be fine, Meg. You go get some work done."

Meg found Bree at the top of the hill, already engaged in a heated discussion with a couple of pickers, whose body language clearly said they disagreed with her. "I don't care if that's the way you've always done it!" Bree said, her voice barely below a shout. "I've tested the sugar three ways, and I say the Cortlands are ready to pick now. The sooner you get started, the sooner you'll be done with them."

Meg hung back until the men had turned away and picked up their bags. "Problems?"

Bree shook her head. "They think they know more than I do. Maybe that's true for

298

some things, but I've been as careful as I know how in choosing what comes next, and they've got to follow my orders. Right?"

"I'm relying on you, Bree. Just try not to piss them off too much, will you? We can't afford to lose any hands at this point."

Bree bristled. "You think I don't know that?"

"Of course you do. Listen, there's something I should tell you. Last night Seth stopped by to pick us up and left his dog Max in the kitchen."

"Whoa, Seth has a dog? When did that happen?"

"Recently. But the point is, when we came back from dinner, the back door was open and Max was running around outside. You didn't by any chance stop by and forget to lock the door?"

"No way. I left before you, remember? And I spent the night in Amherst. You think it was a break-in?"

"Maybe, but nothing was taken, as far as I can see. We told Art, just in case. He didn't seem too worried until I mentioned the break-in at Daniel's house."

"Weird." Bree stated the obvious. "Well, let's get going. I'd like to get this section done before noon."

Meg hoisted her apple bag and hooked

the straps over her shoulders, then headed for the nearest tree.

Bree followed. "You know, if you assume the two break-ins are connected, and nothing was taken, it kind of sounds like somebody was looking for something."

"But what?"

"I dunno. But it's got to be related to the dead guy, whatever it is."

"But why look at my place? I never met the man, and as far as I know, he'd never been in my house."

"Maybe he gave something to your mom, and she brought it back?"

"I think she would have mentioned it by now." Unless it was something intensely personal — but why would a thief know about it, in that case? Or what if it was a piece of jewelry, and Patricia thought she had some claim to it? She could have faked the break-in at her own house, just to hide her tracks. "I'll ask Mother at lunch. That is, if you'll let me take time for lunch?"

"Start picking. We've got a long way to go." Bree marched off to check on the other pickers.

As she began to fill her bag, Meg mulled things over. If the two events were related, then as Bree had pointed out, it had to be somebody looking for something connected to Daniel Weston. But why would anyone have searched at *her* house?

Meg unloaded her bag into the crate a few rows over and returned to her tree. Daniel had been a scholar, and had planned to unveil his discovery at an academic event — one with high visibility. His specialty was Emily Dickinson. Therefore, his discovery was most likely something related to Emily Dickinson.

Dickinson's Farm Stand. Was it coincidence that everything kept coming back to Dickinsons and Emily? Maybe. There were plenty of Dickinsons around the area, past and present. Rachel's husband was a Dickinson. Meg had seen any number of Dickinsons when she had looked at Granford census records. Maybe they were related, maybe not, but the more she dug, the more she found that everybody was related to everybody else in the area.

But what would have brought Daniel to the farm stand? He could have met the person at his home, or at a neutral public place in Amherst. Was he, or the person he was meeting, looking for a quiet place where no one would see them? Why would Daniel have gone along with it, if someone else had asked him? Obviously he *should* have said no. Or had he chosen the spot himself for some reason?

Meg continued picking on autopilot, her mind churning. She felt obscurely relieved: as Elizabeth had told Detective Marcus, it was highly unlikely that her mother would have known about Dickinson's Farm Stand, and Daniel would have had no reason to take her there. According to Elizabeth, they'd already parted ways by then. The hotel could probably confirm when she had returned — didn't they all have keycard access these days? When had Daniel set up this mystery rendezvous? Were there phone records? Cell phone, home phone, office phone? Or face-to-face?

Meg had made an effort to avoid thinking about her mother and Daniel. There was no way she could see her mother as someone's . . . what? Paramour? Lover? Mistress? None of the terms fit, no matter what the relationship. Meg really wanted to believe it was all as innocent as Elizabeth had said. Daniel had heard that Meg lived in the area, and had contacted his old grad school buddies to see if Meg was their daughter. When he'd reached Elizabeth rather than Phillip, he'd issued a casual invitation to come visit, and she, at loose ends with her husband out of town, had said, why not? And that was that. All open and aboveboard, just as Elizabeth had said. They'd had a nice visit, but found they had little in common anymore, and had gone their own ways. Maybe Elizabeth had had different expectations, but nothing had come of them.

But no matter what, Daniel was dead, and the police said he had been murdered. That was one fact that wouldn't go away. And the police weren't likely to let it. A respected professor, killed in a charming college town during new student week? A town that depended on parents sending their little darlings to school there, assuming they'd be safe? No, Detective Marcus was going to keep after this until he came to some resolution, and unfortunately Elizabeth was still in his sights.

Twist, drop, unload; repeat. Meg filled the next couple of hours with picking, until her back hurt and her hands were sore. The sun rose higher in the sky. When Bree passed by, making her supervisory rounds, Meg asked, "Can I stop for lunch, boss? Please?"

Bree surveyed Meg's row of trees. "Looks pretty good. But don't make it a long one — we've got to take advantage of this good weather while we can."

"Yes, ma'am!" Meg slipped out of her apple bag and straightened up with a sigh of relief. "I'll be back at one." She crossed the orchard and started down the hill toward the house, then realized there was a car in the driveway — one she recognized. Her father's.

21

It was all Meg could do to stop herself from running down the hill to the house. How long had it been since she'd seen her father? A year? And maybe now she'd finally get some answers about those "good old days" in Cambridge, when her parents had hung out with the late Daniel Weston.

She paused when she reached the back door: she could see her parents in the kitchen, locked in a close embrace. Elizabeth's head was on Phillip's chest, and he was holding her tight, his chin resting on her head. There was a tenderness in their stance that brought a lump to Meg's throat. Did she really question their feelings for each other? There was certainly no distance between them now, literal or figurative.

Phillip finally looked up and saw Meg hesitating at the door, then released Elizabeth and opened his arms to Meg. "Meggy, my love, you're looking —"

"Like something the cat dragged in, I know. It's so good to see you!" She let herself be enfolded in the warmth of her father's embrace. He smelled of all things familiar, but with an overlay of sea and salt and distant places, as if his recent fishing trip had somehow seeped into his pores. Finally she pulled away. "And where the hell have you been?"

"I was just about to explain. I got home after midnight last night, and when I heard the messages on the phone, I hopped in the car this morning and drove straight up. Can you give a poor man something to eat and drink?"

"I made lunch," Elizabeth said. "Phillip, what would you like to drink?"

"Coffee, if you have it. If I understand several of those phone messages correctly, the local constabulary wants a word with me, so I'd better keep my wits about me."

As Elizabeth moved around the kitchen, Meg studied her father across the table. His skin had a ruddy glow, his nose was peeling, and strands of his graying fair hair were bleached by the sun — obviously he'd been spending time outside.

Elizabeth laid plates on the table, and then a platter of sandwiches. Phillip inhaled a large chunk of sandwich and half his mug of coffee before speaking. "It was that damn boat of Harold's. You remember Harold, don't you, Meg?"

"No."

Seeing her blank look, Phillip went on, "The boat was amazing — really top-of-the-line, what's called a motor yacht. Anyway, Harold said he wanted to move it from New Jersey to his winter place in Florida, and he asked me and a couple other buddies to come along for the ride. You know, one of those trips where we drank a lot, and tossed a line in the water now and then to pretend we were fishing. Real man stuff." Phillip's eyes twinkled. "Besides, we weren't exactly roughing it — the boat had three staterooms, DVD players in each room, and even a washer-dryer. Do you know, Elizabeth, I think it was nicer than our first apartment? Problem was, Harold's a little sloppy about his maintenance schedule, so the motor died on us about halfway there, and of course, he had no idea how to fix it. Luckily we drifted to a nice peaceful island and dropped anchor, but it was days before anybody noticed us — although I'll admit we didn't try very hard to capture anyone's attention, at least for the first day or two. We figured hey, we were on vacation, so none of us worried too much. And at least

Harold had done a bang-up job stocking up on provisions."

"And no phone connections? You didn't have a radio?"

"Well, we could have radioed if there was an emergency, but we weren't in any hurry. Of course, none of us was expecting any frantic phone calls from the police or our wives. Not that Harold has one at the moment." He reached across to Elizabeth and laid a hand over hers. "I would have been here if I'd known — you know that. And I'm sorry I didn't get to see Daniel."

"I know," Elizabeth said. "It was you he asked for when he called." They shared a moment of silent communion, and Meg suddenly felt left out.

"Daddy, can you stay for a few days?" she broke in.

"Did you really think I'd turn around and leave so fast? I want to see what you've done with this place. And we have to sort out this mess with Daniel's death. Is there room for me to stay here? We could always go to a hotel."

"Of course you're welcome here, if you don't mind the simple life. And Mother can tell you that I may not have much time to spend with you, since we're right in the thick of the harvest."

"You're working in the orchard yourself?" Her father sounded mildly incredulous.

"I am. My orchard manager, Bree, broke her wrist last week, and that left us short-handed. I'm picking and making deliveries, since she can't do any heavy lifting for a while. By the way, Bree lives here, too, and there's only one bathroom. You might want to reconsider that hotel."

Phillip smiled. "Darling, I'm here to see you and your mother, not the inside of some anonymous hotel. But if it's inconvenient for you, just say so and we'll get out of your way."

"I'd be happy if you stayed here." Meg realized she meant it — this was her home, and she wanted her family to be part of it.

"Then that's settled!" Phillip clapped his hands together as if to close the subject. "Now, we should go talk to that detective person who's been leaving me messages for days. Right, Elizabeth?"

"Of course — we want to stay on his good side. And I know a lovely restaurant where we can have dinner tonight." Elizabeth winked at Meg.

"Yo, Meg! You coming back?" Bree called out from outside the kitchen door. She walked into the kitchen, then stopped abruptly when she saw Phillip. "Oh, sorry.

Didn't mean to barge in."

"No, you're right — I need to get back to work. Bree, this is my father, Phillip Corey. Daddy, this is my orchard manager, Briona Stewart."

Bree held out a hand, and Phillip rose and shook it. "A pleasure to meet you, my dear. You have a big job here. I hope you're up to it."

Before Bree could take offense, Meg said, "Yes, Daddy, she is — she may be young, but she's smart. Bree, don't be insulted — my father's just an old coot, and a sexist one." She elbowed her father in the ribs, and he laughed.

"Ah, you know me well, my dear. No offense intended, Bree. I'm sure between the two of you, you have that orchard well in hand. Elizabeth, I'll go call the detective now and see when he's available. Meg, I'll see you later. Bree, nice to meet you." Phillip was pulling his cell phone out of his pocket even as he spoke, heading for the door to the dining room.

"You go, dear," Elizabeth told Meg. "I'll call Gran's, if that's all right with you. Unless you'd rather eat here?"

"Go right ahead, Mother. And please be polite to Detective Marcus, and don't let Daddy go all lawyerish on him."

"I think I can manage that. Now, shoo!"

Meg followed an impatient Bree out the door. As they headed up the hill, Bree said, "So, what's his excuse for disappearing?"

"He said his buddy's boat died on them, and they spent a chunk of time partying on a desert island, conveniently out of cell phone range. They were having too much fun to call home."

"You believe him?"

"I think so. Why shouldn't I?"

"Kinda convenient, isn't it? Maybe he and his buddies had something going on, on that fancy boat of theirs. And if they did, I'll betcha his fishing pals would swear they were together the whole time and doing nothing more than fishing."

"Bree, you are a grade-A cynic. Why can't you accept it was a simple fishing trip with the guys?"

Bree threw up her hands. "Okay, okay. Look, it'll be a good thing if they get things squared away with that detective."

"I agree, no question. But, Bree, I haven't seen my father since last year sometime, so I'm going to want to spend a little time with him. I know we've got apples to pick, but cut me some slack, okay?"

"Sorry, Meg. I wasn't thinking about it like that. And I don't usually have to take relatives into account, you know? Look, I know you work hard, and I'm sorry if I sounded like a jerk. But you're paying me to see that these apples get picked."

"And you're doing a great job, under difficult circumstances. Don't worry — I take this seriously, too. Just give me a little time to get this murder mess sorted out."

"You think that's going to happen anytime soon?"

"I certainly hope so. How about this: you can have all my daylight hours, but I reserve the time after dark to spend with my parents?"

They'd reached the top of the hill. "That sounds fine. But now you need to get back to work. You've still got another four, five hours of light."

By dinnertime, Meg stumbled down the hill as the sun was setting. She wanted nothing more than a hot bath and a good meal, but she figured she ought to stop by and warn Seth that her father had finally appeared. There was a light on in the room Seth was using as an office, so she bypassed her back door and climbed the wooden stairs inside the former carpenter's shop. Seth was at work at his chaotic desk, with Max stationed at his feet as if he'd always been there. "Hey, there."

He looked up from the column of figures he was adding. "Hi, Meg. To what do I owe the honor of this visit?" Max came over to sniff her shoes.

"In case you saw the other car in the driveway earlier, I wanted to let you know that my father has arrived."

"Ah." Seth swiveled in his chair to look at her and leaned back. "Is that a good thing?"

"Looks like it. He and my mother were headed off to talk to Detective Marcus this afternoon, and I think we're going to Gran's again for dinner. Look, I want him to meet you, but . . ."

"You need some time alone with him, with them, before you throw me at him? Not a problem."

"Thank you. I didn't want to hurt your feelings." Again. "Tomorrow, maybe?"

"Let me know what the plans are, and I'll see."

Meg felt awkward, leaving things on that note. "Did Art say anything else to you?"

Seth shook his head. "Haven't talked to him since this morning. But you know, if — and that's still a big if — the break-ins at Weston's place and your place were by the same person, that person is probably look-

313

ing for something in particular."

"That's about what I figured, but I have no clue what. Or why. Or where it could be, if it exists. Or who wants it. Not a lot to go on, is it?"

"Let Marcus do his job." Seth stood up, crossed to Meg, and kissed her briefly. "Go and spend some time with your parents. I'll talk to you tomorrow."

"Right. And thanks for understanding."

Gran's was comfortably filled again that evening — there were enough diners chatting that Meg didn't feel they had to watch what they said, for fear of a neighbor overhearing. Not that there was much to say that could be construed as private.

"I was impressed with the detective," Phillip was saying as he enjoyed Nicky's rich butternut squash soup. "All business. Well informed — but clearly frustrated by his lack of progress. It's been, what, ten days now since Daniel died? I take it you know this detective, Meg?"

"Mmmm." Meg suppressed a shudder. Despite their recent truce, those had been less than happy circumstances. "But I agree. Generally he's fair, and he works hard. What did you tell him?"

"I apologized for not returning his calls

and told him why. We talked about how I knew Daniel, and when I'd seen him last. It had been decades, hasn't it, Elizabeth?" He turned to his wife.

She nodded. "Since before he married Patricia. You never met her, did you, Phillip?"

"Not that I can recall. Poor Daniel — I never would have foreseen something like this."

"Are you saying he's not the kind of person you would expect to find murdered?" Meg asked.

"I suppose that's part of it. When we knew him, he was a very happy person — loved what he was working on, loved spending time with his friends. Definitely not the kind of person who would inspire someone to kill him."

"Do you think he changed much?"

"Elizabeth?" Phillip turned to her. "You spent some time with him. What was your assessment?"

"Looking back now, I'd have to say he was perhaps a bit more driven than in the past. After all, he was reaching the end of his career — which by all accounts was successful — but Patricia seemed to think he was hoping for one last hurrah before he retired. Maybe he was onto something, or thought he was. What isn't clear is whether he found what he was looking for. Which may be the same thing the burglar is looking for."

"And yet no one knows what it was. Curious."

"But was it worth killing for?" Meg interrupted. "Although I have to say I'm constantly surprised by what drives people to extremes — things that may seem trivial or irrelevant to others. Everyone keeps telling us that he was a nice guy, people liked him, he was successful at his job, happy in his marriage. So why is he dead?"

"A fair question, my dear. At the risk of sounding like an attorney, perhaps we should ask: who benefits from his death?"

Elizabeth said slowly, "From what little Patricia has said, she doesn't, or not in any significant way — she gets the house and whatever insurance there was, but no million-dollar policies. Apparently his children are well established. The department at the college doesn't benefit, because they've got a hole to fill in the faculty right at the beginning of the school term. A professional colleague maybe? Someone who didn't want to see Daniel succeed where they had failed? Some of them were coming to Amherst for this symposium. Including one of his rivals, Kenneth Henderson, who says they were on friendly terms, which both Patricia and Susan, Daniel's graduate student, say was not true."

"Still, the timing is suggestive," Phillip replied. "And this mysterious 'find' of his — would it have monetary value? Or was it simply a matter of prestige?"

"It's hard to say, since we don't know what it is," Meg replied. "Tell me, Dad, was he the type to play jokes? I mean, was he just building up this thing when maybe it didn't even exist?"

"Do you know, I have some questions about that," Elizabeth said. "He never mentioned it to me, although I don't know why he would have. Of course, he hadn't seen me in years, so we talked about ourselves and our families."

"Changing tacks, your mother mentioned that you had a break-in last night," Phillip parried. "And so did the Westons, the night before. Let's work with the assumption that they're related. Say someone was looking for something in your house."

"But what? Nothing was taken."

"Whoever it was didn't expect to find Max there," Elizabeth added, warming to the subject.

"But that would imply that whoever it was knew I *didn't* have a dog," Meg protested.

"And this person gave up pretty easily — I mean, Max wouldn't hurt a fly, and the burglar could have just shoved him out the door and gone on with his business. He didn't."

"That suggests an amateur," Phillip said. "The question is, what was this person looking for?"

"Meg," Elizabeth said slowly, "the only thing that might have been taken was my genealogy notes. I know that seems silly, but what if there was something in them that the intruder wanted?" She turned to Phillip. "I was spending some time looking at our family history," Elizabeth said, "and the people who built and who lived in our house. I've really only gotten started, but I've been enjoying it, more than I expected. I had printed out a lot of bits and pieces, but I hadn't had time to make any sense of them."

"You've been known to misplace things, my love," Phillip replied.

He and Elizabeth exchanged another fond glance that shut Meg out again briefly. "Wait a minute — didn't you say you'd found some connection between Emily Dickinson and the Granford Dickinsons?" she asked.

"Yes, but only very distantly."

"But think about it. Everything keeps coming back to the Dickinsons — Emily, Dickinson's Farm Stand, local Dickinson families. And you said we're related to Emily?"

"Yes, but it's something ridiculous like fifth cousins five times removed, from what I've found so far. It's not anything like a lineal relationship."

"Listen to you — you've already picked up the jargon," Meg said. "What about the other Granford Dickinsons? Were they closer relatives?"

Elizabeth shrugged. "I can't say yet. I'm pretty new to all of this, and I've just begun to follow the family lines. I'd say no closer than second or third cousins."

Phillip cleared his throat and raised his hand to tick off his points. "This is all very interesting, Meg, but where does it get us? One, Daniel Weston, noted Dickinson scholar, was killed. Two, he was murdered at Dickinson's Farm Stand in the middle of the night. Coincidence? Maybe. Three, some of his fellow scholars were in Amherst for a conference he had organized — which featured Emily Dickinson. Four, he hinted that he had a new discovery to announce, which we might infer relates to Emily Dickinson, his area of specialization. Five, his house was broken into after his death, and the focus was his study. Six, your house was broken into as well and nothing was taken, save perhaps some notes that might or might not have included information on the extended Dickinson family."

"I'm so glad we have a lawyer in our midst," Meg said sarcastically.

"I'm also a fresh eye," her father reminded her.

"That you are. So your theory is that Daniel wanted something related to Emily Dickinson that he was pretty sure existed, and someone thought it, or something leading to it, might be in my house?"

"Exactly."

"So what do we do now?" Meg tried to envision explaining all this to Detective Marcus and quickly abandoned the idea. "Are we supposed to start hunting for this whatever-it-is? We don't even know what we're looking for. If it ever existed," she ended dubiously.

"Apparently Daniel thought, as the mystery burglar may, that there's a chance it still exists. Let me ask you this: if an Emily Dickinson artifact popped up, what would be its monetary value?"

"I have no idea. I'd guess we could look at recent auctions on the Internet, or talk to someone at one of the places that holds her collections."

"Or it might not have been about the monetary value," Elizabeth added. "It might have been about the glory of finding something unknown. I really think Daniel would have cared more about that."

"Which points toward someone who might want the money, if they could sell whatever it is, or toward his professional colleagues, who would prefer the glory of an important discovery," Phillip concluded.

"Exactly," Meg said.

22

"We should examine that assumption," Phillip said.

Elizabeth looked at Meg and grimaced. "Phillip, you're being lawyerly again."

"That's what I do," he replied mildly. "The wife — Patricia? — would no doubt have been a prime suspect for the police. After your mother, of course." He winked at Elizabeth, who swatted his arm affectionately. "Detective Marcus told us they'd looked into Daniel's finances and found nothing unusual, correct?"

Meg nodded.

"So apparently she didn't need the money, although she might have wanted more. They also looked for any hint of sexual misconduct from Daniel and found nothing. My, Daniel sounds rather dull, doesn't he? He must have mellowed since we knew him. What other motive might Patricia have had?"

"She was mildly jealous of Emily Dickinson," Elizabeth said. "She told me so, although she might have been joking. She did think that Daniel was obsessed by her. Maybe Patricia got tired of hearing about Emily all the time and killed him, since it was too late to kill Emily."

Phillip shook his head. "While I'll concede that you may have better insight into her state of mind, I don't see why she would have lured him to the farm stand in the middle of the night."

"I agree — it seems a rather odd choice. Could she have done it to confuse the police? To point attention away from her? It's certainly kept us all guessing," Meg said. "If I'd been in her shoes, I would have dumped him at Emily's house, or next to her grave in the cemetery. Although maybe both were too public, in the middle of town — somebody would have noticed her hauling a body around. Still, she seemed honestly upset about his death, and I don't think she was acting. Does that help or hurt her as a potential suspect?"

"Hard to say. Let's trust that the police have done their homework on her. Now, what about his peers?"

"Kenneth Henderson is the only one we've met, but he's a possibility. We know he was in the area, and we know they had a long-term rivalry. Susan told us that it was more than a friendly competition. But he wouldn't know about the farm stand, unless Daniel took him there, and why would he?" Elizabeth asked.

"Now who's grasping at straws?" Meg chided her father. "What about the break-in at Patricia's? You'd have to assume that either Kenneth did that, too, or that Patricia staged it to shift suspicion away from herself. And don't forget all the people who showed up at the memorial service. The police probably looked at them, too — isn't that standard procedure?"

"We both remember seeing Kenneth there," Elizabeth said. "And he seemed very solicitous of Patricia, even though he said he didn't know her. Maybe they were in on it together?"

Phillip was clearly enjoying this exchange. "Or let's say, for the sake of argument, that Kenneth had grown tired of this constant contest with Daniel, so he came up early and scouted out locations for murder. Maybe he, too, was feeling his advancing years and wanted to commit the perfect crime before he retired."

"Phillip!" Elizabeth protested. "That's absurd."

"Dad, don't even joke about it. That sounds like a bad TV movie. Murder is serious stuff."

Phillip looked contrite, and patted her hand. "I'm sorry, Meg. We shouldn't be taking Daniel's death as a joke. So, where were we? His colleagues, both at the college and those who had assembled for his vaunted symposium."

"We don't know them. That's something the police can handle better than we can. I'm not exactly chummy with the state police, but I know they haven't arrested anybody. There's just no evidence, or not enough." Meg sighed. "This hasn't gotten us very far, has it?"

Phillip sat back in his chair. "Well, I think we should shelve this fruitless discussion and concentrate on our excellent meal. We're not going to solve anything sitting here, and it would be a shame to let the food get cold."

And talk drifted to other matters. Nicky came out briefly to say hello and dimpled at Phillip's compliments. They lingered over coffee until Meg realized her eyelids were drifting down.

Elizabeth noticed. "Phillip, we ought to be getting back. Meg's had a full day, and she's going to be picking again tomorrow. Right, dear?"

"I will. Dad, I'll see if I can break some time loose to show you around, but Bree's got me on a tight leash."

"I understand, my dear. I'm sure your mother and I will find something to keep us busy."

Back at the house Meg played good hostess and let her parents take the first turns in the bathroom. Bree's light was on, but she didn't emerge from her room. Meg sat at the kitchen table, waiting, idly stroking Lolly. She was surprised when her mother emerged silently from the dark dining room and leaned against the doorframe. "I thought you'd go straight to bed," Meg said.

"In a moment. Your father's already dead to the world." Elizabeth smiled. "As usual."

"I'm glad he's here. Are you?"

"Of course I am." Elizabeth took a seat at the table. "Were you really worried about us? Or about me and Daniel?"

Meg was too tired to prevaricate. "I guess so. What you did — coming up here to see him, without telling me — seemed so out of character."

"And you actually thought that we were having a hot and heavy affair while your father was out at sea?" Elizabeth's mouth twitched with amusement. "I'm flattered."

"I wasn't sure — and you did admit you were thinking about it. So you and Daddy are really okay?"

Elizabeth briefly laid her hand over Meg's. "Yes, we are. We have a solid marriage, if that's what you're asking. You know, darling, you don't put much faith in relationships, do you?"

"I guess not. They don't usually work out for me, and I'm not even sure why."

"I think it's a matter of trust," Elizabeth said slowly. "You have to trust yourself, your own instincts, and then you have to trust the other person as well. Your father and I have that. Oh, I'll admit I was tempted — I mean, Daniel was still an attractive and interesting man, even after all these years. But I'll never know if I would really have acted on it if he'd asked. Which he didn't."

"You mean you weren't driven to a psychotic rage when he rejected your unwanted advances?"

Elizabeth smiled at Meg's attempt at humor. "Meg, this is me. I don't do psychotic, in case you haven't noticed. And why on earth would I have killed him at an obscure farm stand in the middle of the night? Even the police had trouble making that fit. Although I will admit that I was a wee bit pleased that they think I'm capable of such a thing. One has so few thrills left at this advanced age." Elizabeth sighed dramatically.

Meg snorted.

Elizabeth began again, "Meg, I don't want to meddle in your love life, but I don't want to think that your view of your father's and my relationship has somehow put you off finding one of your own. As I keep telling you, we have a good marriage. I know it's hard for you to see us as people rather than parents."

"Maybe I didn't look closely enough. Did you say anything to Daddy about Seth?"

"No. I thought it was your business, and you can tell him in your own time. Although he's bound to notice that there's someone else coming and going in your backyard."

"Maybe we can all have dinner together tomorrow? If you'll cook, that is."

"Deal." Elizabeth stood up. "Well, we should both get some sleep. Good night, dear."

Meg was left alone at the table, too tired to move, while Lolly purred contentedly on her lap. Had she really misjudged her parents' relationship so badly? She had always sensed a certain level of reserve between them. They had seldom argued, and when they had, it had been tense and controlled — no throwing of plates or physical blows. But how had that shaped her own concept of a "good" relationship? And how did Seth fit? She had no idea, and this was not the time to try to make sense of it. Bed called.

In the morning she awoke to the sound of male voices outside on the lawn. She recognized her father's — and Seth's? Well, now the decision of how to introduce them had been taken out of her hands. What would her father think of Seth? Or about Seth and his darling daughter as a couple? Was she really worried about his opinion, one way or another? In any event, she had better get herself moving and face . . . whatever.

Ten minutes later she entered the kitchen to find her mother once again dishing up a hearty breakfast, which Bree was already enjoying.

"Hey, slowpoke," Bree greeted Meg. "You're late."

"It was a late night." She glanced at her mother at the stove. "I heard Daddy outside."

Her mother looked up briefly from the eggs she was scrambling and smiled. "Yes, he wanted to go out and survey the domain.

And he ran into Seth."

"So I heard," Meg said.

"Last I heard, Seth was giving him a tour of the barn and his business quarters," Bree said, mopping up eggs with a piece of toast. "Eat up — we've got apples waiting."

"What are you harvesting now?" Elizabeth asked.

"Today, mostly Cortlands, Empires, and McIntoshes," Bree responded promptly. "They're our biggest crop, and the easiest to sell. The Gravensteins are done — they have a real short season. Later in the month we'll be seeing some of the heirlooms — Northern Spy, Esopus Spitzenberg. But the season goes on well into October, even November. The Baldwins come in late, and the Spencers and Rome Beauty."

"What wonderful names they have!"

"Mother, what are you and Daddy doing today?" Meg asked.

Elizabeth brought her coffee mug to the table and sat down. "I thought I'd show your father around the area."

"Watch out for the leaf-peepers," Bree volunteered. "They get so busy looking at pretty trees, they forget to watch the road."

"I'll keep that in mind," Elizabeth said.

Bree drained her coffee mug. "Okay, Meg, enough lollygagging — time to get to work."

"All right, all right. Just let me get a cup of coffee in me. You go ahead. I should say good morning to Daddy, and then I'll join you."

"And check out what he and Seth have been talking about?" Bree smirked. "Just don't take too long. Bye, Mrs. C." She stood up, deposited her dishes in the sink, grabbed a jacket from the hook near the back door, and went out.

Meg stood up more slowly. "Duty calls. So we're having dinner here tonight?"

"That's the plan," Elizabeth said. "Shall I invite Seth?"

Meg hesitated a moment. "Why not? And I'll do it now. Have a nice day sightseeing."

She grabbed her own jacket before heading out the door and found her father and Seth standing in the middle of the driveway together; Seth was pointing at the rambling outbuildings that lay behind the house. Her father noticed Meg first.

"Ah, there you are, darling. Seth has been giving me the nickel tour. Quite a history this place has."

"It does, and I'm still learning about it. I can show you the inside of the house later, and the barn, if you're really interested. I hear you and Mother are playing tourist today?"

331

"That's what I'm told. I'm sorry you can't join us."

"Me, too, but Bree won't let me."

"A real tough one, that young woman."

"That's what I pay her for," Meg said. She turned to Seth. "Seth, would you like to come to dinner tonight? Mother said she would cook."

He glanced briefly at her, trying to assess her intention. "I'd be delighted. When?"

"Seven? Well, I'm going up to the orchard. Have a good day, Daddy." Meg kissed her father on the cheek, briefly contemplated then rejected doing the same to Seth, then headed up the hill. As soon as her back was turned, the two men resumed their discussion of the buildings, and Meg smiled to herself.

23

Meg was so focused on the task in front of her that she didn't notice dark clouds rolling in from the west. Bree stopped her as she unloaded yet another bag of apples into the bin.

"I think we'll have to scrub this afternoon — looks like it's gonna rain," Bree said.

"Does that matter to the apples?" Meg said.

"No, but it does to the pickers, and we can't risk any more accidents. Weather station says it should be over by tonight, so tomorrow will be okay."

Meg stretched and rotated her back. "Does that mean I get to take the afternoon off?"

"Looks like it. Your mom and dad doing all right?"

"Fine, as far as I can tell. But what do I know?"

Bree cocked her head. "You sound pissed

off. Is there a problem?"

"No, I guess it's just that after all these years, I really don't know what makes them tick as a couple."

"Ha! Nobody ever knows what makes couples muddle along. I think your folks are kind of sweet together."

"Sweet? That's not a word I'd pick," Meg replied.

"They give each other space. That's a good thing. But they're tight when it matters. What's your problem? You comparing them to you and Seth?"

"I don't know. I'm just cranky, I guess. I'm tired all the time, and I think my mother — and now my father — want to stick around until Daniel's murder is cleared up. Whenever that is."

"Hey, she's doing a lot of the cooking and cleaning and stuff, which helps. Go get yourself some lunch."

"Where will you be?"

Bree flashed a brief smile. "Thought I'd go see if Michael has a couple of hours to spare. He's pretty busy during harvest season, too, promoting organic crops."

"Well, you two children have fun."

"Will do." Bree turned away to say something to Raynard on the other side of the row, and Meg made her way down the hill.

The house was blissfully quiet when she entered. Even Lolly was asleep, a puddle of fur on the ratty living room rug. How long had it been since she'd had a moment all to herself, in her own house? This farming stuff was hard work, and even once she had more experience under her belt, some parts of it — like picking — were not going to get easier. Maybe by next year she'd have the money to hire more pickers. If there was going to be a next year. That decision rested on how well she did with her crop this year, and that calculation was still a few months off. If she couldn't clear enough money . . . No, there was no point in getting ahead of herself.

What now? Food, then maybe a bath while there was hot water. Meg wondered idly whether her profits, if there were any, would finally allow her to add at least a half bath somewhere in the house. Seth would no doubt give her a good price, but there would still be costs involved. There always were.

Meg had managed to throw together a sandwich when she heard a knocking at the front door. Who? Her mother had a key, and most people she knew came around to the back door. Was it Detective Marcus again? Somebody who hoped to convert her to a new and improved religion? Somebody sell-

ing something? Meg debated ignoring whoever was trying to sabotage her alone time,
but decades of politeness drummed into her
by her mother won out, and she went to
open the door.

It was Susan Keeley, looking both better
and worse than the last time Meg had seen
her, only two days earlier. Her hair was a
few days more unwashed, and she might
have been wearing the same clothes, but at
the same time she was far more animated
than she had been. "Hey, sorry to bother
you, but I think I have an idea about what
Daniel was so excited about. Can I come
in?"

This was unexpected news. "Sure. Do you
want something to eat?"

Susan waved a dismissive hand. "No, no.
Is your mother here?"

"Not right now, but if it starts raining, she
should be back shortly. Why?"

"Because I think you can both help me."
Susan walked past Meg toward the dining
room. "Let me tell you what I'm thinking."

Meg had followed her and gestured toward
the table. "Have a seat. Mind if I finish my
lunch? You sure you don't want coffee or
something?"

"I'm fine. You go ahead."

Meg retrieved her sandwich and now-cold

coffee from the kitchen and returned to the table. Across from her, Susan was almost quivering with excitement. "So, tell me," Meg prompted.

Susan took a deep breath. "Okay, so you know we were wondering if Daniel might have been onto something new, something big?"

"Yes?" Meg said around a mouthful of sandwich.

"So I started thinking, what would be important? Obviously it had to be about Emily. And it had to be something that nobody's found before, something really new."

Meg swallowed. "But hasn't that ground been pretty well covered?"

"Sure, at least the stuff anybody knows about, in collections. But what if this wasn't in a collection, and wasn't published?"

"And you think Daniel found something like that?"

Susan nodded. "I do, or at least he thought it existed. I've been thinking back over the kinds of hints he kept dropping, and I don't think it was simply a new take on her sexuality or her clinical depression or her love of strawberries. I think it's almost got to be something original."

"Okay, but what would it be? You've been

through the major collections of Emily materials?" Great — now she was on a first-name basis with the poet, too.

"Of course. At Amherst, and there's another library in town here that has a decent collection, but there's lots more — at Harvard, Yale, Brown, the Boston Public Library, the New York Public Library, lots of other smaller collections. I've been studying her for years, you know, and I've seen pretty much every surviving piece of paper she ever laid a hand on. Daniel and my other advisors were a big help, pointing me where to go and getting me access to the original documents. You don't just walk in and ask to see special collections in a lot of places."

"So you think that whatever Daniel was working on, it wasn't in anyplace obvious like the collections you've mentioned?"

"Right." Susan nodded again.

"But where is it? It's clearly not at his home or his office."

"I think if Daniel already had it, we would have found it by now. It seems more likely to me that maybe he knew where it was, but he hadn't laid hands on it yet. But he was pretty sure he'd be able to, and maybe he wanted to spring it on the audience at the symposium. That'd really get attention."

"So it had to have been somewhere nearby, right? He didn't have time for an out-of-town trip." Meg was thinking out loud. The fact that he had invited her mother up for a visit certainly reinforced the idea that Daniel wasn't about to leave town. "Okay," she said slowly. "So if it's not in a university library or a well-known collection, are you thinking it's in private hands? Or on eBay or in an auction somewhere?"

"I'm thinking it's somewhere local, and somebody may not even know they have it. But Daniel knew where to look."

Meg sat back and looked at the young woman across the table from her. Obviously she'd convinced herself she was on the trail of something, but Meg still had no idea what or where. "Susan, this is all very interesting, but it's not a lot to go on."

"I'm not done yet. You said you and you mother had been doing some genealogy, right?"

"Yes, but mostly playing around with the easy stuff, what's available on the Internet."

"And your mother said she'd found some Dickinson connections, right?"

"Yes, but only remotely. And as you probably know already, there are Dickinsons all over the place around here. It doesn't necessarily mean they're connected to Emily, any more than everybody's sort of connected around here. What's your plan? Call on every Dickinson, past and present, in the county and ask them if they knew Daniel Weston or if they're sitting on something that belonged to Emily Dickinson?"

"Meg, I don't think it's that complicated," Susan said, her eyes pleading. "Look, what do you know about Emily?"

"The stuff most people know, and what I've learned on the house tour."

"So how did she communicate?"

"Ah, I see what you're getting at. She wrote letters. That's what's in the collections? Her letters?"

"Mostly. Remember, if she didn't go out, the only way she could contact anyone, apart from face-to-face, which she didn't do after about 1860, was to write letters. And she did. For example, there's a big stash of correspondence with her future sister-in-law, Susan Gilbert — there are over three hundred surviving letters to her from Emily. She even wrote letters to her nephew who lived next door. But who's to say that there aren't other letters squirreled away somewhere? You know how exciting that could be, to find a new batch?"

"And you think that's what Daniel thought

he had found?"

"Yes! And it's somewhere in this general area. It's got to be."

Susan was stringing together a lot of assumptions, Meg thought. "That's all very nice, Susan, but what's it got to do with me?"

"I thought that since you know something about genealogy, you could put together a family tree for Emily and the other local Dickinsons, figure out who's connected, and where they were in the 1850s and 1860s."

"Whoa!" Meg held up a hand. "For one thing, I'm a novice at genealogy — I have no idea how long that might take, or even where to start. For another, I don't have the time. I'm running an orchard here."

"You're not out there now," Susan wheedled. "Look, it's pouring!"

She was right, Meg noted when she looked out the window. That should drive her parents home — unless they found a cozy inn to huddle in, in which case who knew when they'd be back.

Susan went on relentlessly. "You've got this afternoon. And your mother can help, right? She was the one who was working on it before. She probably already knows about some of those connections. And there's Alfred Habegger's biography that includes a

341

nice family chart for Emily, so you can start with that and kind of work outward. Please?"

Susan looked like an eager puppy, but Meg could drum up no more than a mild enthusiasm for looking at Emily Dickinson's family ties — heck, she hadn't even worked out her own yet. The real question was, would this bring her any closer to understanding Daniel's murder? "Susan, before I say anything, tell me this: do you think somebody would have been willing to kill Daniel to get hold of whatever it is we're looking for — either to keep it from him, or to claim it himself? I mean, does this kind of thing really go on in the academic world?"

Susan's shoulders slumped. "Maybe. It means a lot to me to be part of that, so of course I don't want to think so. But if this is what Daniel died for, it would be a shame if he didn't get any sort of recognition for it, right? I'd like to look, for his sake. Please?"

That made a certain sense. Meg wondered what her mother would think — and how it would impact her plans for dinner. With Seth. When had her life become so complicated?

"Okay, Susan, let me think about this, and talk it over with my mother. It's not like

342

there's any deadline, is there?" After all, the symposium was over, and Daniel was already in the ground.

"I guess not. Do you mean you'll help?"

"If I can, and if my mother agrees, and if we can find the time. Can I let you know tomorrow? I've got plans for tonight."

Susan stood up abruptly and unexpectedly hugged Meg. "Oh, thank you, Meg — you're the best! I'd do it myself, but I've never done that kind of research, and I figured you could do it faster than I could. I'll get out of your hair now."

When Meg shut the door behind Susan's retreating back, she turned to Lolly, perched on the back of one of the decrepit armchairs. "What? Like I don't have enough to keep me busy? Let's see what Mother thinks about all this before we decide anything."

Lolly went back to sleep, and Meg went to take a bath and soak her aching muscles.

24

As Meg came down the stairs after her bath, Elizabeth and Phillip came through the back door, laughing and dripping.

"Hi, Meg," her mother said, shaking water from her coat. "I didn't think New England weather could change so fast! One minute it was lovely, and the next, whoosh!"

"You should have been here for the hail-storm last month," Meg said.

"Good heavens! How frightening. Was there any damage?"

"No, my orchard came through all right, but there were others that weren't so lucky."

"Drat!" Phillip stopped in the midst of removing his coat. "I forgot to stop at the liquor store."

"Did you remember groceries?" Meg asked.

"Of course, dear. We're all set for dinner. Phillip, why don't you bring in the food and then you can go find a liquor store? Meg, where would the nearest one be?"

"Go out to the highway and turn left, toward Holyoke. There are a couple along that road."

"Anything in particular you want, Meg? What does your young man drink?"

My young man? "Beer and wine mostly. You can pick something that goes with the meal."

"I won't be long, ladies." Phillip retrieved the groceries, then took off again. Elizabeth bustled around Meg's kitchen, looking quite at home.

"Your father does like to keep busy, and I wanted him out from underfoot. I thought I'd make a roast chicken. Will Bree be joining us?"

"No, she went looking for Michael when it started raining and we had to halt the picking."

"You're done for the day?"

"Yes, Bree let me off the hook. But it's supposed to be nice tomorrow, so this is a short break. Listen, Mother, I need to talk to you about something."

"If it's about Seth, I didn't tell your father anything, I swear. But he's not blind, you know, and he figured it out for himself."

Meg really didn't want to get into that now. "No, it's not that. Susan Keeley

345

stopped by while you were out and asked if we could help her. She's got an idea about what Daniel was so excited about."

"And she thinks *we* can help?" Elizabeth hadn't stopped moving around the kitchen, checking the oven and assembling supplies.

"Yes, she wants us to do a little genealogy work on Emily Dickinson and her local connections. Susan thinks that Daniel's surprise could be an unknown cache of letters from Emily."

"Interesting." Elizabeth took a chair opposite Meg. "I know I've seen the Dickinson name on a lot of the online lists that I've been looking at, but I'm not sure I'm qualified to sort out who's who and how they're connected. Did Susan have any suggestions about how to narrow the search?"

"She thinks it's got to be close, in this area, near Amherst, because Daniel seemed confident that he could lay hands on whatever it is quickly."

"And why would nobody have come across this before?"

Meg shrugged. "I don't know. This is Susan's theory. She seems very eager to do it for his sake. Maybe she's chasing smoke, but it couldn't hurt to put together a family tree. You said you'd already found some connections between the Dickinsons and the Warren family?"

"Yes, but very distant. It was more an exercise in 'find the famous relative.' We're about as closely related to Ethan Allen and Johnny Appleseed."

"Well, Christopher Ramsdell once told me that it's altogether possible that some of the apple trees in the orchard are descended from old Johnny's trees, so maybe that's not so far-fetched. Are you up for it?"

"Can I get dinner started first?"

"I wouldn't stand in your way on that, believe me. And I don't think there's any big hurry. I told Susan I'd call her tomorrow, after I'd talked to you." Meg watched as Elizabeth lined up the ingredients for stuffing a chicken. "What did you see today?"

"Oh, mostly we drove around on back roads. It was rather nice, just wandering. And I'd forgotten how pretty it is around here. If you're just sitting there, you can make yourself useful. Grease this cake pan for me, will you, please?"

Elizabeth soon had a ginger cake in the oven, with the timer set. She washed her hands, took off her apron, and said, "Why don't we sit down and go over this family tree stuff? Your laptop's still in the dining room, isn't it?"

"It is. And while I think of it, I've also got some old maps from the Historical Society, and a lot of them have the names of property owners on them."

"Well, let's see how much we can get done while the cake bakes. When it comes out, I'll have to put the chicken in."

Half an hour later, Meg had decided that what they really needed was a giant piece of paper so that they could map out all the connections between Dickinsons. There certainly were plenty, scattered all over Hampshire and Hampden counties — no way was she going to look any farther afield than that. It was daunting. "I think I've got a big piece of Tyvek somewhere, and we could sketch this out on that. Maybe it would look clearer to us if we could see it, rather than trying to keep all these people straight in our heads."

Elizabeth shook her head. "I've got to take the cake out, and I could use a break anyway. Do you think Susan had any idea of the scope of what she was asking us to do?"

"Probably. Did you see anything like Emily's family tree lurking among Daniel's papers?"

"Not that I remember, but I certainly wasn't looking for anything like that. Or it could have been on his computer. Do you really think this will lead to anything?"

"I don't know, but it can't hurt, I guess. And you can learn a lot about the Warren family while you're at it." Meg followed her mother into the kitchen. "It's kind of sad that the line dwindled out like that. From what little I've seen, there were Warrens all over Granford, especially within a mile or two of here, and most of them were related. And they all had plenty of kids. Mother, why didn't you and Daddy have more kids?" A question that Meg had somehow never asked.

Elizabeth stopped what she was doing and turned to Meg, leaning against the counter. "We tried. It never happened. And we were happy with you, with the way things were. Maybe that was selfish of us, but we rationalized that we could give you more — more things, more attention — as an only child. I can see that it might have been lonely for you. But does that affect how you feel about having children?"

"To be honest, I've never felt a burning need to have kids, or even one kid. Maybe there's something wrong with me, to feel like that."

"Don't you like children?"

"I do, but as people, not as generic things.

349

Look, if the circumstances were right, I'd certainly consider it, but right now I don't feel deprived by not having children."

Elizabeth turned back to rubbing herbs and butter on the chicken. "Seth doesn't have children, does he?" she said.

"No. He was married once before, but no kids." Although Meg had to admit she had thought Seth would make an admirable father.

As if echoing her thoughts, her mother said, "I think he'd be a great father."

Phillip's car pulled into the driveway, and a minute later he bustled in the back door. "Success! Your local selection leaves something to be desired, but I think we should find something we all like here. Do I smell ginger cake?" He put down the clinking bags and gave Elizabeth an enthusiastic kiss.

"You do," Elizabeth replied, "and I'm all buttery from the chicken, so watch out for your sweater. Do you want to join us here, or do you want to go find something manly to do?"

"I *can* chop a mean vegetable. But actually, I'd love to see some more of the house, if you don't need Meg."

"I'll let Mother wrestle with the naked chicken. I'd love to show you the house, Dad. I have no clue what's in the attic, but

350

you should enjoy the basement — you can still see some of the original logs, and there's a well under the kitchen here."

"Basement it is. Lead on, my dear."

Meg dutifully led the way down the narrow stairs from the dining room to the basement. Parts of the floor had received a thin and patchy layer of concrete over the years, but there were still areas of bare dirt. The center was occupied by a massive brick structure, and Phillip made a beeline for it. "What on earth . . . ?"

"That was built to support the original fireplaces, which were in the middle of the house. I've been told that the space in the center was used as a smokehouse, but that may be fanciful — I'd say it's more likely that when the fireplaces upstairs were rearranged in the nineteenth century, somebody thought this would make good storage. I don't know — I've been so busy I haven't done as much as I could to learn about the history of the place."

Phillip wandered to another corner. "And this would be the well you mentioned? I thought it would be bricked over."

Meg followed him. "No, it's still open, and there's still water in it. I guess if I ever had to fend off a siege, I'd be all set. If you look up, you can see the patch in the subflooring

351

above it there — once upon a time they could probably lower a bucket and pull water right up into the kitchen. Very forward-thinking."

"Indeed." Phillip turned then to look at her. "What a wonderful house this is — so much history!" He paused briefly. "Are you happy here, Meg?"

Where did that come from? "I suppose. Why do you ask?"

"I know it's been a hard year for you, with a lot of changes. I want you to know that I'm proud of you, and so is your mother. You could have walked away from all this, but you chose to stick it out, to try something new. I respect that."

Meg felt a surprising prick of tears. "I kind of fell into it, and things kept happening . . . But I guess I am enjoying it, even though it's hard work. I like the town, and the people. Living here seems more 'real' than living in Boston did." Meg hesitated, but if they were being honest, here in the dim and damp basement . . . "Daddy, were you really okay about Daniel, about Mother coming up on her own to see him?"

A pained expression passed quickly over Phillip's face and vanished. "I wish I had been here. We were all good friends once. Long ago. I'm sorry that Daniel's dead."

He didn't exactly answer my question, Meg thought. But she suspected that it was the best she was going to get.

"So what's going on with you and this Seth Chapin?" her father asked.

Meg could feel herself blushing. "I don't know. Something. But I'm not rushing into anything."

"That's fine. I just didn't want to put my foot in my mouth at dinner. He seems like a nice fellow." Phillip checked his watch by the dim light from the small cellar window. "What about the rest of the house? I'd like to squeeze in a nap before dinner."

Relieved by the sudden diversion, Meg said, "Sure. Let's go upstairs."

She led him up to the second floor, where they spent a happy few minutes talking about woodworking and the drawbacks of multipaned sash windows, but the tour didn't take long. They ended up in front of the guest room. At the door Phillip stopped and turned to Meg. "I mean what I said. You've become a fine young woman, and I'm very proud of you. Wake me up at six thirty, will you?"

He slipped into the bedroom and closed the door, leaving Meg gaping. She had probably engaged in more intimate conversations with her parents in the past few days than in the decade that preceded it. Were they getting old? Or had she really changed?

Seth arrived promptly at seven, armed with another bottle of wine and a potted chrysanthemum, and Meg met him at the back door.

"Right on time," she said. "Trying to impress?"

"I'm always on time, in case you haven't noticed. How is everything? I saw that the pickers quit early."

"Yes, Bree said we shouldn't work in the rain and dismissed us. And then Susan Keeley, Daniel Weston's grad student, came by and gave Mother and me a research project — we'll tell you all about it over dinner."

Seth followed Meg into the kitchen, where Elizabeth was setting the chicken on a platter. "Hello, Seth — nice to see you. Phillip, would you prefer to carve in the kitchen or the dining room?" she called out.

Phillip came into the kitchen, his damp hair still bearing the tracks of the comb. "In here — then you don't have to watch me make a fool of myself. I never can find the joints on a bird and I end up mangling the poor beast. Seth, good to see you again!"

"You, too, sir."

And the evening rolled on. Sometime

halfway through dinner, Meg wondered why she had ever been worried about getting these people together. They were talking with enthusiastic gestures, and Meg felt warm and happy. Probably the wine she had drunk played some role in that, but it was not the only reason. Her father had asked earlier if she was happy; at this moment, she would say yes.

"Meg said Susan had asked you for something?" Seth asked Elizabeth.

"Yes, apparently Susan asked if Meg and I could do some basic research on Dickinson family connections in this area, on the chance that their descendants might have some material that had come down from Emily Dickinson. She thinks it could be related to whatever Daniel was so excited about, and it may have been a factor in his death, so I'm more than willing to help her. We won't know unless and until we find out what it is, though."

"Interesting. Well, there's no shortage of Dickinsons around, even today. Not many in Granford, though."

"I saw several on the old Granford maps. Have they've all died out?" Meg asked.

"Like the Warrens," Seth agreed. "Maybe you should check the local cemetery."

"They won't talk to us," Meg said, and

giggled. "Seth, do you memorize phones books in your spare time?"

"No, but I've lived here all my life, and I've worked with some of the Dickinsons in Amherst. And of course, my sister married into one of the Dickinson branches, though my brother-in-law's family connection is pretty minor."

"The closest connection I've found between us and the famous Emily is fifth cousin," Elizabeth said. "That's not exactly an intimate link either. But I'm nowhere near finished. I do hope Susan isn't in a hurry, because it's slow going."

"I'll have to leave it to you, Mother, because if the sun is shining tomorrow, I'll be in the orchard. Dad, does having Mother chained to the computer mess up your plans?"

"If there's anything I can do to help, I'd be delighted. And if this will help solve Daniel's murder, I want to be a part of it. Would you like me to clear the table and bring in the cake now, Elizabeth?"

"That would be much appreciated, Phillip." Elizabeth winked at Meg.

The evening wound down happily, and it was after ten when Meg found herself saying good night to Seth outside the back door. The rain had stopped, and Meg could smell earth and damp, and heard the occasional drip from the trees onto the growing pile of leaves that would probably turn into mulch by the time she got around to raking them. She was pleasantly tired and still buzzed from the wine. "That went well." She leaned against Seth in the dark.

"What did you expect?" He wrapped his arms around her.

"I don't know. I never brought any boyfriends home to meet the family."

"You were afraid your parents would eat them alive?"

"Nope, no boyfriends."

"I find that hard to believe."

"Thank you. That's nice." Meg reveled in his embrace just a bit longer, then pushed back. "I'd better go back in. Tomorrow's going to be busy."

"I'll let you go." He kissed her gently. "And thank you."

"For what?"

"For getting all of us together. Good night, Meg."

25

Elizabeth was already at the computer when Meg came down the next morning. She barely looked up when Meg entered the dining room. "I made coffee," she said, waving vaguely at the kitchen.

"Thanks. Have you seen Bree?"

"No. And I didn't see her car in the driveway. She must have spent the night at Michael's."

"Need any help there?"

"Thanks, but I think I have the hang of it. I want to get done as much as I can before your father comes down."

"He's still asleep?"

"Dozing, I'd say. He gets tired more easily than he used to, although he tries to pretend he doesn't. He's past sixty, you know."

Meg had done her best to avoid thinking of her parents as "old," but the math was inescapable. "What were you going to do today?"

"I've gotten rather intrigued by this research, and I'm afraid if I leave it, it will all get muddled in my head. Do you think maybe you could take your father up to the orchard and show him that? Maybe you could persuade him to pick apples or something. I think I'll have a much better idea of where all these Dickinsons fit by lunchtime."

"I'll do my best." Meg meandered into the kitchen, where Lolly greeted her lazily, meowing for breakfast. She poured coffee, popped a bagel in the toaster, and then stood by the sink to eat it as she admired the view out the kitchen window. The sun hadn't yet burned the September mist off the Great Meadow. What was it that Keats had said? Something like "season of mists and mellow fruitfulness"? That certainly fit: she was staring at the mist, and the "fruitfulness" was waiting for her up the hill.

As she watched, Bree's car pulled in and she clambered out. She caught sight of Meg at the window. "Yo, Meg! You ready?"

"Just waiting for my father to come down," Meg called back. "Will he be in the way if he joins us in the orchard?"

"Can you show him how to pick?" Bree said as she came into the kitchen and helped herself to coffee.

"I think so. I'm sure he'd be careful. My

mother wants some free time to work on the family history."

"She's really getting into it, huh? Next thing you know she'll be joining the DAR."

"Is that such a bad thing? From what I've heard, the Daughters of the American Revolution aren't the blue-blood snobs people think they are. And I gather that most of the patriots were ordinary citizens — farmers mostly. Probably the Warren who built this house fought in the Revolution, because most able-bodied men did then."

"Hey, you don't have to lecture me. I'm sure your mom would fit right in."

"Good morning, ladies," Phillip boomed as he arrived in the kitchen. "What a marvelous day!"

"Hi, Dad. I was going to ask if you wanted to come up to the orchard with me this morning. I can show you what goes on with the picking."

"That sounds grand, once I've had my caffeine. You're quite a stern taskmaster, Bree — or should I say taskmistress? It's so hard to know what's politically correct these days."

"Manager will do just fine, Mr. Corey. Gender-neutral, you know."

"Of course. You're mother seems quite absorbed, Meg. More genealogy?"

"I warned her it was addictive. There's always just one more thing to check. But she said she might have some results on the Dickinsons by lunch."

"So she asked you to entertain me? I understand. Anyway, I'd love to see the orchard."

"I'll put you to work," Meg warned.

"All the better. Must keep fit." Phillip patted his still-flat stomach.

"Did you actually do any fishing on your trip, or was it mostly lounging around with a cold beer?" Meg said.

"My dear, fishing was not the main objective, although we did have some grand meals al fresco. Mainly we figured we old coots wouldn't have too many more chances to play hooky like that."

"Don't you have work to get back to?"

"Nothing urgent. I'd cleared my calendar for the boat trip, and it's not like any of my corporate clients need me to defend them on murder charges or any other pressing issues. One of the reasons why I didn't go into criminal law, which is so unpredictable."

"Well, I'm told that learning something new helps keep you young. Apple picking should be an interesting addition to your résumé."

"Meg?" her mother called out from the dining room. "Can you help me for a moment?"

Meg cast a helpless glance at Bree. "One minute, I promise." She joined her mother. "What do you need?"

Elizabeth barely looked up from the sheets in front of her. "I won't keep you, but you said you had some nineteenth-century maps? And could you print out the local censuses for 1850 through 1870?"

Clearly Elizabeth was getting the hang of this fast. "How many towns? I've already got them for Granford, and I can show you how to access the rest online. Let me find the files." Meg rummaged through the file boxes she had stacked against the wall, drew out several manila folders, and handed them to her mother. "We're heading up the hill now, okay? Daddy's coming with us. We'll be back down for lunch."

"Fine, dear," Elizabeth said absently, leafing through a folder. "Have a nice time."

Up the hill in the orchard, Meg introduced her father to Raynard. She was glad to see that Phillip wasn't too winded by the climb — he seemed reasonably fit. She picked up one of the apple bags and showed him how it worked, slipping her arms through the straps and demonstrating the drawstring at the bottom that released the apples into the bin. "You have to be careful that you don't bruise the apples, Dad — that lowers their value, and also makes them susceptible to rot. You want to try?"

"Certainly, my dear. Lead me to a tree."

Meg fastened the bag on him. "Now remember — twist gently, don't pull. I don't want to damage the branches."

"No ladders?" Phillip asked, surveying the row of trees.

"Not often. Modern trees are grown on dwarf rootstock, to keep the size down and make the apples easier to pick. We do have a few older trees, where we still need ladders."

"But how does that affect the apple varieties?" he asked.

"The variety depends on the graft, not the rootstock." Meg settled her own bag on her shoulders and, as they worked side by side, explained to him the traditions and science of modern apple cultivation, checking periodically to see if he actually was interested and not just humoring her. He seemed to be following, and he was filling his bag carefully with apples.

"What are these?" he asked after Meg wound down.

"Empires. They're a relatively new variety,

about fifty years old. It's a cross between Delicious and McIntosh but it's better than either one, and it holds well."

Phillip asked some intelligent questions and then said, "My bag is full. What do I do now?"

Meg pointed. "The apples go in that bin over there, which is then hauled down the hill. From there, it depends on who's buying the apples, and also on what variety they are. I sell mainly to small grocers and farmers' markets around here. And to the restaurant. Did Seth show you the storage chambers in the barn?"

"He did — he seemed quite proud of them. He's certainly a busy young man — running his own business, serving the town. Spending time with his family. When do you ever find time to be together?"

"We kind of grab it on the run. Daddy . . . are you all right with this?"

"With you and Seth? Why on earth would I not be?"

Meg focused on twisting another apple off the tree, avoiding her father's eyes. "Well, often fathers seem to think that no one is good enough for their darling daughters."

Phillip laughed. "I raised you to think for yourself, love. I never assumed I had veto power over your choice in men, although I can't speak for your mother. Is that why you waited so long to tell us about Seth?"

"I wasn't sure what there was to tell. And I haven't spoken to either of you much lately — I've been so busy here."

"Meg," he said gently, "are you making excuses? Are you not sure where this relationship may be going?"

"Maybe. I was so wrong about Chandler."

"Well, then — learn from your mistakes. From all I've heard — and seen — Seth is nothing like Chandler. He seems like a good man who cares for you, and that's all I'm going to say. You're going to have to work things out for yourselves."

"Thanks — I guess. At least for letting me blunder along my own way. Now, let's get some more apples picked. If Mother finds anything useful, she's going to want to share it with us, and Bree will be on my back if I take too much time away from the trees."

"How long will this cruel pace continue?" Phillip kidded.

"Until all the apples are picked," Meg replied.

"Well, then, let's see how much we can get done today."

Elizabeth was sitting in the same spot where they'd left her several hours earlier, although there were more piles of paper spread across the dining room table, and her hair was standing on end as though she had been running her hands through it.

She dragged her eyes away from the computer monitor when she heard them come in. "Oh, please don't tell me it's noon already! This is going to drive me crazy!"

"Welcome to the wonderful world of genealogy, Mother," Meg said with a smile. "Maybe a food break would help?"

"Maybe if I stood up and moved around, the blood would return to my head. Sorry, I didn't make anything to eat."

"We'll survive. Did you find out anything interesting?"

Elizabeth gave an unladylike snort. "I found out that the Dickinsons, like almost everybody else in past centuries, reproduced like rabbits and kept moving around. Oh, and they liked to recycle the same names among family members."

"That sounds about right." Meg smiled at her mother. "Anything pop out at you, though?"

Elizabeth sighed. "Plenty. In Granford alone I counted at least six Dickinson families in 1860, scattered all over the place. It's just as bad in the other towns. And none of them are any closer than second cousins to the famous Emily. Does that count?"

"It's hard to say. I get the feeling that the way we use the term 'cousin' isn't at all like it was in the nineteenth century. Maybe we should all take a break, and you can let your subconscious work on it?"

"I could use a break. Any ideas for lunch?"

Phillip rubbed his hands together. "Why don't I take you lovely ladies out to lunch? Meg, your mother tells me there are some delightful places in Northampton. That's not far, is it?"

"Why don't we drive to Amherst instead? Then you can see just how far we are from Emily's home. And remember, they had to hitch up a horse and buggy to go anywhere, so going calling was not taken lightly. And you were supposed to offer hospitality to your guests, which meant you usually had to keep some baked goods handy, in case somebody dropped by. You couldn't call ahead."

"Amherst it is. I promise I won't keep you away from the orchard for too long."

In the car, sitting in the backseat, Meg leaned forward and asked her mother, "Are you ready to talk to Susan? She's been studying Emily for years, so maybe some of these names will ring a bell."

Elizabeth turned in her seat, as far as her

seat belt would allow. "I think that's a good idea — I've done the first round, and I'd hate to waste time looking at dead ends, if she can help us avoid them. Emily must have mentioned other people in her known correspondence, and I'll bet somebody's done research on who was who. Susan should know."

"We can call her from lunch. And maybe we should stop by and say hello to Emily?"

"Excuse me?"

"She's buried in Amherst, within sight of the family home, remember? Maybe she can give us some spectral insight."

"I'll take all the help I can get," Elizabeth said fervently. "Now, where shall we eat?"

After a quick meal in one of Amherst's smaller restaurants, Meg led her parents to the cemetery that lay a few hundred feet to the north of the former Dickinson home. "There she is," she announced.

Elizabeth and Phillip exchanged an amused glance. "Uh, are we supposed to make a plea or something?"

Meg laughed. "No, Mother, I haven't gone over the edge. I just thought you'd like to put her in some sort of context. You've seen the house, and she didn't get very far even after her death. This was the extent of her world. Once her mother fell ill, she more or less limited herself to Amherst, and then to her room in the house."

Her mother looked at the tombstone silently. "Sad," she said finally. She took a breath. "Emily, if you'd like to help us, I'd appreciate it." She glanced at Meg and her mouth twitched. "Should I expect a roll of thunder, or maybe a bird will land on my head?"

Meg laughed. "No, I don't think it works that way. Let me call Susan and see if she can help us. At least she's still among the living."

26

When Elizabeth called her, Susan agreed to meet them back at the house in Granford, and arrived no more than five minutes after they did. "Have you found something?" she asked eagerly before she was in the door.

Elizabeth laughed. "I've found lots of somethings, and I'm hoping you can help to sort things out. Meg, dear, I don't want to keep you if Bree needs you up the hill. I'm sure it will take Susan and me some time to go through all this." Elizabeth waved her hand over the drifts of papers that covered the dining room table.

Meg was torn: part of her wanted to stay, and in fact, she felt rather proprietary about the history of the town and its people. On the other hand, as a responsible farmer she had work to do, and she couldn't just drop it to follow a whim, even one that might lead to solving a murder. "You're right. But I'll take my cell phone along, in case you need me."

"That's fine, dear." Elizabeth's attention was already focused on the papers, and she began explaining to Susan how she had arranged the piles.

Meg and her father shared a complicit look. "Well, I guess I'm going back to work. Daddy, do you want to keep on picking, or do you have something else to keep you busy?"

"I'm sure I'll manage to occupy myself. You go on."

Meg climbed the hill reluctantly, feeling left out. At the top of the hill Bree greeted her. "You're late."

"I know. We stopped by to say hello to Emily Dickinson."

"You do know she's dead, right? You planning a séance anytime soon?"

"Ha ha. Let's get to work."

With the sun warm on her back, Meg fell into a rhythm picking her apples. Her hands were busy, but her mind was free to wander. What would it be like to have all the intimate and ordinary details of your life raked over by generations of scholars? Of course, Emily didn't know, since she was dead. Would she have lived differently if she had anticipated that kind of scrutiny? And why were people so fascinated by her? She had lived a simple life, and had written simple poetry, and had never really expected to share it with the world. Were her letters anything like her poetry? Or had she written mainly about her sister's cats and what was blooming in her garden and what was on the menu for dinner on any given day? Meg tried to conceive of a world without electronic communication, something she and her peers took for granted. Certainly letters in the nineteenth century would have held greater value in the scheme of things, keeping scattered families up-to-date on personal events — births, marriages, deaths. Local events, crop failures.

Maybe if she read more of Emily's letters — surely some had been published? — she would have a better idea where to look. But she didn't have the luxury of time to sit and read. If for some reason the hypothetical unknown letters were connected, directly or indirectly, to Daniel Weston's death, the sooner they were found, the sooner the investigation could move forward. It had already been almost two weeks since his death. What would Emily Dickinson think about someone having died for her letters a hundred-plus years after she had written them? Maybe Elizabeth was right: poor Emily.

Meg's phone didn't ring. The sun sank over the hill, and her back muscles were telling her it was time to call it a day when she saw her father walking up the hill toward the orchard.

"Hi, Daddy," she called out. "Any news?"

Her father smiled. "Much gnashing of teeth and pulling of hair, but that's about all. I got bored — it looks like they'll be at it awhile longer. Need any help up here?"

Meg scanned the orchard, looking for Bree. She caught sight of her at the opposite corner. Meg waved; Bree gave her a thumbs-up and waved her away. "I guess not. Looks like I can quit now."

Phillip followed her gaze and gave a mock salute to Bree. "Do you want to jump into the Dickinson hunt, or would you rather find something else to do?"

"We should think about dinner. I guess I can cook tonight — I'd hate to interrupt Mother if she's onto something."

"Can't we get takeout?"

"Sure, if you want to drive twenty minutes in any direction. You've seen Gran's — that's the best and only real restaurant we have in Granford. There's a small place in the new shopping center on the highway, but that's open only for breakfast and lunch."

"It's a wonder all you hardy pioneers have survived this long!" Phillip said. "I'll volunteer to make a foray to the market for provisions, if you'll point the way again."

"Deal." They'd reached the back door of the house, and Meg pulled open the door. "Anybody home?"

"In here," came her mother's voice from the dining room. Meg followed the sound, trailed by her father.

"Hi, Mother, Susan. Any breakthroughs?"

"Some. Susan, tell her what you told me. Phillip, don't disappear — we need all the brains we can muster to hear this."

"Happy to be of service," Phillip said, taking a seat.

"I went back through my notes," Susan began, "and I think I may have found the flip side of some of Emily's correspondence — the letters she received. They were in a subcollection at Amherst College — one of those that's labeled something like 'Miscellaneous Correspondence.' Nobody paid much attention to them because they weren't from anybody important, so they just dumped them all together. There weren't a whole lot — maybe thirty — and I grouped them together by sender. Some of them were easy to eliminate, because they were from too far away. But there's this one

374

group of a dozen or so" — Susan opened a folder and retrieved a batch of photocopies — "and I wanted you to take a look at them. The envelopes were long gone, not that they would have done much good in that era. Some are dated, but they say only things like 'Tuesday the twelfth.' No year, or even month. You can infer the time of year, at least, from what the correspondent talks about — like what's blooming, or what they've harvested."

"And how are they signed?"

" 'Ellen.' First name only. Sometimes 'your friend Ellen.' So no surname, no town, no year. No wonder nobody's done much with them."

"And you think we're looking for the letters that Emily sent to this person?"

"That's my guess. I'm pretty sure that Daniel had some copies of the ones she sent. We didn't see them when we went through his stuff, Elizabeth, but I may have seen them earlier. Maybe someone took them?"

"So now what? We do a search for everybody named Ellen in several counties over a couple of decades?" Meg knew it was possible, but it would take a lot of time.

"No, Meg, I think we can narrow it down a bit further," her mother jumped in.

Susan pushed a couple of photocopies to Meg. "Take a look at the handwriting — it's kind of immature, don't you think?"

Meg flipped through the pages. "If you say so. I don't know much about nineteenth-century handwriting."

"I've seen plenty. I'm guessing this is a girl or young woman, maybe fifteen to twenty, with some education — she probably attended one of the local academies. You can see that she can spell. From what she talks about, though, it sounds as though she lived on a farm, rather than in a city or town. But what's more valuable is the other people she mentions. Yes, I know — mostly it's 'mother' or 'father,' but she does refer to brothers and some friends or relatives. So that narrows the age range, and gives us other family members to look for. This Ellen was living with her parents and at least two brothers in a rural community at the time she was writing. So now your search is for an Ellen who would have been between fifteen and twenty sometime before 1860 — when Emily stopped leaving her house — with some connection to Emily Dickinson."

Meg was impressed by Susan's logic. "You sound like a detective. Do the letters tell you much about what kind of terms she and Emily were on? Was the tone familiar, casual? I know Emily wasn't a celebrity at the time, so it's not like a fan letter, but do you think they knew each other well? Was this Ellen a relative of hers?"

Susan smiled. "Could be, but not necessarily. Ellen did seem comfortable writing to her."

"Over what time interval — months, years?"

"I don't know. As I said, the letters aren't dated."

"But you're guessing what? The eighteen fifties?" When Susan nodded, Meg added, "Okay, that means we can search censuses. Starting in 1850 they include a lot of family information — ages, relationships. And they're searchable, so if you want to find an Ellen born in Massachusetts between a certain age range, you can do that. Do you want me to show you?"

"Please, dear. I'm afraid my eyes are crossing," her mother said.

Phillip interrupted. "Do you need me for this, or shall I go find us something to eat? Susan, will you be staying for dinner?"

Susan looked startled by the unexpected invitation. "If you want me to."

Meg said, "The more, the merrier. And I expect that Bree will be joining us, too, so that's five. I'll cook, Mother, if you want to keep going once I show you how the census hunt works."

"That's fine. Give your father a detailed list — he tends to forget the essentials and come home with capers and smoked salmon, but no main course." She smiled fondly at Phillip.

"You cut me to the quick," he responded, returning her smile. "Meg, let's check what you have, and then I'll go and let you get back to your searches."

In the kitchen, Meg opened her refrigerator and stared helplessly at the meager contents. "What do you feel like eating, Daddy?"

"Whatever's simple. Do you have a grill?"

Meg shut the refrigerator and turned to him. "I do. Burgers and the works?"

"I think I can manage that. I'll get some charcoal, too. Now, how do I get to the market again?"

Meg explained and sent him on his way. She returned to the dining room, where Susan and Elizabeth were waiting patiently.

"Okay, give me the laptop." Meg logged on to the site and wove her way through the options until she reached the 1860 census search page. "Okay, let's put in first name 'Ellen,' birth year 1845 plus or minus five years, born in Massachusetts, lived in Massachusetts, gender female, and see what we get." She hit the search button and then sat back and laughed. "That gives us over four thousand possibilities. Looks like Ellen was a popular name."

"We can't possibly go through all four thousand," Elizabeth said, dismayed. "Can you narrow the search?"

"I can. Let me put in Hampshire County." Meg did that, hit search again. "Much better. There are about one hundred and seventy-five Ellens of the right age in Hampshire County including, uh" — she keyed in a few more details — "sixteen in Amherst."

Elizabeth sighed. "That's still a lot of names. How do we look at each one?"

"Just click on the record, and a list of household members will come up. You can eliminate the ones who are living in boardinghouses or with someone who isn't a family member, at least for the first pass. And someone who's married, probably. Courage! Who said this was going to be easy?"

"Can I look, too?" Susan asked.

"Not at the same time. I've got only the one subscription, and I can't log in twice. But you can look over Mother's shoulder and help her eliminate possibilities."

Susan and Elizabeth focused on the computer screen in front of them, and Meg went back to the kitchen. She fed Lolly, then started hunting for condiments and plates and such. Should she ask Seth to join them? No, he'd probably be bored silly by all this genealogy talk. Funny how this turned out to be a lot like a detective search, as she'd told Susan. Of course, you had to make assumptions to narrow the search, and there was always the possibility that you had inadvertently eliminated a likely candidate. But you had to start somewhere.

Her father returned, laden with goodies, and they spent a companionable half hour assembling burgers. He'd bought potato salad and coleslaw, and he'd even remembered buns. He volunteered to get the fire going, and Meg directed him to the grill in the covered shed. Elizabeth and Susan remained engrossed in their chase, and Meg heard a steady stream of low comments issuing from the dining room.

Bree emerged from the barn and greeted Phillip. "Hey, something smells good. Am I invited?"

"Of course. We've made enough for an army," Meg heard her father say. "The others are inside looking at census records."

"Hi, Meg," Bree said when she walked into the kitchen. "I'm parched."

"There's plenty of stuff in the fridge,"

Meg said. "Dad did the shopping. I think he was worried about us starving to death — we may not have to shop for a month."

"Sounds good. Where we going to eat? The kitchen table's kind of crowded with five of us."

"Good point. I'll see if Mother and Susan can clear off the dining room table."

When Meg went to the door leading to the dining room, she almost collided with her mother. "Whoa! You look excited."

"I am!" Elizabeth said triumphantly. "We've gone through all the local Ellens and found a few likely possibilities. But guess what? One of them, Ellen Warren, lived right here, in this house! What are the odds of that?"

Meg wanted to share her mother's elation, but at the same time she felt an unexpected sense of foreboding. Could Daniel — or whoever had broken into her house last week — have come to the same conclusions? If Daniel had laid hands on Ellen's letters, and had covered the same genealogy ground, would that have pointed him to the Warren house? And was that why he had suddenly contacted Elizabeth after so many years — to get to this house?

She couldn't bring that up now; she needed time to think about it. Meg plastered on a smile. "That's intriguing. You'll have to show me. But Dad's itching to put the burgers on the grill, and we need a place to eat. Can you clear off the table, just for a while?"

"I guess so." Elizabeth's good cheer was not diminished. "And after we've eaten, we can show you what we found."

Over dinner Elizabeth and Susan recapped their deductions and the results of their search. Bree was properly skeptical. "Give me a break. How likely is it that you'd find whatever it is you're looking for right here? I mean, it would be nice, but you've got to look at the other possibilities."

Meg agreed; it did seem far-fetched that some Warren daughter had carried on a correspondence with Emily Dickinson. Why would she have known her? Meg comforted herself with thinking that they really needed to find that link before focusing solely on that one person. But Daniel Weston's sudden rekindling of interest in her family just before his death troubled her. Susan seemed to think that he had known about the letters for some time. He had certainly seemed sure of his results, if he had planned to announce his find at the symposium.

"You're quiet, Meg." Phillip's voice interrupted her meandering thoughts.

"I'm just trying to work out what else we

need to know. I love the idea that Emily knew this house, but why would she? Mother, you said you'd found some Dickinsons up the line, but none of them were particularly close."

"I know, dear — we're getting ahead of ourselves. We don't even know whether any letters from Emily to Ellen exist, and if they do, where they might be — if they survived. But this Ellen Warren is at least a possibility."

"Was there another Ellen connection at the Dickinson Farm Stand?" Could that explain why Daniel was there in the middle of the night? They'd already proved that "Ellen" was a very common name at the time.

It occurred to Meg that apparently Daniel had been working under multiple assumptions: that Emily's letters to Ellen existed; that Ellen had kept them; and that somehow, somewhere, the letters had survived. There were buildings at the farm stand that looked to be old enough to come from the right time period, but what had Daniel hoped to find? Letters stuffed in the wall? It seems unlikely that they would have survived there, in a shed.

"And even if there was an Ellen there," Meg said slowly, "are we really supposed to believe that this Ellen left the letters in a wall somewhere, and Daniel was going to find them just waiting for him? Susan, was he that obsessed, or did he have something more to go on?"

Susan shrugged. "I really don't know. Obsessed? Maybe. He'd spent most of his life doing research, talking, publishing about Emily. He took pride in knowing even the smallest details about her. I mean, he was *the* expert. Maybe he had more pieces of the puzzle, which he didn't share with anyone else." She drooped in her chair. "Maybe this is all just castles in the air. Maybe he'd finally lost it, lost his grip on reality."

Elizabeth laid a hand on Susan's arm. "I don't think so. I spent time with him, and he seemed quite rational. Funny, charming, interesting. And we didn't even talk about Emily, except in passing. So I wouldn't call him obsessed."

"Then he had to know something else," Meg said. "And maybe it was based on the genealogy."

The plates were empty, and it was dark outside. Meg was tired, and her brain was working slowly, which didn't bode well for working out complicated nineteenth-century family relationships.

"I thought you'd be more excited, Meg," her mother said almost petulantly. "And don't forget — if we can figure this out, we might know why Daniel was killed."

Who was she to rain on her mother's enthusiasm? "Okay, here's what I'd suggest. I'll clear the table, and then you can show us who was related to who, and maybe we'll see a connection. You've got a lot of information, between the censuses and the maps. If nothing jumps out at you, then maybe we can go a level deeper — tomorrow, I'm afraid. I'm wiped out."

"Poor darling, I can see that. All right, we'll give it another couple of hours, and if we don't turn anything up tonight, we can start again tomorrow with fresh eyes. Susan, does that work for you?"

"Sure. I want to see where this goes — for Daniel's sake."

27

Meg woke the next morning to the sound of rain. She allowed herself a guilty moment of relief: no picking today, which was good news for the Emily hunt. Meg figured that her mother and Susan hadn't made any important discoveries the night before, because surely her mother would have woken her to share the news regardless of the hour. Meg vaguely remembered hearing Susan's car start up and pull away sometime during the night.

She'd called this a wild-goose chase, and a hunt for a needle in a haystack. They were looking for some pieces of paper that, if they even existed, hadn't been seen in a century. Paper was fragile, easy to destroy or lose. What were the odds that anything had survived, undiscovered, all these years? Slim to none.

But still, Daniel Weston had been killed, presumably over these mysterious letters.

Where did that fit? He was a dedicated scholar, so it was at least conceivable that he had gone haring off to a locked building in the middle of the night, in search of what he believed were these lost documents. Maybe. Meg had trouble getting her head around the idea that academic discoveries could inspire enough strong feeling that someone would kill for them. But nobody had any better theories, including, it seemed, the police. Daniel had been dead nearly two weeks, and no one had been arrested.

With a sigh, Meg hauled herself out of bed and dressed. Downstairs she found her mother in the kitchen, drinking coffee and reading the paper, Lolly purring on her lap. Meg poured a cup and joined her. "So, no big breakthroughs?"

"No, not yet. It's complicated, isn't it? You'd think censuses would get things right, but the spelling of people's names changes from one to the next, and their birth years are all over the place. Do you think people lied to the census takers? Or maybe they were all deaf."

Meg smiled. "I sometimes wonder that myself. So, what's on for today?"

"Susan said she'd be coming back around ten. Are you picking today?"

"I doubt it, given the rain, but I'll wait for Bree to tell me. You know, I was thinking about Ellen Warren. From what I've learned about the Warren family in the nineteenth century, there's nothing to eliminate her as a candidate for the Ellen who wrote to Emily. Ellen Warren lived here all her life with her parents, and she had brothers. I'll have to show you her father Eli's will — it's very funny. It sounds as though the family was a bit dysfunctional." Meg swallowed some coffee. "Although I won't hold my breath about finding the letters. Hold on a minute." Meg went to the dining room and retrieved her printout of Eli Warren's family tree. "Here, these are the people we're talking about. Ellen Warren was Eli's daughter by his first wife. Her father remarried and had some more kids. After her father died, Ellen ended up living in the house with her stepmother and a passel of half-siblings. So let's put ourselves in the head of a fifteen-year-old girl, back in those days. She's living in a crowded house — this house — most likely sharing a room with a few siblings. Say she wants to keep something secret, something personal. What would she do?"

"Shouldn't we wonder why she would

have met Emily Dickinson in the first place?"

"We can work that out later. But right now I'm more interested in what a girl would do with her treasures."

"Hide them from prying eyes, you mean? Somewhere in the house . . . Darling, how much of the house has changed since her day?"

"Not much. Ellen's brother's grandchildren ended up with the house — Lula and Nettie. You know how little they did to the place. Then you rented it out, and nobody made any real improvements. Some cosmetic stuff, most of which I've stripped away. I should ask Seth — he knows more about old houses, including this one, than either of us. He can probably tell us which bits are original and which are replacements. But for the sake of argument, let's assume that physically everything here is much the way it was in Ellen's day. Where would she hide something?"

"Where snoopy siblings wouldn't find it? Out of sight. In the floor or walls. The attic, the basement. Probably not in an outbuilding, because there it would be vulnerable to the weather."

Meg nodded. "Good. I'd rule out the basement, because it's dark and damp, and

I can't see a girl tiptoeing down there to visit her treasures."

Phillip ambled into the kitchen. "Good morning, ladies. You look like you're plotting and scheming."

"We are. We're trying to get into the head of a girl in 1855, and where she might have hidden something."

Phillip poured himself a cup of coffee and joined them at the table. "So you're going forward with your theory that there are letters hidden in this house?"

"Let's say we haven't eliminated the possibility," Meg said.

Bree clattered down the back stairs and drained the remains of the coffeepot into a mug. "Meg, you're off the hook for picking today. What's up?"

"I think we're planning to go on a treasure hunt. We have a theory that letters from Emily Dickinson might be hidden somewhere in the house."

"Cool," Bree said. "Is that what the professor was looking for?"

"Maybe. Susan thinks it's possible."

"What's she going to do if you find them?"

"I don't know. I didn't think to ask. Announce the discovery herself, since he can't?"

"Convenient, isn't it? Nice way to make a

name for yourself."

Meg stilled. Her mother turned back from the stove and met her eyes. "You don't think . . . ?" Elizabeth said.

Phillip picked up her thought. "That we should take a harder look at Susan?"

"But how? And why? Why would she want to kill Daniel? She said herself that his death only makes things harder for her. Didn't she need his support if she ever hoped to find a teaching job?" Elizabeth's forehead furrowed.

"Wouldn't a significant discovery like some lost letters of Emily Dickinson be a big boost for her job search? What do you know about Susan?" Phillip went into his lawyer mode once again.

"She's a graduate student at UMass, writing a dissertation about Emily Dickinson, and Daniel was a member of her thesis committee — but one of several."

"And she has had access to Daniel's office, his home, and to this place."

"She had been here before the break-in," Meg said slowly, "and she did know we were working on our genealogy."

"And maybe she knows more about these letters than she's told us," Elizabeth added.

"Did the police interview her?" Phillip asked.

Meg shrugged. "I don't know. They may have, but I never thought to ask. Bree, you're closer to her age than we are. What do you think? Can you see any reason why Susan would have wanted Daniel Weston to die?"

Bree sat back in her chair and crossed her arms. "Huh. That's a tough one. He was on her thesis committee, but that's usually not enough to drive someone to murder — although I've heard some students say they'd like to kill their advisors when they ask for one more piece of research or one more rewrite. Not that anybody's rushing to jump into the job market these days, so there's no hurry to finish their degree. But Mr. Corey has a point. If she did something newsworthy, she'd get attention, and it might make it a lot easier to find a job."

"Which gives her an incentive to find those letters. It comes back to the letters that she's so eager to find," Phillip said. "She's planning to come back here this morning?"

"Yes, that's what we arranged," Elizabeth replied.

"Then perhaps we'd better look around before she arrives," Phillip said. "Meg, you were going to ask Seth if he could help?"

"Right — I'll see if he's in his office." Meg

went out the back door and crossed the driveway to Seth's office, dashing through the steady drizzle and up the interior stairs.

Seth looked up when she came in. "Hi. What's up?"

"Listen, I need your help for a treasure hunt. Or wild-goose chase. What do you get when you combine those?"

"Got me. A goose that lays golden eggs? What's this about?"

"We're looking for letters from Emily Dickinson, and there's a chance they're in the house somewhere."

"That sounds like a lot more fun than these invoices. What do you need me for?"

"Advice. If a sneaky teenager wanted to hide something from her family in a crowded house during the 1850s, where would she put it? I thought you might be able to tell us which parts of the house date to the right time period, and what's been muddled around with."

"I'd be happy to help." Seth stood up and put on a waterproof jacket. "Lead the way."

Back in the kitchen, Elizabeth was piling scrambled eggs and stacks of bacon on a platter. "Good morning, Seth," she said. "Did Meg explain what we're up to?"

"She did. I'm intrigued. But how likely is it that these letters are in the house?"

Elizabeth pulled toast out of the toaster. "I'm not sure. Susan and I spent yesterday afternoon working out who the Ellen who wrote to Emily Dickinson might have been, and we narrowed it down to a list of perhaps twenty possibilities in this general area, one of whom, Ellen Warren, turns out to have lived in this house. And if it was her, whether she might have had — and saved — letters from Emily somewhere in the house." She hesitated a moment before adding, "I'm beginning to suspect that Daniel may have covered the same ground, and that might have triggered his belated interest in renewing contact with Phillip and me. It did seem to come out of nowhere."

Meg wondered how hard it was for her mother to admit that. Elizabeth had hoped for something different, and now she had to face that Daniel could have been using her and nothing more.

Her thoughts were interrupted when Seth asked, "Because he knew, or at least suspected, that it was your daughter, Meg, who was living in this house?"

"One of the small bonuses of local notoriety," Meg deadpanned.

Elizabeth set the platter of bacon and eggs on the kitchen table. "Please, dig in. And I'm afraid there's more to the story."

"What?"

Meg answered for her mother. "We're beginning to wonder how long Susan may have been aware of this, and if she might have had something to do with Daniel's death."

Everyone was silent for a few moments. Finally Meg spoke again, "So, Seth, what we need to know is where the likely hiding places in the house might be."

"Interesting question," Seth said, taking another helping of eggs. "Colonial houses are fairly simple in construction. Assuming Ellen wanted reasonably easy access to whatever she was hiding, she wouldn't have put it behind a plaster wall, for instance. That pretty much leaves the woodwork."

"Has much been changed since 1860?"

"Yes and no," Seth said. "Eli Warren was the carpenter, and he did some renovations in the later nineteenth century. You know, Meg — he's the one who reconfigured the fireplaces and added the existing stairway in the hall."

"Eli was Ellen's father. Should we figure that anything he worked on is ruled out, because he would have found Ellen's cache?"

"Probably, unless she found a new spot after he was finished. How big a stash are you thinking?"

Meg and her mother exchanged glances. "We hadn't thought about that," Elizabeth said. "A wooden or metal box, about the size of a shoe box, I'd guess? I can't imagine that she would have kept the letters loose, or just bundled up with a ribbon."

"Okay, so you had four bedrooms upstairs — five, if you count the room that's now a bathroom. Do you know who was living in the house at the time?"

"Ellen, her father, her stepmother — who was apparently pregnant for most of the 1850s, so lots of other half-siblings — and her older brother."

"So most likely the parents had one room, with maybe another serving as a nursery, and the rest of the kids would have had the other two. The fifth room — Bree's room — was probably for a hired hand or two who helped with the farm."

"When did the indoor plumbing go in?" Phillip asked.

"Sometime after 1900, and I'd guess that went into what had been the nursery. But you're right — that would have disrupted some part of the rooms upstairs. When did Ellen die?"

"Before the 1920 census," Elizabeth replied promptly.

"Then she was likely still here when the bathroom was built. She probably would have remembered her childhood cache and moved it, if that was a problem. It seems less likely that Ellen would have hidden something downstairs initially, since those were the public rooms, and there probably would have been someone around most of the time."

"So you're saying we need to look at any wooden moldings or structures in the upstairs bedrooms," Elizabeth said, "and skip over the bathroom?"

"That's about right. Loose boards, dead spaces in the walls, built-ins with false floors or backs, anything like that. Who knows what we might find?"

"All right, then," Meg said. "Mother, you and I can take the front bedrooms. Bree, you check your own room, and Daddy, can you take the fourth? Seth, you're on call if we find a likely place. And it shouldn't be anything where we'd need a crowbar, right?"

"No crowbars," Seth agreed. "But maybe a box knife or a putty knife — there may be a lot of paint layers to get through. We're looking for someplace a girl could access without too much difficulty, but possibly cleverly hidden. So let's go."

Swabbing the last of the eggs from her

plate, Meg said, "I agree. We have only an hour or so before Susan arrives, and I guess I'd like to know before she gets here." Although, she realized, if they found nothing, would she still report her suspicions to the police? They had so little to go on. It would be better to gauge Susan's reactions before taking it any further.

Meg headed toward the front bedroom that she had been using, while her mother went to the guest room across the hall. If Seth had guessed correctly, Meg's room had been the master bedroom; the adjacent bathroom filled what had once been a nursery. She had mixed feelings about this hunt: she wasn't sure whether she wanted to find anything or not. In her room she stood in the center and turned in a full circle, studying the structure. The plaster walls were original and intact, so she could eliminate those. There was what was laughingly called a closet, less than a hanger's width deep, ringed inside with Victorian iron hooks. Another of Eli's additions? Outside her room in the hall, the adjoining space was filled by an equally shallow bookcase set into the wall, so there was little room left over to conceal a box. The baseboards offered some possibilities, but most were single board lengths and, judging by the layers of paint, hadn't been moved in decades. Surely young Ellen wouldn't have been moving ten-foot boards around? That left the floor.

Many of the wide floorboards were long, almost the full length of the room, but in some cases there were short pieces at the edges, extending under the baseboards. Meg sat down on the floor and contemplated the short bits. The boards were about eight inches wide, maybe two feet long, and were held in by a couple of old nails on the end closer to her. She dug a fingernail under the nearest one and found it firmly attached. She slid over to the next one: the same thing. The board was rock solid.

There was only one left, at the front corner of the room, one board in from the edge. Funny, this one seemed to be missing any nails, and there was a small irregular notch on the near end of the board, which her finger fit neatly into. She pried up the board, dislodging a century's worth of caked dirt, and slid it out. Between the joists nestled a rectangular wooden box with carved initials: ESW.

28

Meg sat back on her heels and drew a long breath before calling out, "Hey, guys? I think I've got something."

Her mother was the first to arrive, from across the hall. "You found something?" She stopped in her tracks when she saw the dusty hole in the floor in front of Meg. Bree, following Elizabeth, all but bumped into her.

"So it appears," Meg responded, her eyes still on the box. "From the layer of dust on it, I'd say nobody's handled this for quite a while."

"Should we touch it?" Elizabeth leaned over Meg for a closer look. "Or maybe we should take some photos first, just in case."

"In case of what?"

"Well, it could be evidence in a murder investigation."

"I doubt the box itself is. As I said, it hasn't been touched for a very long time. If this had something to do with Daniel's death, it's only because someone *wanted* to find it, and obviously they didn't. But sure, why not take pictures? We might need to establish provenance."

"Huh?" Bree said.

"If there's any question about the source of . . . whatever might be inside, we should document where we found it," Meg said.

Phillip and Seth were the last to join the group, and Meg's bedroom was crowded now, with everyone staring over Meg's shoulder. "I'll get my camera," Bree volunteered, and went down the hall to her room.

Meg found to her surprise that she was reluctant to take the next step. She wasn't sure what she wanted to find. If Emily's letters were there, what would it mean? And if they weren't, did that mean Daniel died for nothing?

Bree returned with a small digital camera. Meg stood up, brushing the dust bunnies off the seat of her pants, and stepped back to give her a clear view. Bree snapped a variety of shots — wide shots showing the corner of the room and close-ups showing the box with its undisturbed dust. Then she retreated and said, "Well, isn't anybody going to open it?"

Meg hesitated. "Mother, do you want to

do the honors? It's your house, too."

"Sweetheart, you found it. I think you should have that privilege."

Meg knelt down. The group waited silently as she reached into the void and pulled out the box. It was solidly made, with a simple brass clasp on the front. Meg could hear some small objects shifting around inside as she lifted it. "If there is anything valuable inside, we should be careful how we open it — you know, wash our hands, open it in a clean area."

"The dining room table," Elizabeth said. "I'll go clear it off."

After she left, the rest of them stood around awkwardly. Meg still held the box, unsure what to do next. It felt kind of ridiculous to be so uncertain. It was just a box, after all, and it probably held a few simple trinkets, of historical interest but no particular value. Why didn't she believe that? Because Daniel was dead.

"Shall we?" Her father gestured toward the door, and Meg finally moved, followed by Bree and Seth. Downstairs, her mother had cleared off the tabletop and spread out a sheet. Meg set the box down, and they all stood in a circle around the table and stared at it.

They were interrupted by a knock at the

front door. Meg jumped at the sound. "That must be Susan. Do we tell her?"

"I think we have to. Don't you?" Elizabeth replied.

Meg nodded, then went to the door. When she opened it, Susan took one look at her dusty clothes and said, "You've been searching." Then she saw Meg's face. "You found something!"

Meg stepped back to let Susan pass, and she made a beeline for the table, oblivious to the others in the room. "Oh," she breathed. "I can't believe it. It's real." Then she looked at the others. "You haven't opened it?"

"We just found it."

Susan looked at Meg with an obvious plea, but Meg was reluctant to give up first rights. Her house, her discovery. Her parents' friend, dead. This was something she realized that she wanted, needed to do herself.

"I'm just going to wash my hands first," she said, escaping to the kitchen. Seth followed. "You okay with all this?" he asked her.

Meg kept her eyes on her hands, soaping them, rinsing, drying, slowly and carefully. "I feel weird about it. I mean, what are we going to find in there? And regardless, how on earth did Emily Dickinson and a murder somehow come together — even theoretically — in this house?"

"Hard to say, but nothing surprises me, particularly where old houses are concerned. They've probably witnessed a lot more than we suspect."

"Nothing new under the sun, eh?" Meg produced a wavering smile for him. "Then let's do it."

In the dining room, the other three had closed ranks, flanking Susan. To restrain her from running off with the box? Meg had brought a clean towel with her from the kitchen, and gently wiped the encrusted dust from the box. "No lock, just the latch," she said. She took a breath, then slipped the latch from its loop and opened the box. As one they all peered in.

It was about two-thirds filled. "Bree, can you get a picture of this?" Meg asked.

"I'm on it." Bree pulled the camera out of her pocket and snapped a few quick pictures.

When Bree was finished, Meg reached out a tentative hand, then stopped. "One more thing." She fished through one of the boxes of documents from the Historical Society that she had been cataloging and pulled out a pair of white cotton gloves, and slid them

404

on her hands. The others looked quizzically at her. "This is how you handle old documents — the oil from your skin can damage them. Susan knows that." Susan didn't respond, all her attention still focused on the box.

Meg turned back to the box and its contents. On top of the small pile inside the box was a long-dead flower, which crumbled when Meg touched it. A scrap of embroidery had fared better, and she set that on the table next to the box. A child-size ring, red-gold, set with what looked like tiny turquoise chips and a seed pearl. A small doll, leather-bodied with a hand-painted china head, which Meg laid gently next to the embroidery. And in the bottom, a small stack of folded papers, bound together with a ribbon that might once have been blue but which was now faded to a dull gray.

Before she reached to extricate them, Meg glanced at Susan. There was excitement in her face — but there was also pain. This meant so much to her. Why?

Meg pulled out the slender bundle. The paper appeared to have aged well, though Meg could see that the folded pages had been much-handled, because they bore obvious marks of wear around the edges. The moment of truth: were these old love letters — or something much more important to literature scholars? Meg untied the small bow holding the paper together and unfolded the top document, smoothing it out gently on the table.

There was no question: this was a handwriting she had seen before, on websites, in books, and all over the town of Amherst. That idiosyncratic rolling stroke, the broad spacing of letters and words, so unlike the prim formal style of the day, the frequent long dashes, could only belong to Emily Dickinson. The penciled signature at the bottom of the page, "Your dear Friend Emily," was only icing on the cake.

"Wow!" breathed Bree. "It really is. Isn't it?"

Meg looked up at the people around her, and saw that Susan's face was wet with tears. Susan held out a hand. "May I? Please?"

Meg nodded, and handed her a second pair of gloves. Then she stepped away, watching. Susan took the piece of paper as though it might crumble in her hand. She ran a tentative finger across a line of text, then down to the signature. "I knew it," she whispered. "He was right . . ." She stopped abruptly and looked up, to find everyone watching her. She finally locked eyes with Meg.

And Meg knew what she had to ask. "You *knew* Daniel was looking for these letters?" She wasn't sure she wanted to hear the answer.

Susan dropped heavily into the nearest chair and nodded. Everyone else followed suit. The box sat in the middle of the table like a silent accusation. "There are more letters from Ellen to Emily than the ones in libraries. I have them, because they came down through my family — but I only found out about them recently. Nobody else knows about them, except Daniel — I told him about them. So he knew about them for a little while, except for where they were. Here."

29

Meg stood up abruptly and stripped off her gloves. "I have a feeling that this is going to be a complicated story. Right, Susan?"

"Yes," she whispered.

The next question was obvious. Meg said gently, "Susan, should we be talking to the police?"

Susan stared at her for a long moment, and then she nodded silently.

Meg looked at the people around the table, all showing signs of shock. "Then I'd better call Detective Marcus. Susan, why don't you wait to explain things until he arrives? Then you'll only have to do it once." She snatched up her cell phone from the sideboard and went to the kitchen to make the call.

It took Detective Marcus half an hour to arrive at Meg's front door. Meg had told him the bare minimum on the phone: that she had new information about Daniel

408

Weston's death, and she thought he should hear it from the source. If it had been anyone but her, he might have laughed or pawned her off to a subordinate. Instead Marcus had sighed and told her that he was leaving immediately.

When Meg let him in, he drew her aside into the little-used parlor on the west side of the house. "Okay, what's going on?"

"I'll give you the short form. We've found what we believe is a batch of letters written by Emily Dickinson to someone who lived in this house in the nineteenth century. We also think that the letters were the catalyst for Daniel Weston's death."

"Why?"

"Because" — Meg swallowed — "I think his graduate student Susan Keeley had something to do with his death. She's here, and she's willing to talk to you."

"What did she tell you?"

"Nothing. I stopped her before she could say anything. You can take it from here."

"She in there?" He nodded toward the other side of the house.

"In the dining room."

Marcus turned and strode toward the dining room, stopping when he realized that there was already a small crowd of people there. Meg, trailing behind, caught up with him and said, "I think you know everyone here, except Susan."

"I do. Ms. Keeley, I understand you have something to tell me?"

Susan nodded. "I do. Can everyone else stay? I want everyone to hear what I have to say." She paused while everyone found a chair, except for Seth, who opted to lean against the doorframe, his arms crossed. Phillip took a chair on Susan's right, while Meg sat across from her so she could watch her face. The open box and its stack of letters sat in the middle of the table. "It was an accident," Susan began.

"Tell me what happened," Marcus said, not unkindly.

Phillip interrupted. "Susan, you don't have to tell him anything."

"Mr. Corey, she's not under arrest. Are you her attorney?"

"I will represent Susan if that's what she wants. Susan?"

Susan glanced up at him. "No, it's okay. I want everyone to know what happened."

Susan turned back to face Marcus. "I really want to get this over with. I've felt so awful, ever since . . . I'd better start at the beginning." Susan folded her hands in front of her and began talking. "I'm writing my PhD thesis about Emily Dickinson. Daniel

Weston was on my thesis committee as an outside advisor, and we met maybe a couple of times a month, over the past year. I grew up in Amherst, so I've kind of been living with Emily Dickinson all my life. Plus I had another connection — my great-grandmother worked for Emily's brother next door, and his widow, Susan, after that. After Emily's brother died, Susan and their daughter were the ones who first published Emily's poetry. But Susan did a lot of editing, and she tossed a lot of stuff, too. It looks like my great-grandmother kind of kept a lot of what she found in the trash, don't ask me why.

"But I only found that out recently. You see, my grandmother has Alzheimer's, and she's in a home now, and my mother finally decided to clear her stuff out of her house. She found this box of papers and told me she thought I might be interested in them, because I liked old stuff. I don't think she ever looked at them. Could I have some water, please?"

"I'll get it," Seth volunteered.

Susan resumed. "So one night I went through them and I found a bunch of letters, and when I started reading them, I realized what they were, or what they might be. I was so excited! I mean, it was unreal

— letters that had actually belonged to Emily Dickinson, and I had them right in my hand. Of course, I had to do some research to be sure, but it's all there in the censuses — my great-grandmother, called 'servant,' right next door to Emily's house. My mother didn't even know, and it was too late to ask Nana if she remembered anything. But I had the letters, so of course I took them to Daniel right away and showed them to him. And he got excited, too. And then he said, you know what this means? That there may be letters from Emily to this Ellen somewhere. And I said, well, why haven't they been found? And he said, maybe because no one was looking?"

Seth reappeared and silently handed Susan a glass of water. She drank gratefully.

"When was this?" Detective Marcus asked.

Susan frowned in thought. "Not long ago — maybe last month? And I told Daniel about it a couple of days after I found the letters."

"And what did Professor Weston do?"

"He said we should look for Emily's letters, and he had some ideas about how to do it." Susan gave a short, bitter laugh. "Turns out mine weren't the only letters from Ellen — I didn't know about the ones in the Amherst College collection. Daniel had already seen those. He showed them to me and said maybe if we combined the information from all the letters, we'd have a better idea where to look."

"Wait a moment," Elizabeth interrupted. "You mean you and he had already done all this genealogy?"

"No, no. Daniel knew Emily's life backward and forward, so he could point to where she visited, who she'd known, at least in known sources. But it hadn't occurred to him to look for relatives, especially the ones where a Dickinson woman married someone else, and you don't always see the surname. He just wasn't into all that. Looking at the extended family connections was my idea."

"And you continued to share information with him?" the detective asked.

"Yes, of course. I thought we might actually find the letters, and if we did, maybe we could publish the results jointly. You know how great that would be for my career, to start out with something like that?"

"So that's what took him to Dickinson's Farm Stand? You were there?"

Susan nodded. "We figured out some of the Amherst Dickinsons, and he knew that the buildings at the farm were probably from the right time period. He told me to meet him there that night, when nobody would be around."

"Why on earth didn't you go by daylight, when you could see what you were doing?" Elizabeth asked.

"I don't know. He was really paranoid that someone would figure out what we were looking for. He said that Professor Henderson was crazy enough to follow him around and spy on him. Plus we were running out of time, but I didn't know that until we got there and he told me what he was going to do."

"Which was?"

"That he was going to announce finding the Emily letters at the symposium. He was pretty sure he knew where they were, thanks to my letters and the research I'd done. They weren't at the farm stand — there was something about the configuration of buildings that Ellen had mentioned that didn't fit Dickinson's. But he said he'd have them soon, and he was going to stand up at the symposium and tell the world about his great find, and take the credit for it. He said he'd be sure to give me a footnote when he published his discovery."

"What happened that night?" Marcus asked.

414

"I met Daniel at the farm stand, around ten o'clock. We looked at the layout, and he pointed out the parts that didn't jibe with Ellen's descriptions. But he didn't seem too disappointed, and when I asked why, he said he thought he knew a more likely place — he was just confirming that he could cross Dickinson's off the list. I asked him where, and he wouldn't tell me. That's when he told me he was going ahead without me.

"You can imagine how I felt. I mean, I've got all these student loans, and I really need a job when I get done, and it's not easy to find one these days because nobody has any openings and they can't even afford to fill the ones they do have . . ."

Meg reached out and touched Susan's hand. "Slow down, Susan. Take a drink of water."

Susan complied, then resumed in a calmer tone. "I told him, 'You can't do that!' I was the one who brought him the letters, and I should get equal credit. And he looked down his nose at me and said, 'You're only a student. As your advisor, I can claim whatever I choose. I'll be happy to give you a nod — in a footnote.'

"I argued with him, but he said, who was going to believe me if I went around saying that I had made this big discovery and he said it wasn't true? He was the expert, and I was nobody. He just wouldn't listen, and I got so mad . . . I hit him."

"You hit him?" Marcus prompted. "With what?"

"With my fist. I just hauled off and socked him, right in the stomach. I've never done anything like that before in my life, but I'd been so happy, and for him to do that to me . . ." She swallowed, fighting for composure. "And he fell down. I just stood there and stared for a while, I don't know how long, waiting for him to get up. But then I realized he wasn't moving, and when I checked, he wasn't even breathing. As far as I could tell, he was dead. I'd never even seen a dead person. How was I supposed to know? I mean, maybe I should have called someone for help, but I really couldn't believe it, and I guess I was in shock or something, but I just kind of sat down and waited. It was dark, and really quiet. If Daniel had been breathing, I would have heard it. But he wasn't." She swallowed a sob. "It took me a while before I could think straight. I'd killed him, even if I didn't mean to."

She took a deep breath. "I know what I did next doesn't make me look too good. But I figured if I told the police I'd killed him, I'd be kissing my career good-bye, and then nobody would find the Emily letters. I couldn't take back what I'd done, but at least I could finish what Daniel and I had started. He'd said he was pretty sure he knew where to look, so I figured I'd just retrace his logic. And then I found out about you, Elizabeth, and I realized that if he'd asked you here at this particular time, there must have been a good reason."

"Wait — how did you know who I was and that I was here?" Elizabeth asked.

"You had dinner with him right before we met that Sunday night. He told me he'd seen you, and that you held a key to the puzzle. He was really stoked by then. That's why I volunteered to go through his papers with you, and why I asked you to help me out with the genealogy. I knew there had to be some connection, and I had to spend time with you to figure out what it was. And I was right."

Elizabeth nodded. "And when I think about it now, he did spend a lot of time talking about Meg and how he didn't realize we had roots in the area, let alone an old house in the family. He was probably angling to get into the house."

"That's what I'd guess," Susan said. "I think he'd eliminated most of the other possible hiding places anyway — either they didn't fit, or they were long gone. Maybe you were his last shot at finding the letters, but he seemed pretty excited after he'd seen you."

"Obviously he was right, although we'll probably never know why," Elizabeth said.

Phillip cleared his throat. "Detective, it sounds as though this was a tragic accident. Susan here was wrong not to come forward, but she had no intention of killing the man."

"Be that as it may, Mr. Corey, but at the moment I need to take her in. We can discuss this there."

Five minutes later Detective Marcus left with Susan in tow.

"I'll follow you in Northampton, Susan," Phillip told her. "Don't say anything else until I get there."

"I'm coming with you, Phillip," Elizabeth said.

They departed in Phillip's car a few minutes later, leaving Meg, Seth, and Bree alone in the house — with the letters.

"Well," Meg began, and stopped. She had no idea what to say.

"We should put this stuff someplace safe." Seth waved at the items on the table.

"Oh. Right. Of course." Meg carefully pulled on the gloves and slipped the letters back into their box, and added the other items on top, much as they had been stored since who knew how long. "Where should I put them?"

"Do you have a safe-deposit box?"

"No."

"Seems like a good time to get one."

EPILOGUE

"You'll be back for Thanksgiving?" Meg asked, hugging her mother hard.

"Of course we will. I can't wait for us to share a real New England Thanksgiving in this house."

"You, too, Dad?" Meg let go of her mother and hugged her father.

"Wouldn't miss it. Don't you work too hard between now and then."

"At least the picking should be over by the time you come back. And thank you for helping Susan."

"She's not a bad person — she just got herself into an unfortunate situation. Something like I imagine you did?"

"You're right, and I'm glad she had someone like you on her side. I can't bring myself to be angry at her. She saw her chances slipping away when Daniel betrayed her, and she just lashed out."

"I have to agree that he treated her rather

420

shabbily at the end there. Maybe he was feeling that his time had passed, and he wanted one more success before it was too late." Phillip turned to Seth, waiting behind Meg. "Seth, a pleasure to meet you. I hope we'll be seeing more of you?"

"I hope so, too, sir." The men shook hands while Elizabeth and Meg exchanged an amused glance.

"Drive safely, both of you. And let me know when you get home," Meg cautioned.

"Yes, dear," her mother said. "We've been driving for, oh, forty years now. I think we can manage. Take care, darling, and we'll see you soon."

Meg watched as her parents pulled out of the driveway in tandem. She sighed and sat down on the granite step outside the kitchen door, where Seth joined her.

"Relieved?" Seth asked.

"Yes. And no. What an odd couple of weeks it's been!"

"Your folks seem nice."

"They are. It was good to see them, despite all the mess."

"Which came out as well as could be expected. Did anyone ever figure out how Emily Dickinson knew Ellen Warren?"

"We've got a good guess, based on the letters and on some research Mother did. She couldn't let it go last night, so she kept working on it. It turns out that one of Emily's nearer cousins married a man down the road, and her husband was Eli's cousin, though the cousin was a lot older than Eli, so Eli helped him out with a lot of the heavier chores. That turned up in one of the letters, but it took a bit of digging to figure out who was who. So it's quite likely that Emily called on them, back before she became housebound, and that's how she met a young girl from down the road."

"You read all the letters?"

"Of course — very carefully. How could we not? Don't worry, I'll take them to the bank this morning. I'd hate to see anything happen to them now."

"Does your father think Susan will get off? And did Marcus believe her story?"

"I think he did. He told us that Daniel technically died of something called 'commodio cordis.' You see it most often in young athletes who are hit in the chest playing sports. But if you happen to hit someone in just the right place on the sternum, it can stop the heart, even in someone who's healthy. Susan was plain unlucky. But she never meant to kill him."

"What happens to the letters now?"

"I'm really not sure — I plan to ask a

lawyer. Since my mother inherited the house, presumably they're hers."

"What do you two plan to do with them?"

"I'm going to think about it for a bit."

"They should be worth some money."

"I know. I hate to benefit from something like this, under the circumstances, though. I could give them to the Granford Historical Society, or Amherst College, if that's legal. But on the other hand, I could use the money. I don't have to decide right away. Maybe after the harvest is over, and I see how much money I've made, or not made." Then she smiled. "But there's one I know I want to keep. Here, I made a copy." She handed a piece of paper to Seth.

He read it and smiled. "I can see why."

A purple light announces dawn —
the day — in Eider — soon to break.
And some deep warren underground —
where rabbits slumber — darkly waits.
And shoulder'd there — as cousins —
an orchard thick with fruit
Whose branches tremble — tunneling —
reaching toward the Firmament.

RECIPES

Ginger Cake

Meg's mother, Elizabeth, enjoys making this flavorful and delightfully rich cake. The two gingers give it a distinctive flavor, and sprinkling the pan with coarse sugar provides an interesting crunch.

The recipe calls for a 12-cup tube pan, but it can easily be cut in half — use a 6-cup pan and watch your baking time so that it doesn't become too dry.

softened butter (for pan)
1/2 cup raw sugar (also called turbinado sugar)
2 1/4 cups flour
4 teaspoons ground ginger
2 teaspoons baking powder
1/2 teaspoon salt
1 cup unsalted butter, room temperature

2 cups sugar
4 large eggs
1 large egg yolk
2 teaspoons vanilla extract
1 cup sour cream
1 cup chopped crystallized ginger (you may chop this as fine as you like, depending on how much you like crystallized ginger)

Place a rack in the center of the oven and preheat the oven to 350 degrees.

Generously butter the inside of a 12-cup tube pan (you can use a bundt pan). Sprinkle raw sugar over the butter, coating the pan completely.

Whisk together the flour, ground ginger, baking powder, and salt in a medium bowl.

Using an electric mixer or stand mixer, beat the butter in a large bowl until smooth. Gradually add the sugar, and beat at medium-high speed until blended, about 2 minutes. Add the eggs one at a time, beating well after each addition. Beat in extra egg yolk and vanilla.

Add the flour mixture in 3 additions, alternating with the sour cream, beating on low speed until just blended after each. Mix in the chopped crystallized ginger.

Spread the batter in the prepared pan, being careful not to dislodge the raw sugar.

Bake the cake until the top is light brown and a tester comes out with just a few crumbs, about 55 minutes. Transfer to a rack and cool in the pan for 15 minutes.

Invert the pan and tap the edge carefully on a work surface until the cake loosens. Place cake on rack and cool completely.

Slice and serve! This cake doesn't need any embellishment. It also keeps well and travels well.

KIELBASA WITH APPLES AND CABBAGE
Another hearty but simple dish for a nippy night.

Serves 4–6

2 tablespoons olive oil
2 medium onions, thinly sliced
2 cloves garlic, minced (or use a garlic press)
1 medium red cabbage, coarsely shredded
4 apples (you want a relatively firm apple, like a Fuji or a Braeburn), peeled, cored, and sliced
1 whole kielbasa, about 21/2 pounds (you may substitute the smaller individual-size ones if you prefer)
1 bay leaf
1 teaspoon dried thyme, or two sprigs fresh thyme

1/2 teaspoon freshly ground black pepper
1/2 cup stock (you may use beef, chicken, or vegetable)
1 tablespoon red wine or apple cider vinegar

Heat the oil in a large kettle and sauté the sliced onions and the garlic for 5 minutes, until soft but not brown.

Stir the shredded cabbage into the onions and cook for 5 minutes over medium heat.

Add the sliced apples to the cabbage and onion mixture.

Lay the kielbasa in the pot with the vegetables, and add the herbs and spices.

Add the stock and vinegar. Cover the pot and bring to a boil. Reduce heat to low and simmer for 30 to 40 minutes.

When cooked, remove the kielbasa (if whole) and cut into serving-size pieces. Arrange the cooked vegetables on a platter and top with the kielbasa.

Serve this with boiled potatoes.

WHITE CHICKEN CHILI
This recipe has traveled a long way from its Southwestern origins, but it's a satisfying dish for a chilly autumn night.

1 15-ounce can navy beans

1 large onion, chopped
1 stick (1/2 cup) unsalted butter
1/4 cup all-purpose flour
3/4 cup chicken broth
2 cups half-and-half
1 1/2 teaspoons chili powder
1 teaspoon ground cumin
1/2 teaspoon salt, or to taste
1/2 teaspoon white pepper, or to taste
2 4-ounce cans chopped mild green chilies, drained
2 pounds (approximately) boneless, skinless chicken breasts, cooked and cut into half-inch pieces
1 1/2 cups, about 6 ounces, grated or shredded Monterey Jack
1/2 cup sour cream

Drain the beans in a colander and rinse them.

In a skillet cook the chopped onion in 2 tablespoons of the butter over moderate heat until softened.

In a 6- to 8-quart heavy kettle, melt the remaining 6 tablespoons of butter over moderately low heat and whisk in the flour. Cook the roux, whisking constantly, about 3 minutes (make sure it doesn't brown). Stir in the cooked onion and gradually add broth and half-and-half, whisking constantly until the mixture is smooth.

Bring the mixture to a boil, then lower the heat and simmer, stirring occasionally for 5 minutes or until it thickens. Stir in the chili powder, cumin, salt, and white pepper (you may adjust the amount of seasoning to your taste).

Add the beans, chilis, chicken, and cheese and cook over low heat, stirring occasionally for 20 minutes. Stir in the sour cream just before serving.

You may serve this alone or over cooked rice.

ABOUT THE AUTHOR

Sheila Connolly has been nominated for an Agatha award for the Glassblowing Mysteries she writes as Sarah Atwell. She has taught art history, structured and marketed municipal bonds for major cities, worked as a staff member on two statewide political campaigns, and served as a fund raiser for several nonprofit organizations. She also managed her own consulting company, providing genealogical research services. In addition to genealogy, Sheila loves restoring old houses, visiting cemeteries, and traveling. Now a full time writer, she thinks writing mysteries is a lot more fun than any of her previous occupations.

She is married and has one daughter and three cats. Visit her website at: www.sheila connolly.com.

We hope you have enjoyed this Large Print book. Other Thorndike, Wheeler, Kennebec, and Chivers Press Large Print books are available at your library or directly from the publishers.

For information about current and upcoming titles, please call or write, without obligation, to:

Publisher
Thorndike Press
295 Kennedy Memorial Drive
Waterville, ME 04901
Tel. (800) 223-1244

or visit our Web site at:

http://gale.cengage.com/thorndike

OR

Chivers Large Print
published by AudioGo Ltd
St James House, The Square
Lower Bristol Road
Bath BA2 3SB
England
Tel. +44(0) 800 136919
email: info@audiogo.co.uk
www.audiogo.co.uk

All our Large Print titles are designed for easy reading, and all our books are made to last.

435